Praise

"Extraordinary...Once again, the authors color-fully integrate authentic archaeological and anthropological details with a captivating story replete with romance, intrigue, mayhem, and a nail-biting climax."

— *Library Journal*

"It is fascinating to see how much like us these early tribesmen, and that the more things change, the more they stay the same."

— *Romantic Times*

The Poison Bride

Also by W. Michael Gear and Kathleen O'Neal Gear

Big Horn Legacy

Dark Inheritance

The Foundation

Fracture Event

Long Ride Home

The Mourning War

Raising Abel

Rebel Hearts Anthology

Sand in the Wind

Thin Moon and Cold Mist

Black Falcon Nation Series

Flight of the Hawk Series

The Moundville Duology

Saga of a Mountain Sage Series

The Wyoming Chronicles

The Anasazi Mysteries

The Peacemaker's Tales

The Poison Bride

The Earliest Americans
Book 3

W. Michael Gear

Kathleen O'Neal Gear

WOLFPACK
PUBLISHING
— EST 2013 —

The Poison Bride
Paperback Edition
Copyright © 2025 (As Revised) by W. Michael Gear and
Kathleen O'Neal Gear

Wolfpack Publishing
1707 E. Diana Street
Tampa, FL 33610

www.wolfpackpublishing.com

Illustrations by Ellisa Mitchel.

Paperback ISBN 979-8-89567-135-1
Ebook ISBN 979-8-89567-027-9

With special thanks to the Chamberlin Inn in Cody, Wyoming, for providing us a refuge every time we need a quiet, beautiful place to discuss the plot and characters of our next literary project.

Acknowledgments

This book was inspired by Dennis Labatt during our visits to the Poverty Point site. Every North American archaeological site should have such a dedicated and enthusiastic supervisor. We would like to thank Robert Connolly, Lisa Wright, Linda York, and Kay Corley for their assistance during our visits and for their cooperation in providing Poverty Point Objects—cooking clays—for our ongoing research in prehistoric starch, phytolith, and pollen analysis at Poverty Point.

We would especially like to acknowledge the work of Dr. Jon L. Gibson, who has dedicated so much of his life to the interpretation of Poverty Point's archaeology.

Once more, we would like to thank our longtime friend and colleague, Dr. Linda Scott Cummings, for her endless enthusiasm and pioneering ethnobotanical research. Working with us, she has recovered the first starches, pollens, and phytoliths from Poverty Point cooking clays. Now, when we say they were cooking foods like yellow lotus and little barley in the earth ovens, we can prove it. Thanks, Linda.

Nonfiction Foreword

Ask any American to name the oldest city in the United States and he might tell you St. Augustine, Florida (A. D. 1565). Among an enlightened few, the name Old Oraibi (A. D. 1240), in the Hopi Mesas, might pop up. But, with apologies to both of these places, we wish to point out that North America's oldest city was not located in Florida—or even in the Southwest—nor was it built around St. Louis, or in the fertile valleys of Ohio. Rather, to find it, you must journey to northeastern Louisiana, just outside of the small town of Epps. There, under the superb management of the state of Louisiana, you can still walk the stunning earthworks of Poverty Point, North America's first true city.

While earthen mound construction begins over six thousand years ago in North America, Poverty Point was inhabited between 3,750 and 3,350 years before present. From radiocarbon dates, most of Poverty Point's incredible earthworks were created during the last century of occupation. At its height, a permanent population of several thousand people lived on Poverty

Point's curving ridges. They traded for goods as far north as Wisconsin and Ohio. Materials were imported to Poverty Point across nearly fifteen hundred miles of Archaic wilderness.

The site itself is huge. From Lower Jackson Mound on the south to Motley Mound on the north is a little over five miles. The main earthworks cover more than four hundred acres and may contain as much as *one million cubic yards* of earth that was dug out of the ground and packed on human backs to build this leviathan. In sheer size, it would remain unmatched for another fifteen hundred years.

We agree with Jon Gibson that Poverty Point is a grand-scale projection of the human mind onto the landscape. Its form was not accidental or random, but a reflection of a shared vision of their physical as well as spiritual world, their kinship systems, and creation mythology.

A note on kinship: Non-Western societies organize their social structure in many different ways. What we see reflected in Poverty Point's architecture suggests two moieties, or social divisions, that contain three clans each. We have utilized a matrilineal matrilocal kinship system since that was present throughout the south.

Our reconstruction of prehistoric cosmology in *People of the Owl* must remain tentative, but we have looked for constants in South and Central Eastern Woodland mythology and oral tradition. We discarded elements that reflect later Mississippian—*People of the River*—agricultural traits. What is left is a shared tripartite belief in the surface of the earth, the sky above, and the underworld.

We have used real places as a setting for the story.

Poverty Point is Sun Town. The Panther's Bones is set at the Caney Mounds (site 16CT5) in Catahoula County. When Saw Back is exiled, it is to the Jaketown site in Mississippi. Twin Circles references the Clairborae Site near the mouth of the Pearl River in southern Mississippi. While we did not extensively explore distant Poverty Point settlements in *People of the Owl,* sites containing Poverty Point's distinctive artifacts have been found as far away as the Florida Gulf Coast.

So, what explains this spectacular thirty-five-hundred-year-old cultural fluorescence? These people were hunter-gatherers. Intensive corn agriculture wouldn't catch on for another two thousand years. The answer seems to lie in the richness of the Lower Mississippi Valley and its yearly floods. The people at Poverty Point ate everything that walked, crawled, swam, burrowed, and grew in their benevolent food-rich environment. In short, the Lower Mississippi Valley provided the surplus in resources that allowed remarkable cultural achievements.

In the coming years, we hope to learn a great deal more. As of this writing, one-half of one percent of the site has been excavated. In our own research with Linda Scott Cummings on Poverty Point Objects—PPOs— or cooking clays, we have recovered the first starches, phytoliths, and pollen residue from the food they cooked in their earth ovens thirty-five hundred years ago. As more research is tackled, our view of this complex site is going to change substantially. It will be important research. We believe that Poverty Point was to North America what the Fertile Crescent was to Europe: *the place that generated and disseminated cultural concepts that would influence subsequent cultures across the eastern woodlands.*

Information on the site is as close as your computer: povertypoint@crt.la.us. Jon Gibson's excellent read, *The Ancient Mounds of Poverty Point*, is available from the University Press of Florida. For an overview of the whole of North American archaeology, we recommend Brian Fagan's *Ancient North America* published by Thames and Hudson. At the end of *People of the Owl* you will find a selected bibliography. Finally, we urge you to visit the Poverty Point State Commemorative Area in person. Until you experience the wonder of it yourself, you will never fully understand the magic.

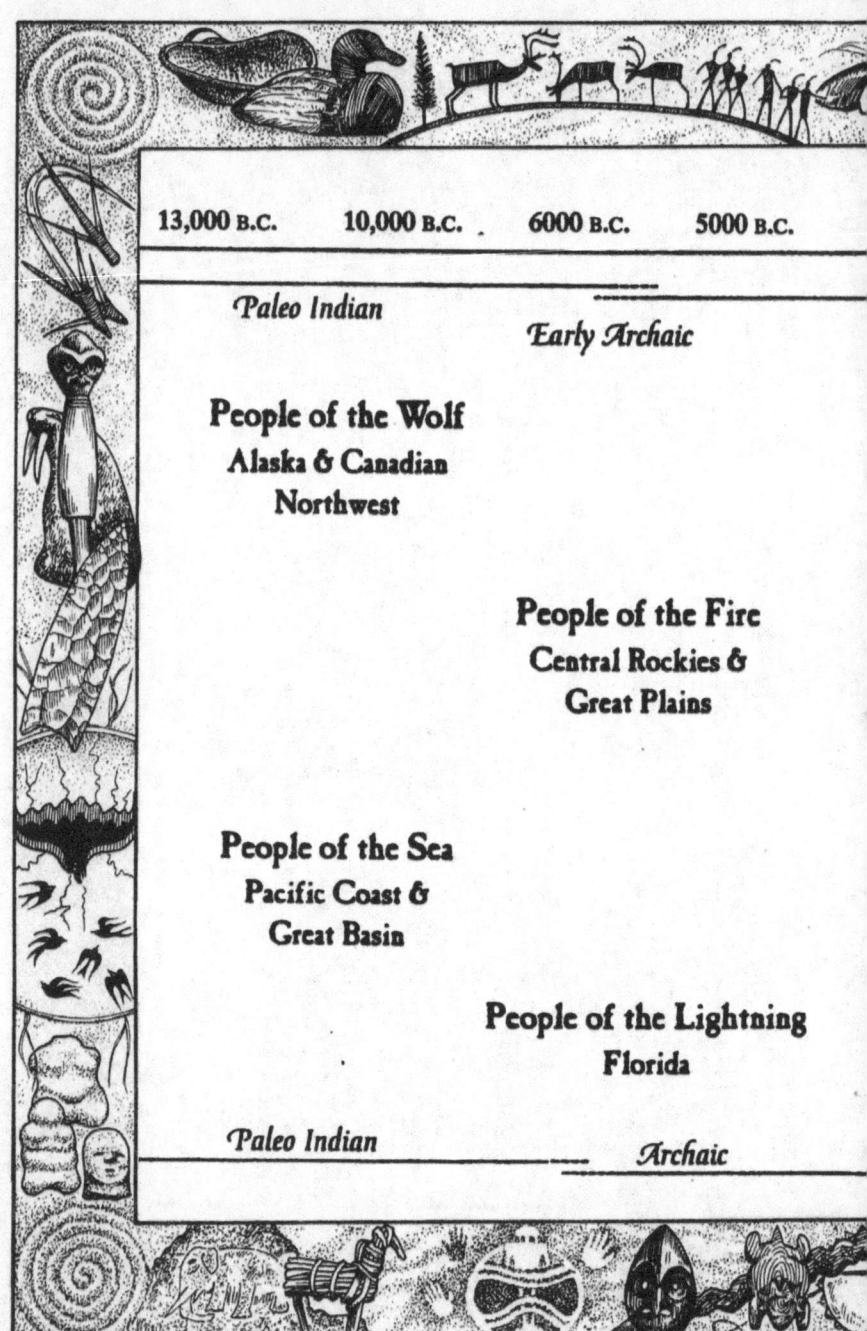

13,000 B.C.	10,000 B.C.	6000 B.C.	5000 B.C.

Paleo Indian

Early Archaic

People of the Wolf
Alaska & Canadian
Northwest

People of the Fire
Central Rockies &
Great Plains

People of the Sea
Pacific Coast &
Great Basin

People of the Lightning
Florida

Paleo Indian

Archaic

00 B.C.   1500 B.C.   100 A.D.   800 A.D.   1000 A.D.   1300 A.D.

Archaic   *Woodland*   *Mississippian*

People of the Earth   **People of the Mist**
Northern Plains   Chesapeake Bay
& Basins

                     People of the River
                     Mississippi Valley

         People of the Masks
              Ontario &
            Upstate New York

         People of the Lakes
         East Central Woodlands
              & Great Lakes

People of the Owl   **People of the Silence**
Lower Mississippi   Southwest Anasazi
Valley

       Basketmaker   *Pueblo*

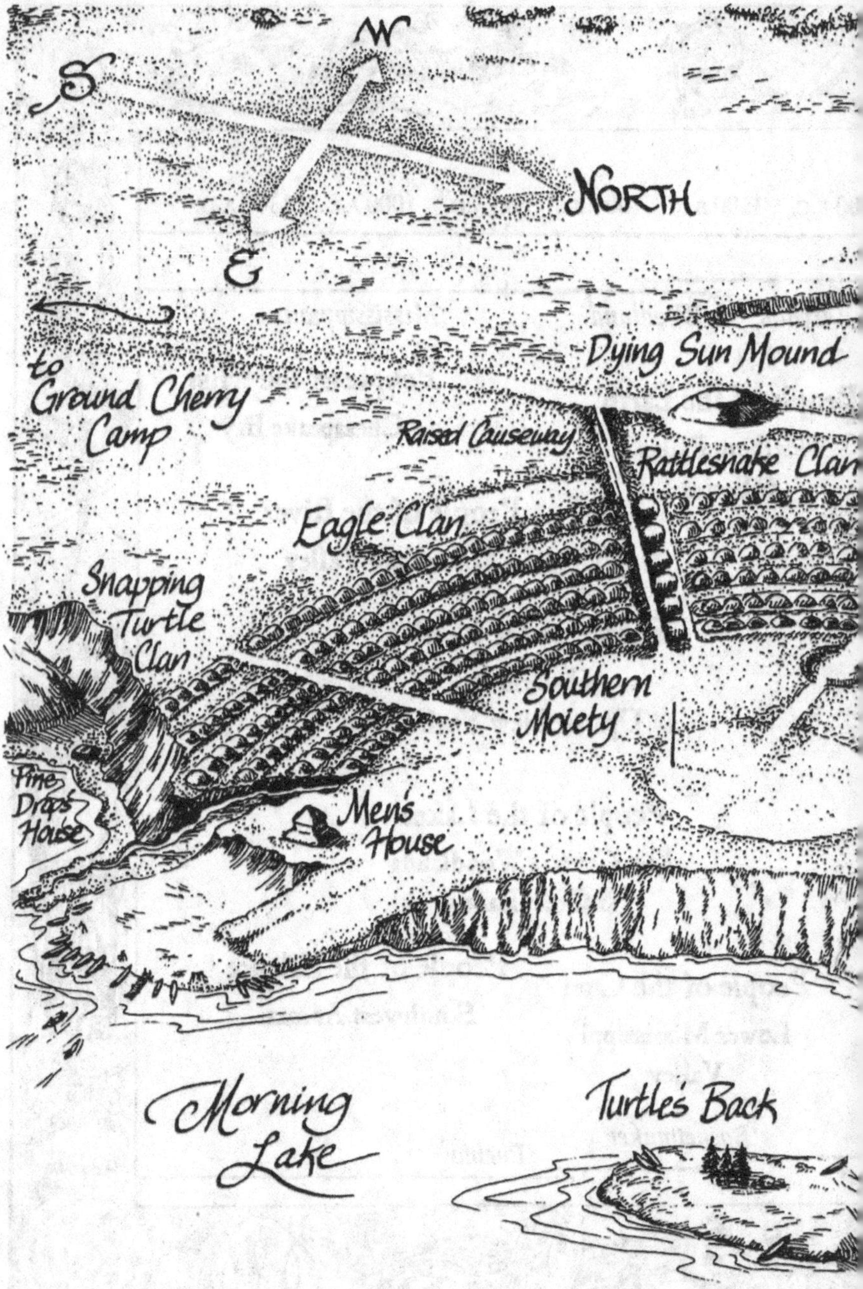

S
W
E
NORTH
to Ground Cherry Camp
Dying Sun Mound
Raised Causeway
Rattlesnake Clan
Eagle Clan
Snapping Turtle Clan
Southern Moiety
Pine Drops House
Men's House
Morning Lake
Turtle's Back

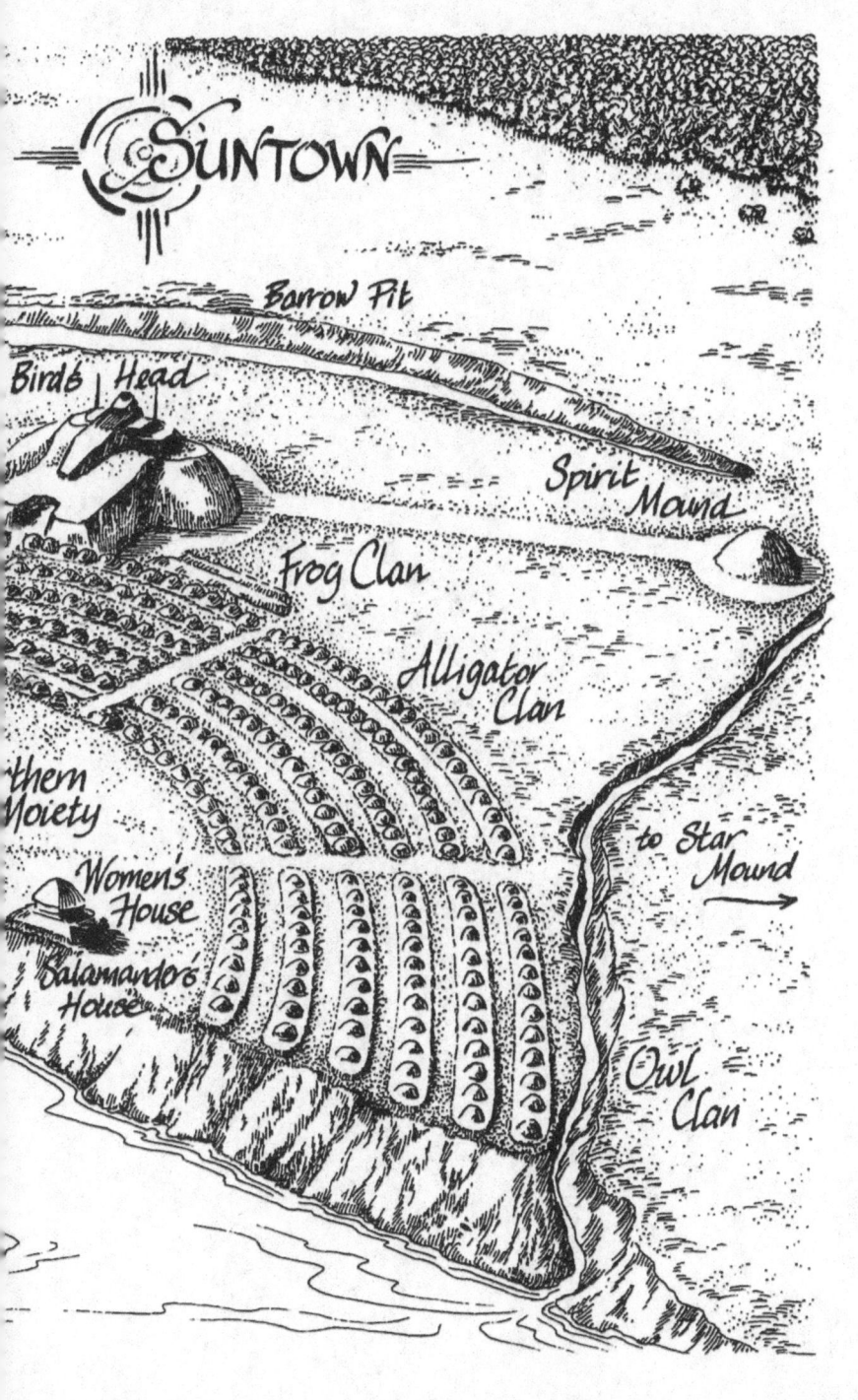

SUNTOWN

Barrow Pit

Birds Head

Spirit Mound

Frog Clan

Alligator Clan

...thern Moiety

to Star Mound

Women's House

Salamander's House

Owl Clan

Land of the
Wolf People

Great East River

NORTH

Father Water

Wash'ta
People

Yellow Mud
Camp

Suntown

Ground Cherry
Camp
Diving Eagle
Lake
Panther's
Bones

Twin Circle
Camp

The Poison Bride

Chapter One

Night Rain squatted to relieve herself at the edge of the borrow ditch below her sister's house. The night was still, cold. Only the distant barking of one of the camp dogs broke the silence. Smoke hung low, its odor tickling her nostrils. When she looked up it was to see a white ghosting of stars across the night sky. Father Moon still hid in shame below the horizon, and Bird Man's path across the sky glowed with an eerie luminescence.

As she started to stand, a hand reached out from behind to grab her. That touch brought a squeal from her frightened lungs.

"*Hush!*" the familiar voice ordered. "What's going on?"

"Uncle?" her voice failed, breath short in her panicked lungs. Mud Stalker wheeled her around to face him, his crushing grip hurting her elbow.

"What is your game, Niece? Who are you playing against whom? Deep Hunter against Salamander? Deep Hunter against me? What's your sister's role in this? What were you doing out there with Saw Back? Rutting, like everyone says? That I don't doubt! But why didn't you tell me?"

"Uncle, please!" She squirmed away from the pain.

"You tell me, woman. You start at the beginning, and you tell me."

"Uncle, honestly, I didn't do anything..." His hard slap sent her stumbling. She slipped, falling backward into her damp urine.

"Don't lie to me!"

She caught her breath, swallowed hard, and cast a desperate glance at the dark shape of her house up on the ridgetop. Pine Drop would be asleep, ignorant of her plight. Not that it would matter, not even Pine Drop would interfere with their uncle over clan business.

"Please don't hurt me."

"I'll beat you until your souls cling to your body by a thread!"

He drew back a foot, as if to kick her. She scrambled back, hands and feet sliding in the mud. "I swear, I did nothing against the clan. I just wanted Saw Back! You know that! You know I've always been in love with him!"

Mud Stalker loomed over her. "Deep Hunter knew I was going to offer Eats Wood for Green Beetle. He beat me to it, offered Thunder Tail his cousin, Needs Two, and access to a root ground before I could take the Speaker out to that bear tree. I couldn't figure it out. But after the Council meeting, and what Pine Drop did, I finally understand. You were there, you heard me discuss it that night with your mother."

"I *didn't*, I swear!" She was suddenly thankful for

the darkness. He couldn't see her face, couldn't read the lie in her expression.

"Why did Salamander take you back? Why didn't he just throw you out like the punky worm-riddled piece of wood you are?"

"I don't know! You'd have to ask him. He's...he's..."

"What?"

"Odd, Uncle. Strange. He hears things, has Dreams." She lurched backward like a crawfish on land as he stepped nearer. "I don't know what possesses his souls to make him do the things he does."

"What does the barbarian hold over him? Is she a witch? Does she control his souls?"

"I don't think so. She's just mean. She hates us. You heard Eats Wood, he says she's the one White Bird caught. You've seen those scars on her skin? We did that to her when she was a prisoner."

"Why did you betray me to Deep Hunter?" His voice sounded tired now, wounded.

"Uncle, I didn't. You have to believe me."

"I shouldn't have trusted you. You were too young, not smart enough. I see that now. Snakes! What was I to do? Don't you understand, woman? We're almost at the top! We've worked all of our lives to see our clan become preeminent. The gains we have made can disappear from beneath us like water from a puddle, and you let a little pleasure in your canoe, and the promises of a crafty lizard like Deep Hunter, turn you against your own family!"

"Uncle, I swear!"

She squatted there, her butt in the mud, waiting as his dark body hulked against the stars. The silence grew interminable.

W. Michael Gear & Kathleen O'Neal Gear

When he finally broke it, he asked, "What part did Salamander play in all this? What did he do to get Pine Drop to support him in the Council?"

"He asked her to trust him," she whispered, unable to see what it would hurt. "That it would explode like a chert nodule in a fire if she didn't."

She could see him, a dark blot against the sky as he fingered the scars on his maimed arm.

"Salamander was trying to keep our clan from fighting with Alligator Clan." There, would that mollify him?

"Why? What difference does it make to him?"

"We're his wives." She swallowed hard, trying to find the right answer. "He cares for us. For me."

The kick caught her by surprise. His foot slammed into her ribs, rolling her. She yelped at the pain, frightened by the hollow thump.

"You're *stupid*, Night Rain! No one cares for a woman like you." Mud Stalker turned his head and spat. "Least of all your skinny, witless husband." A pause. "No, this is something else. Some plotting he must be doing at the behest of that Panther witch who wraps him around her bony fingers."

"Uncle, I—"

"Shut up! I'm thinking, trying to understand."

"Please, Uncle, I didn't do *anything*."

"You betrayed me. You and Pine Drop. But don't think I haven't learned, Niece. Indeed, I have learned a great deal about you— and your husband. I've underestimated him. I won't do that again."

She could feel his gaze as he studied her. She wanted to shrink, to shrivel up and burrow into the waste-tainted mud.

4

"In the future when I come to you, you will tell me the truth, Night Rain. And someday, to make up for this humiliation to Snapping Turtle Clan, to your lineage, and me, I am going to ask you for something. When I do, you are going to do as I say, or I am going to break your head with a stone-headed hammer. Do you understand?"

"Yes, Uncle." Her voice came as a hoarse whisper.

"In the meantime, stay out of my sight."

He turned, walking wearily away—head down, shoulders bowed. He plodded up past her house and headed east on the ridge.

She closed her eyes and sagged into the stinking mud.

Branches, like gray fuzz, softened the distant border between the forest and sky as if one faded into the other. The morning was cold, silent but for the calls of the winter birds. Not even the ducks stirred when Anhinga's canoe slipped silently down the channel.

Her breath puffed whitely. Despite the cold she paddled with her cloak thrown back over her shoulders, as her muscles provided enough warmth. On the still water the cold seemed thicker, sticky, ready to sap a body's heat. She glanced at the canebrakes, tawny and gray. The banks were brown, the trees black, their fringe of branches lonely and longing for spring.

"You shouldn't be taking this trip," Pine Drop had warned the night before.

As if I need advice from her! Anhinga made a face, feeling the cold in her cheeks. The bulge of her belly made sitting in the canoe awkward, but she needed time away. Besides which, her brother, Striped Dart, would be coming to meet her this time. Half a cycle had passed since she had seen him last. He would be bursting with news about people at the Panther's Bones. She, in turn, had so much to tell him about the Sun People, and Night Rain, about smacking Saw Back, and the ruckus she had stirred in the Council as a result.

Thinking about Saw Back brought a shudder to her. The side of his face looked horrible. In the weeks since the incident, he had healed, but her axe had peeled a long scar that ran from beside his navel to just under his left nipple. The thin arch of bone ahead of his ear had been crushed. Had she not turned the axe at the last moment the blow would surely have penetrated his skull.

When he, or any of his clan, looked at her now, it was with a simmering hatred.

He attacked me. That memory clung to her like summer cobwebs. The incident filled her thoughts, recurring in her Dreams.

By the Panther's Bones, that had been a close one. But for her quick wits, it could have turned out worse than it had. Oddly, she rather enjoyed having put Night Rain in her place. Over the long term, however, she had a hunch that her actions that morning would come to haunt her.

Overhead a V of geese crossed above the web of branches. The swish of their wings and the lonely honking were the only sounds outside of the water gurgling around her paddle.

She glanced up at the banks—just enough higher

that each tangle of dormant honeysuckle or nightshade could conceal a crouching warrior. She could imagine Saw Back's smile of anticipation as her slim canoe coasted within range. He would feel the joy of revenge in his breast as he rose, sighted, and drove a dart through her body.

He will kill my baby. Her mouth went dry. Panther! Why hadn't that thought occurred to her? It wasn't just her anymore. If anything, the baby was even more of a temptation to Saw Back. He could kill her and Salamander's child in one stroke. He could wreak his retribution on her while repaying Salamander for his trickery in allowing Jaguar Hide to escape: two for one.

A stick cracked in the forest. A squirrel dropping a nut? Or the weighty step of a man's foot?

The silence pressed down upon her. As the canoe coasted she pulled her atlatl and darts closer to hand. Next she slipped her axe through the belt of her kirtle.

Ghostly fingers of breeze stirred the quiet air. She whirled, rocking the canoe. The channel behind her lay empty, her wake spreading toward the banks. In the cold winter sun the water had a silver sheen. She couldn't see far, the channel twisted and looped, choked with cypress, tupelo, and water oak. The trees watched her, silent, as if their ancient souls were waiting.

Eyes, a thousand of them! She glanced around, looking up in the branches where brown-tinted hanging moss drooped wearily. Her quickened imagination saw faces leering out from the patterns of dry vegetation.

Swallowing, she picked up the paddle and drove her canoe forward. *Hurry! Just leave this place behind. If he is after you, outrun him. Paddle like you have never paddled before.* The canoe flew ahead.

7

He could be just behind her, and knowing these passages, he could beach his canoe, cut across a narrow neck of land, and ambush her from any patch of tangled brush.

Flee, you have no other choice. She couldn't go back, not and take the chance of running headlong into him.

She tightened her hands on the paddle handle. *You're being silly, Anhinga. You have no proof that he's behind you. No proof that he's after you at all.*

She was just jittery. Her imagination was teasing her. The strain had begun to make itself felt in her shoulders and arms.

I would be out hunting, if I were he.

She couldn't help but remember that she herself, smarting from injustice, had brought a war party north to avenge Bowfin's death. Perhaps Saw Back wasn't as impetuous as she, but could she take the chance? How many eyes had been watching that morning as Salamander saw her off from the landing?

Paddle! A new surge of fear drove her onward. They would know she would have taken this channel south. It was the most direct way through the bottomlands paralleling Sun Town's high silt bluff. If she made it to the rendezvous alive, she could always take another route home. It might be longer, out of the way, but a hunter wouldn't know when or where to expect her.

If I go home. That thought caught her by surprise. She didn't have to go back. Not after the affair with Saw Back. Uncle wouldn't expect her to and neither would Striped Dart. They would rather have her safe, especially carrying her clan's child.

She shot a quick look over her shoulder again.

Nothing. Her wake was undisturbed by so much as a fish jumping.

Salamander would approve of her caution. In the gray dawn of the canoe landing she had seen the worry in her husband's eyes.

"I have to go," she had told him simply. "They will be waiting for me. If I don't show up, they will worry. It might lead them to foolishness. We both know how dangerous it would be if they came here looking for me. Only Owl Clan is bound by your word of peace."

He had nodded, a terrible reluctance reflected in the set of his mouth. "I need you to come back to me."

Impulsively she had reached out and drawn him to her in a desperate hug. She had held his thin body against hers, her swollen belly pressing the hollow of his. Then she had turned, grateful for his help as she awkwardly pushed the canoe into the cold water and climbed in.

I hugged him. Panther's blood, why? It isn't as if I really care for him. He's the enemy. No matter that he severed my bonds one night.

Was it her imagination, or had something about Salamander changed over the moons? Men, she had heard, acted differently after they planted a child and could see it growing in their wives. Or was it that she had fought for him, for his honor, that day when she surprised Saw Back and Night Rain?

You didn't mean to, she argued with herself. *It was expedient to shame Night Rain that way. If you'd killed them both, you would have been finished in Sun Town.*

She no longer went out alone to gather firewood, or collect nuts, or check the snares. Somehow, Pine Drop,

Salamander, or Water Petal always seemed to be ready to accompany her.

Night Rain had surprised them all, demurely taking her place like a proper wife. Anhinga suspected that she buried herself in household activities to avoid facing people. Laughter still broke out at the sight of her, and occasional calls followed her around Sun Town, asking if she needed to borrow any clothing. The teasing would eventually die off like fall grass. Night Rain need only wait it out.

He is a better man than I would be in his place, she concluded. Indeed, she'd have thrown the little witch out. Salamander, however, had acted as if nothing had happened, welcoming Night Rain into his house and his bed with great dignity.

How many nights had Anhinga lain in her bed, hearing their whispered conversation? Something was being forged between them, although Night Rain still shot her looks that bordered on the murderous.

At the end of the next strait, Anhinga glanced back, barely catching movement behind a distant cypress knee. She blinked hard to clear her eyes and stared. What was that dark blot behind the old roots? A man, or a shadow? Her canoe almost drifted into the bank before she straightened it.

Imagination, or trick of the light? She dared not take the chance, and drove her paddle into the water with renewed fury.

She shot out of the narrow channel and into one of the wide, shallow swamps. Her flying canoe sailed into the maze of trees as she followed her way south. A lightning-blasted cypress marked the entrance to the far channel, and gratefully she cast a final glance over her shoulders. Nothing. No. Wait. Movement, there, back in the trees! But was it a man, or an animal? Before she could determine, her canoe coasted into the channel, the banks obscuring her view.

Desperate again, panting, she drove herself onward. A red smear caught her eye as she shifted her grip on the paddle. When had her palm blistered and broken? Compared to the ache in her forearms and shoulders, it was nothing.

Time collapsed into fear, pain, and exhaustion as she raced her canoe down the winding passage. A hand of time later she emerged into a familiar swamp and marked her progress. Known landmarks, fallen trees, stumps, and oddly shaped cypress knees guided her through the brackish shallows.

She cried out with relief as she drove her narrow craft onto the muddy shore of the little island. For long moments, she could only sit there and gasp for breath. Her arms barely supported her as she tried to get up. She propped herself on the gunwales and struggled against the bulk of her swollen abdomen.

Coming within a hair of capsizing herself into the muddy shallows, she stepped into the water, staggered sideways, and caught her balance.

As her legs came alive, she turned and looked back at the silent swamp. Nothing moved, not even birds, usually ever-present in the winter moons. The water reflected the sky's dull gray sheen, motionless, heavy.

Slogging out of the water she rolled her arms, wincing. Tomorrow would be agony. Bending over her girth, she pushed the canoe higher up the bank and grabbed the sack of supplies she had brought. The drinking bowl that she normally filled before arriving here was empty, forgotten in the frantic flight.

She collected her atlatl and darts, tapping her axe with reassured fingers. Let him come. Here, on dry land, she could vanquish any fool who paddled a canoe up to the island.

Walking through knee-high dry grass, she stepped into the beaten campsite she had shared over the moons with her relatives. A few damp pieces of wood lay on the wet ground. Looking around, it appeared that no one had been here since she and Uncle had left.

"You need dry wood. This won't do to make a fire." She kicked the wet wood and started off through the grass in search of old flood-deposited flotsam. She stopped and inspected a large branch. Thick as a man's thigh, it had fallen from a water oak. Partially protected by the overhanging branches, the wood felt moderately dry to her touch. She looked around at the brown grass and weeds. Hip high, they masked her movements. The island slept, dormant and silent.

She laid her atlatl and darts to one side and worked her tired fingers, feeling the joints ache. It would take two hands to drag this back. The smaller branches would make kindling, and she could talk Striped Dart into hacking up the rest when he arrived.

She bent, got a grip, and heaved. The branch moved, and like some ungainly turtle, she dragged it one pull at a time toward her camp. With each tug, she took a moment to rise and peer out at the swamp. No movement marred the surface. No sound intruded on the normal noises.

As she bent once again and pulled, she caught a blur at the corner of her eye. Something struck her from behind, knocked her forward over the branch. The hard wood smashed her chin and left breast.

For a terrified instant her thoughts scrambled, then she rolled onto her back, staring up in disbelief. For a moment, she could not place his face. "You?"

She was gasping, her heart pounding as Eats Wood grinned down at her. "Hello, bitch. Snakes, it's been a long time that I have been waiting to do this."

"What are you doing here?" She remembered him, remembered his fingers twisting her left nipple as he carried her from the canoe landing up to the Men's House. His leer brought back all the terrible memories of that day.

"It took me a while to work out your trail. I learned a little more every time you left. Never followed you all the way. Just a bit at a time. And what should I find? You, bending your head with Jaguar Hide, planning ways to hurt us all."

"He is my uncle!" She managed to brace her elbows under her. Eats Wood held a stone-headed axe in one gnarled fist. He swung it back and forth, each swing promising pain.

"He is our enemy." He smiled down at her. "You made good time today. Jaguar Hide shouldn't be arriving here for at least another hand of time."

"What are you going to do?" Her atlatl lay back at the tree. Her axe, however, was pinned under her hip. Had he seen it hanging from her kirtle?

"What I wanted to do the first time I saw you." He tilted his head to the side, eyes half-lidded. "I'll bet you don't remember me."

"I remember you," she spat. "You and your grasping hands."

"I'm going to grasp you again," he told her. "I'll consider it a warm-up before your uncle gets here. He'll see the canoe, be expecting you. I might even be done with you and have a fire going before he gets here. Jaguar Hide's head will be on Deep Hunter's hearth by nightfall. A gift from my clan to his. He will be obliged to me and to Snapping Turtle Clan. I suppose you know, a great many good things come to a hunter who has a Speaker obliged to him."

"I'm carrying a child!"

"Not after today," he told her offhandedly. "I haven't decided yet whether I'll cut it out of you, or just leave it to rot in your body."

"Salamander is married to your kinswomen!"

"No one will know what happens here. Besides, the Speaker and Clan Elder will be making other arrangements for Pine Drop and Night Rain. They're too valuable to waste on your silly Salamander. So, are we going to do this easily, or am I going to have to soften you up a little? Conscious or knocked dumb, it won't matter to me." With one hand he pulled the knot loose that held his breechcloth. The fabric fell away from his erect penis.

"Do as you will," she murmured, trying to sound broken, wondering how she could turn to lay her fingers on the axe.

"Toss it away." He wiggled his club. "The axe you are wearing. I'm not the fool Saw Back was. Toss it to one side, or the first blow I land will be right in the middle of that big belly of yours."

She bit her lip, a sinking sensation folding around her hammering heart. With half-numb fingers, she pulled the axe free, giving it a weak-hearted toss. Was it still close enough?

"Prepare to die, you stinking barbarian bitch." He leered at her, dropped to his knees, and slapped her legs apart. He was reaching for the hem of her kirtle when movement flashed in the corner of Anhinga's vision.

She barely recognized Salamander as he rose behind Eats Wood and swung a stone-headed axe down onto the crown of the man's head. Bone snapped. A violent shiver shot through Eats Wood's body. His eyes popped in surprise. A spasmodic jerk of his legs drove his face into the crushed grass between Anhinga's tense thighs.

She gaped, speechless, glancing back and forth between her husband and the jerking body. Blood, bright and red, welled from the oblong hole in Eats Wood's head. His hair soaked it up like a vibrating brush as his twitching worsened. A gasping rattle came from his throat.

"Are you all right?" Salamander stepped over the man's body.

"I..." Words were dead inside her. She could only nod, her eyes fixed on Eats Wood's quivering body. She almost collapsed again when Salamander pulled her to her feet. She shrank against him, burying her face in the hollow of his shoulder and bursting into tears.

Chapter Two

S pots of blue broke the overcast of gray winter clouds. The island, normally her refuge against the world, now felt oppressive and dangerous. Anhinga's souls kept flashing images of the assault. The leering expression on Eats Wood's face hung behind her eyes. She could glance over her shoulder to see the tree. Beneath those branches, Eats Wood's body was growing cold, his empty eyes turning gray.

His angry and frightened souls are rising, staring at me from among those naked branches. A shiver traced down her muscles, as if he were reaching out for her with ghostly fingers.

She didn't feel better. Not even Striped Dart's arrival, a half hand of time ago, reassured her. Salamander sat close beside her. He kept reaching out, patting her in reassurance. When she looked into his eyes, though, she could see the disquiet he tried so hard to hide.

Panther's blood! Why am I still scared? After all I've been through, I shouldn't be shaken by anything!

"Anhinga?" Salamander asked as he leaned forward, searching her face.

"I thought it would be Saw Back," she whispered.

The fire popped, blue smoke rising from the fire pit that separated her from Striped Dart. Her brother looked anything but happy, the deep grooves of worry might have been carved into his forehead. She could tell he didn't approve of the situation. His expression darkened at Salamander's solicitation, as if he begrudged this stranger's intimacy with his sister.

Salamander made a face as he scrubbed Eats Wood's blood from his axe. He kept shooting curious glances at Striped Dart.

In the moons since Anhinga had seen him last, Striped Dart, too, had changed. She didn't remember this long-boned young man, his hair coiled tightly on top of his head. He wore a new puma hide. The gray-brown pelt hung over his shoulders with white belly fur gleaming in the gray light. He had a triangular face, attractive, much like hers but with harder, masculine lines. A stifled anger burned behind his brown eyes and reflected in the set of his jaw. He held an axe in his hand and slapped it against his calloused palm.

"I thought I saw movement behind me." Anhinga closed her eyes and hugged her bulging belly protectively.

"I didn't want to get too close," Salamander told her. "It was difficult, racing after you, then having to slow down and wait for you to get out of sight."

"Why didn't you call to me?"

He made a dismissive gesture. "If you had been safe, I would have turned around and left." He inspected his axe, picking at bits of dark red in the binding. "You didn't ask me to come here, Anhinga. This is your time with your own people."

She stared. *Why would you do that? Surely you know I come here to plot against you!* Aloud, she said, "I don't understand."

His dark brown eyes seemed to see right through her. Another shiver ran down her spine as he said, "You must be free to follow your heart, Wife. Wherever that takes you. Whatever the price."

By the Sky Beings, what did he mean by that?

"She could have been killed," Striped Dart's accented voice interrupted. "This is too dangerous."

"What do we do, Brother-in-law?" Salamander asked. "If you come farther north, someone—like Eats Wood—will take the opportunity to kill you."

Anhinga glanced back at the oak, feeling the presence of the corpse lying there in the blood-soaked grass. *Snakes! What is Pine Drop going to say? Eats Wood is her cousin.*

Striped Dart finally said, "If she will not come home with me to the Panther's Bones, she is safer staying in Sun Town until the child is born." He looked up at Salamander and smiled. "It would seem that you are more than capable of protecting her."

"When she's not battering her enemies herself," Salamander replied. She could tell from his expression that he didn't feel the levity he projected.

"I was told that you were a fool." Thick muscles slid under Striped Dart's smooth brown skin. "But my uncle, he sees things differently than I do."

"Many people call me a fool," Salamander replied.

"But you're not, are you?" Striped Dart asked.

Salamander's lips twitched. "Can any of us truly

know that he is not a fool, Brother-in-law? I doubt myself all the time."

Anhinga blinked, as if seeing her husband anew. He seemed so controlled, possessed of a calm sadness. He had just killed his first man—one of his own, someone he knew, not a stranger. He sat across from an enemy, yet he might have been comfortably at his mother's fire rather than deep in Swamp Panther territory with the corpse of Pine Drop's cousin weighing on his souls.

Striped Dart's eyes narrowed. "I did not approve of Anhinga going north. I did not approve of this *peace* of his. Our sandstone is ours, given to us by the Creator at the beginning of the world." Striped Dart shot Salamander a steely look, daring him to disagree.

"You speak truthfully, Striped Dart. I cannot second-guess the Creator's reasons for placing things where he did when he made the world." Salamander stood and slashed his axe through the air to fling the water off, then walked over to lower himself beside Anhinga. He took her hand, rubbing his fingers across her soft brown skin. The touch soothed her as he added, "In Sun Town, we have a need for sandstone."

Striped Dart said bitterly. "Along with your thefts, your people killed my brother—and countless others over the turnings of the seasons!"

"We were wrong." His dark brown eyes seemed to suck up her souls. She felt a tingle run through her as he said, "For that, I apologize." He turned his attention to her brother. "Looking back, Striped Dart, one cannot say who started this or who is more wronged. The sandstone is yours. For now Jaguar Hide has offered us safe passage to take one canoe load each moon."

Anhinga took a deep breath, relieved at the cool air

pumping into her oddly starved lungs. *Salamander saved my life. This is the second time. I owe him for that.* But how did she balance that against her vow to strike back in the names of Bowfin and her friends? Just being here, in the presence of her brother, rubbed the wound raw again.

Striped Dart was giving Salamander a hot look. "I tell you now—do not come for sandstone again, *Brother-in-law*. My people will kill yours." He made a dismissive gesture. "It is *our* sandstone. Why should we allow you to have it just because you promise not to kill us while you help yourselves?"

"We have a peace," Salamander reminded, "but for one, I do not wish to send my kinsmen where they are not wanted." He steepled his fingers, thinking. "Jaguar Hide told me that we could have one canoe load per moon, but that if we wanted to take two, we would have to send a load of gifts." He glanced at Striped Dart. "You are right, Brother-in-law, it is not equitable."

What are you saying? Anhinga wondered. *That sandstone is one of the few things Owl Clan has left to barter with for obligation!*

Striped Dart opened his mouth, but the hot retort died on his tongue. "I'm right?"

Salamander nodded. "Of course you are. We are getting many things for nothing. I have a beautiful wife, a canoe load of sandstone each moon, and peace. You, my friend, just have the peace from one clan. Mine. It is not fair."

"What are you saying?" Anhinga snapped.

"I'm saying we should renegotiate." Salamander spread his hands wide. "Striped Dart, what if we sent a load of gifts with each trip? What would your people like?"

"Fabrics," Anhinga said quickly. "No one makes fabrics like Sun Town. And dyes. You make the most beautiful dyes. Smoked meat, like the buffalo and elk you have Traded for. My people don't get such luxuries."

"Stone?" Salamander asked, indicating the sharp green stone celt hafted onto his axe.

"No. We have plenty of our own," Striped Dart answered. "Trading rocks for rocks sounds silly. But these other things?" He looked genuinely interested. "You would do that when you didn't have to?"

"I would, Brother-in-law. I would simply because it is right. And we have to consider safety." Salamander jerked his head toward where Eats Wood lay out in the weeds. "Someday soon, someone like Eats Wood, from one of the other Sun Town clans, will come to raid and steal sandstone. He will come to break the peace, not because he hates the Swamp Panthers, but because it is a way to hurt my clan."

Anhinga asked, "So what will you do? Kill him, too?"

"No, Wife. I will try to be smarter than my enemies." Salamander's brows lowered. "I will only send a canoe on the full moon, Striped Dart. I will always send someone you know: Yellow Spider, Bluefin, one of my kinsmen. If you see a canoe with strangers in it, be wary. My advice would be to avoid it."

"Why? It is our territory. Why should we put up with raiders?"

Salamander let that strange brown gaze of his bore

into Striped Dart. To Anhinga's amazement, her brother squirmed, then lowered his eyes.

Salamander spoke in a respectful tone. "The decision is yours, Brother-in-law. I cannot tell you whether or not to attack them, but I would have you consider that so long as this peace lasts between you and me, it is a thorn in the side of the other Sun Town clans. If we break it, they will have won...and you won't get fine fabrics and exotic foods in return for your stone."

Anhinga shook her head. "Striped Dart, you can't make this agreement. It is up to Uncle. He is our Elder! When he hears, he'll be furious! He already distrusts you."

"He and I think differently, Sister." Striped Dart had pursed his lips. "I had to beg to get this chance to see you alone. He has the winter solstice to plan for, or he would be here, telling me *no*. I'm not a child any more than you are. One day, I will be Elder. I want to be a good one."

"We need not tell Jaguar Hide," Salamander said easily. "If there is trouble over the Trade, simply say that Anhinga has talked me into sending it as a *gift* to my wife's people. Such things are done." His expression went solemn again. "Like you, I am planning not just for this moon, but for many moons in the future."

Striped Dart smiled, reaching out with a strong hand. "Done." Then his smile slipped. "We have one other thing to settle between us. The child."

"Yes?"

"It is ours. A member of my clan. I want my nephew to be raised as a Panther, not as a Sun person. He is to learn our ways, and I am to teach him."

"And if it's a girl?" Anhinga asked.

"Then she is to be raised by Mother."

"Our child will be raised by me!" Anhinga told him sharply. "I will see to its needs." What was she saying? She wasn't going to be in Sun Town for much longer. All she needed was Jaguar Hide's order to act, and she would implement the plan she had in mind. Immediately she would take a canoe, head for home, and her clan would raise the child.

"You are going to teach my nephew to hunt?" Striped Dart cried. "How to fish and stalk enemies?"

Salamander raised his hands. "This is a matter between the two of you. But know this, Striped Dart, if anything should happen to Anhinga, I will bring you the child as soon as I safely can."

"Why?"

"Because it will be your kin, Striped Dart."

Striped Dart looked confused, as if he fished for thoughts in his head. He asked, "Do you fear me? Is that why you do this?"

Salamander shook his head. "You do not scare me. No, just the opposite. I think that you and I could become great friends in spite of what our peoples have done to each other in the past."

A crooked grin crossed Striped Dart's lips. "You are *not* what I expected." He paused. "I think you should keep my sister safe until the child is born."

"No!" Anhinga started to say. "I have..." Her voice trailed off as both men gave her an inquiring stare. To say more was to give away everything. "Very well, tell Uncle I will come after the child is born." Somehow she had been outmaneuvered, placed in a position she didn't want to be in.

Salamander said, "I will send word with the sandstone boat when she will be coming to meet you again. And perhaps I shall send an escort, trusted warriors who will deliver her safely, then stand off. This place"—he gestured around—"is too well known now."

"We think alike." Striped Dart's eyes were hooded. "I didn't agree with Uncle's plan in the beginning. You, Speaker, have shown me that it is good."

"If I can be of service, Striped Dart, if a problem should develop, send word with the stone shipment. Give me a time, and I will meet you here, or send a known representative if I cannot come."

Salamander stood. "I will leave you now. You probably have family matters to discuss."

"You're leaving?" Anhinga cried as she struggled to her feet. "Now?"

"I must get back." He jerked a nod toward the body. "There are things I have to deal with."

Worry tightened in her breast. He couldn't just up and leave her. Not on this island, not with Eats Wood's souls lingering about. "What will you tell Pine Drop and Night Rain?"

"Nothing, Anhinga. I am going to load his body into my canoe. Somewhere, out there"—he indicated the swamp—"he might slip off the side. That's all."

"You can't just ignore it." She thumped her breast in emphasis. "You killed to protect your family! Your child and your honor!"

"Do you think I should announce myself at the Men's House and demand a warrior's tattoos?" He smiled sadly, reaching out and running his fingertips along her cheeks. "This must remain our secret."

"He *attacked* me!"

"Put yourself in Pine Drop and Night Rain's position. I have killed their kinsman. You know the pressure Mud Stalker and Sweet Root are already putting on them. No matter what, Anhinga, I will spare them."

She could only stare in disbelief. He did everything for others. Did he do nothing for himself?

"Wait!" Anhinga turned, looking at Striped Dart. "I am going back with my husband. Brother, take the body, dump it on the way home. Someplace where no Sun Person can stumble across it. That way no blood-stains will be on our canoes when we get back to Sun Town."

"And his canoe?" Salamander pointed to the craft they'd found hidden in the grass.

"Take it, Striped Dart. But you must promise me that you will destroy it." She walked up to him as he rose to his feet. "Do you understand why that is so important to me?"

He nodded. "No one must recognize anything of his in the future. He will just have vanished." A grim smile played on his lips. "Perhaps some large cat was out hunting?"

"You must tell no tales!" she reminded, shaking a finger in his face. "Not one, nothing about what happened here today."

Striped Dart offered his hand to Salamander again. "You have my silence, Speaker, and my sister's respect. A rare combination." A veiled look crossed his eyes. "I look forward to dealing with you in the future."

Salamander reached into his belt pouch. "A token," he offered. "My Spirit Helper. If you ever need anything, send me this carving of Masked Owl."

Striped Dart studied the little potbellied owl he

held between thumb and forefinger. "It looks as pregnant as my sister."

"Come, Husband." Anhinga studied the brooding sky. The patches of blue had vanished, and the clouds had taken on a heaviness. "I think it will rain, and in this weather that will be most uncomfortable."

The Serpent

I am coming to the end of words.

    I breathe slowly. I feel the way I am lying on the floor. I see the unchanging inner stillness that lives in my heart, and like a deer dying in the forest, I find myself absorbed by it. My attention focuses solely on these final moments. My chest rises and falls. My heartbeat pulses in my ears. The voices around me are faint, but pleasing. I thank the ancestors that I am not alone.

    There is only one thing I have done in my life that I am truly proud of.

    I have tried to be a teacher.

    I think some of my students actually heard me, though the gods know, listening is not easy. The greatest danger for the Student is thinking he has heard everything perfectly. It takes a long time to understand that the wisest words are not rolls of thunder. They don't strike at the heart like lightning. They are whispers, softly spoken into the ear, easily ignored by the spiritually intoxicated.

    Oh, I am old, but I remember that intoxication, that

heady rush of certainty. Even now, just thinking about it, I'm a little tipsy.

That's why wisdom sneaks by. We're tipsy. We can feel revelation surging in our veins. Who has time for whispers when the whole world is a divine shout?

Unfortunately, shouts are just air. Genuine spiritual awareness is hard work. It's like quarrying stone beneath a blazing sun, day after day. A man gets tired.

So very tired.

It is just easier to sit down, smile, and think great thoughts in the shade.

The truth, you see, is that revelation isn't fun. Revelation is pain.

I close my eyes. My vision is growing dim.

I hear voices calling to me from far away. I think I recognize my mother's voice. I force myself to listen. I listen for a long, long time. And finally...I swear to you, I do hear the whispers.

Chapter Three

In the Serpent's central fire pit, flames flickered and cast their warm light. Smoke rose, pooling around the rafters and the sacked herbs hanging from the roof.

In the wavering yellow glow, Bobcat sat on his haunches, forearms propped on his knees. A worried look filled his moon-shaped face with its odd, beaklike nose. His mild brown eyes communicated his concern as he looked at the Serpent.

Salamander tried to breathe in shallow gasps. The stench of feces, clotted blood, and closing death permeated the air. Even now, after having been smothered with it for days, it clung in his nostrils.

Death was everywhere. It filled his dreams, creeping out of the corners of his souls. It showed him Eats Wood's face as it rotted in some secret location. In his dreams, he watched the flesh turn brown, soften, and slip from the skull. In off moments, he felt the cracking of bone through the handle as he drove his axe through the top of Eats Wood's head. His souls flinched as the corpse twitched in his memory.

He hadn't expected killing to be like that. Not after the way the warriors spoke. He had found no glory in the murder of Eats Wood. Instead, he was plagued by an aching hollowness, the lingering nightmares, loss, and the bruise of regret.

Now Death lurked here, Dancing with the firelight, slipping among the shadows. It hovered with the smoke in the rafters, clinging to the sooty cane poles as it peered down at the dying Serpent with liquid black eyes.

My friend is dying. Who am I going to talk to now? Salamander's souls ached in anticipation of the coming loneliness.

The Serpent lay on his back, faceup, mouth gaping. Rasping air passed back and forth between his dry lips. His body was little more than bones with a thin leathery skin sagging off them. Only his belly, just left of the navel, was swollen. Scabs showed where Bobcat had punctured the skin, using a stone sucking tube to try and draw out the evil. When Salamander touched the lump, he discovered it was hard, like a rock.

"He said that it entered him sometime ago," Salamander replied wearily. "How could it beat him? He is the strongest of us."

"Sometimes evil is the strongest of all." Bobcat laced his fingers together.

They waited.

The Serpent muttered, half of the words garbled, but now and then a name would come out: that of someone long dead. Or a snatch of conversation, one-sided, as the Serpent babbled to someone only his frantically jerking eyes could see. At other times his limbs moved. He might have been walking in some distant time or place.

"He's talking to the Dead," Bobcat said. "It won't be long now, Salamander."

"Then they are all around us." He looked up at the cloudy smoke, hearing the rain pattering in puddles as it trickled off the roof. Ghosts? All around? Who were they? Was his uncle there? Did White Bird circle in the hazy smoke, looking down at Salamander?

Hello, Brother! Hello, Uncle. Are you there? His souls ached to speak with them again.

Bobcat reached into a bowl of filthy water and squeezed out a red-brown-stained cloth. The stench strengthened in the air. Raising the Serpent's stick of a leg, he wiped at the man's fouled anus and cleaned the slight dribble of urine from his thigh. Finished, Bobcat dropped the cloth back in the water.

"Wolf Dream," the old man gasped suddenly, his eyes flickering. He began to mumble:

> *"Raise the infants to the god in the sky.*
> *Earth, hey, Earth, from it spread,*
> *Raise the Underworld of the Dead."*

A rattle sounded in his throat before he added:

> *"Flight of the bird, so big, so loud.*
> *Calls the lightning from the cloud."*

"What is he saying?" Bobcat watched the old man as his mouth opened and closed, the tongue moving pink and silent behind his toothless gums.

Salamander leaned forward. "Serpent, are you saying that Masked Owl calls the lightning?" Coldness ran through him. "Did Masked Owl kill my brother?"

"Yes...coming...for the seeds..."

"The goosefoot seeds?"

The old man's eyes flickered weakly from side to side, the muscles spasming this way and that. "Not time..."

"Not time for what?" Salamander asked.

"We don't understand, Elder," Bobcat cried. "What are you trying to tell us?"

Muscles tensed in the Serpent's legs, his limbs pumping weakly then going still. His fingers nibbled, like a dog after a louse.

"Take...care, Salamander...between the gods." The Serpent shuddered, a croaking in his throat. "To see... mushrooms..."

The eyes rolled back, whites showing a tracery of blood vessels as the old man's shallow breathing came in weak gasps.

"Mushrooms?" Bobcat turned uneasy eyes on Salamander. "You have journeyed?"

"I rode the clouds with Masked Owl," Salamander replied absently, his souls locked on the Serpent's revelation. "My Spirit Helper? He killed my brother?"

Bobcat had a sick look on his face. "You should be the next Serpent, Salamander. The Elder always favored you."

"You know I cannot, Bobcat. Nothing has changed since the last time we had this conversation. I don't know the Songs, the ceremonies, or the rites. Power wants something different from me." He looked across at the young man, seeing the uncertainty in his eyes, the fear of the future falling so rapidly toward them. "You are the Serpent."

"But this thing between you and Masked Owl? You ride the sky with his wings? You are touched, Salamander. Power has woven itself through your life. You are part of things I cannot comprehend."

"Nor can I. However, I can tell you from my souls, you *must* be the Serpent. For all I know, I may be dead soon."

"Dead?"

Salamander rubbed his face wearily. "When one is caught between warring Powers, one can't count on digesting supper, let alone savoring its taste."

"What do you know?"

Salamander shook his head. "I can feel Death, sense it stalking me. In bits and fragments of Dreams, I am dead, Bobcat. It is coming so quickly—and I have only recently discovered what it means to be alive."

"You look frightened. I'm not used to that in you."

"I just don't know, Bobcat. That is the part that is driving me crazy! What am I supposed to do? What does Power want with me? Why *me,* of all the people to chose from?"

"If the Serpent knows, he's taking the answer with him to the Land of the Dead." Bobcat reached for the smelly cloth and cleaned the old man's anus again.

"The Land of the Dead," Salamander mused, his eyes straying to the lines of pots, stone bowls, and bags with their carefully tended herbs. Reaching over he lifted a thin bit of dried plant from one of the stone bowls, and stared at it with worried eyes.

"You're not thinking of going after him, are you?" Bobcat asked as he recognized the dried mushroom cap.

"I need answers, Bobcat."

"Are you willing to take the risk of losing your souls to get them?"

The Serpent whispered, "...*Sing, Sun God, blood rises...stingers...in the sky...*"

Stingers in the sky? The words rolled around Salamander's soul as he fingered the desiccated mushroom cap. *Do the answers lie there? Is that what you are trying to tell me, Serpent?*

A softening of the rattle in the Serpent's lungs was accompanied by a relaxation of his arms and legs.

The old man died.

Rain slanted down. Bobcat's breath fogged as he pranced around the Serpent's house and shook his painted turtle rattle. He Sang in the old tongue. In better weather he would have carried a torch with him, but the constant drizzle and intermittent rain hadn't let up for days. Clouds hung low overhead, heavy and dark with moisture.

Clan Elders and Speakers were gathered in the front of the crowd, breath misting as they stamped their cold feet in the mud. Cane Frog, Thunder Tail, Sweet Root, Clay Fat: they were all here, clustered around Pine Drop and Salamander to mourn the passing of the Serpent.

Pine Drop's heart ached at the expression on her husband's face. How did he deal with the terrible load that Power had placed upon his shoulders? She had come, hearing that Salamander and Bobcat had finished with the ceremonial preparation of the Serpent's corpse. When she had walked up to Salamander, she might have discovered another person inhabiting her husband's body.

Pine Drop shivered and reached out to take Salamander's hand. What was wrong with him? She had never seen him look so odd. He seemed hardly to be aware of the weather, of her, or the people around him. He was wet and clammy, his fabric cloak soaked. Rain dripped from the back of his square bark hat. He looked slack, unresponsive. Unshed tears pooled within his souls. When his eyes met hers, they had a liquid quality that unnerved her.

"Go free, Serpent!" Bobcat called as he ended the Song. Then he ducked into the doorway.

Because of Salamander's prestige as Speaker, he and Pine Drop stood in the front of the crowd and could see inside the low doorway. Bobcat lit a pine-tar torch from the central fire. In the flickering light, the Serpent's carefuly stripped bones gleamed where they rested on a wooden rick inside.

Bobcat raised the torch, holding it high so that it ignited the soot-stained interior thatch. For long moments, nothing seemed to happen, then blue smoke began welling out of the gaps between the roof and walls.

Bobcat ducked out, coughing, as thick smoke bellowed from the doorway behind him. He gasped mouthfuls of the cold clear air and sniffed before turning back to watch.

The fuel load overcame the saturated thatch, and a spear of yellow fire leaped up from the dark roof to challenge the sky. Steam hissed and popped. A huge plume rose as a low roar built, and sparks gyrated upward in the white-gray column.

"Goodbye to you, too, old friend." Salamander might have been answering an unheard speaker. He leaned his head back and let the rain pelt his face. "Yes, I hear you just fine. Your words are clear, Serpent. Look at you flying! Take him, Masked Owl. Bless his souls and fly with him to the One."

She glanced around uneasily and squeezed Salamander's hand. "Shhh! People are listening." *Snakes! What is he hearing?* Pine Drop considered the words, wondering what the One was. Then her husband shivered, and she could see pimpled flesh on his thin arms. The welling heat from the burning structure barely seemed to dent the cold.

Clay Fat stood just to their right, his round stomach dwarfing her pregnant belly. He was watching Salamander, puzzlement on his face.

"We'll miss him," Pine Drop said, trying to act as if nothing had happened.

"There won't be another like him anytime soon," Clay Fat replied, then looked up at the spiraling white plume that carried the Serpent's souls to freedom.

"A Serpent is a Serpent," Cane Frog muttered, her unseeing white eye blinking as she reached a hand out to feel the heat.

"Mother!" Three Moss hissed. "Keep your voice down!"

Pine Drop arched a slim eyebrow. *And they think Salamander is an idiot?*

"They think many things, Wife. It is a clutter. Hear them? Like a thousand birds." Salamander turned those eerie wounded eyes on hers.

Surely her thoughts hadn't sent that painful sliver into his souls?

Salamander tilted his head back to stare into the leaden sky. He didn't seem to mind the rain pattering on his open eyes. "One man's idiocy is another's Dream." A pause. "They have never seen the world from above."

Was anyone else hearing this? She looked past Salamander to where Mud Stalker stood with his mangled arm wrapped in warm fox hide. Uncle wore a conical hat that shed rain in all directions. His prune-sour expression reflected distaste at the event, the weather, and life in general. Everyone's spirits were down, as waterlogged as everything else in their world during the endless winter rain.

Deep Hunter and Thunder Tail stood next in line. It seemed like everywhere Thunder Tail went, Deep Hunter showed up.

He is being wooed. That knowledge sobered her. Too many things were changing. Even Mud Stalker and Deep Hunter—who had been lifelong rivals, barely sharing a civil word—stood together like brothers.

"They are hardly brothers, Wife," Salamander said absently, his dreamy eyes on the rising smoke and steam.

Snakes! I never spoke!

Salamander's tongue stumbled over the words. "You Dreamed it."

A sudden fear tightened around her souls as her eyes darted warily around. Her heart began to race, a fear, colder than the rain, tickling her skin.

Chapter Four

With a whoosh, one-half of the Serpent's roof let go. People stepped back as sparks and bits of burning thatch began sprinkling down from the sky.

"Come," Pine Drop said, tightening her grip on Salamander's hand. "You are cold, Husband. You have been up caring for the Serpent for a night and a day without sleep. You have done your duty."

"He's here. See him flying? Right here around us." Salamander raised his other hand, his finger pointing up into the rain. "Go in peace, my old friend."

Pine Drop jerked him hard enough to pull him off-balance. It took all of her strength to keep him from falling into the mud. People were watching, curiosity in their somber black eyes.

"What's wrong with you?" Pine Drop demanded as she tried to lead him away with some semblance of dignity.

"He was the only one who..." He caught himself, pinching his mouth closed.

"Who could understand?" she asked. "Is that what you were trying to say?"

He clamped his jaws, his huge glazed eyes looking back at the flames. Thunder! What was he seeing? Surely nothing of this world.

"Nothing of this world," he whispered.

She tugged insistently on his arm, desperate to get him away as fast as his ill-balanced tottering feet would carry him. By force of will she overpowered his reluctance to leave.

"Salamander, I would talk to you." She kept glancing around, trying to hide her fear, telling herself it was nothing. He was tired. That was all. Grief left him dazed, his souls crying for his lost teacher and friend.

Snakes help them if anyone heard his disjointed rambling!

"You have done enough! Come home. Anhinga and Night Rain have fixed something special."

"There is no hurry. The buffalo tongue hasn't baked all the way through yet." He might have been talking to a shadow. "I just have to make sure that he knows..."

"He knows, Husband. You and Bobcat made sure." She nearly jerked him off his feet again, aware of the stare that Clay Fat and Three Moss gave them. The latter had already leaned to whisper into Cane Frog's ear. When the old woman died, would Three Moss continue leaning over to whisper, even if only the empty air heard?

"It is her way," Salamander said simply.

The roar inside the Serpent's house was dying as Pine Drop pulled him down the ridge, their feet slopping in the silt. As they passed, rain dribbled from house roofs to patter into ring-shaped puddles around the walls. Wet dogs lay in the scant shelter of the over-hang before the house doors, looking cold, miserable, and starved.

"He told me so many things," Salamander said half to himself. "He opened my eyes to the One."

"The One?" He seemed to be half out of his head. Snakes, his souls weren't coming loose like his mother's, were they?

"The One," he whispered in assent. "The Dance. The place where Dreams cross." He smiled sadly. "What I would give! Oh, Pine Drop, I don't want to die. If I could only rise and fly away from all this. Just spread my wings...and fly!"

"I think your souls are loose enough already." She tightened her grip on his hand. She had to tug to keep him moving as they passed the head of the second ridge. His house huddled in the rain before them, faint threads of smoke lost in the downpour. She had kindled a fire there, just in case the rain stiffened. As it had.

She led him to the door and set it aside, ducked into the dark interior with him, and reset the cane door behind them. In the gloom she stepped over to the wood-pile. Placing several lengths on the glowing coals, she made the awkward descent around her pregnant belly to blow the embers to life. As the flames licked the logs with yellow light, she looked up. His eyes were large and hollow, his expression vacant. Water dripped off him to spatter on the ash-stained floor in little round star bursts.

She grunted as she stood up. He seemed oblivious, so she took the rain hat off his head. "You are soaked clear through, Salamander."

"His souls were loose," he said in that oddly

detached voice. "He didn't know who we were. One minute he was fighting evil spirits, the next he was grinning, curing people long dead. He was talking to the Dream Souls of the Dead. I never really understood. They're here, right in the air around us."

She took the wet cloak from his shoulders, shocked by its sodden weight, and laid it next to the fire to dry. She plucked the knot loose on his breechcloth and pulled the wet fabric from between his legs. Setting it aside, she positioned him over the fire, where the warm heat and smoke rose along his shivering naked body. Trickles of water ran down his skin, reflecting like silver veins in the firelight. Droplets beaded silver in his pubic hair.

"Stand there while I find you dry things." She waddled around to his bed and retrieved his buffalo hide. Wrapping it across his shoulders, she made sure the edges were well clear of the flames and backed onto the bench. Stripping off her own cloak, she realized she was as wet as he.

"Snakes, it feels good to be alone with you again." She glanced at him. "What is happening to you? Salamander? Please, tell me."

"You said Anhinga and Night Rain were expecting us?" At least that thought was lucid. Maybe his belly was eating through his grief.

"They are at my house. We thought it better. The food is there." *And I have you alone for the first time in weeks.*

"They do not expect us yet. Night Rain has just stepped outside. She can see the smoke plume through the rain."

W. Michael Gear & Kathleen O'Neal Gear

"How do you know that? You can't see through walls—let alone that far across the plaza."

"She doesn't think we're coming yet. She's ducking inside, telling Anhinga we will be longer."

"Salamander, you are frightening me! It's as if you can hear my thoughts. Talk to me. Are you well?" *Just tell me that the spirits haven't taken possession of your souls!*

The corners of his lips curled, threads of smoke rising from the confines of the tentlike buffalo hide. "I am the only one in possession of my souls. They bind me like rawhide. They suffocate me. It is so hard to breathe."

"What?" She placed a hand to her breast, searching his eyes for an answer.

"My souls are cages, like fish traps. I can't get free of them."

"I don't understand."

"You've never flown," he whispered sadly and closed his eyes.

"Flown?" she asked. "How did you fly?"

"Masked Owl comes. He shows me the way." His eyes were still closed, expression turning blissful. "Why can't I ever do it on my own? Why can't I break the cages that surround my souls?"

"Because you'll die," she cried.

"Death is release." He smiled. "I never understood until the Serpent told me."

"You really did talk to his souls?"

"It isn't like speaking, Pine Drop. It's different. Dreaming. I Dreamed him. I Dreamed them all. Saw into their souls."

42

"What do you mean, Dreamed them all? The other Speakers? The Clan Elders?"

"They are so bitter. Their souls taste like green walnut rind. They leave a yellow cast within me."

She nodded. "So many hands are raised against you, and I never hear a cross word, never see your temper flash. And sometimes, like today, you are gone somewhere, flying on Masked Owl's wings, I think."

She saw his smile growing. Her words had touched him.

"Salamander? They are drawing the net around you. You know that, don't you?"

He gave the barest nod.

"You can't just let them trap you."

"I am who I am." He was talking to emptiness again, eyes still closed. "I learn, watch, and absorb the lessons. I am Salamander, the one never seen. I have Danced with the mushrooms. I am floating."

"Mushrooms?" she asked, heart tapping hard against her breastbone. "What mushrooms?"

"I see your soul, Pine Drop. I see our daughter's life, glowing like an ember inside you."

You really are scaring me.

"I'm sorry. You have no reason to fear me."

Are you a mystic, or an idiot?

"You must understand: I am caught between Masked Owl and Many Colored Crow. The Serpent told me the night he died. Masked Owl killed White Bird."

"What?" She was suddenly oblivious to the water that ran down her forearms from the soggy fabric.

"He was warned, but his pride wouldn't let him stop. The goosefoot seeds, they would have changed this place. Changed us as a people. Masked Owl doesn't think it's time. So he killed White Bird."

"What are you talking about?"

"The Brothers, the Hero Twins. Born of Light, Born of Dark. Wolf Dreamer, Raven Hunter: the Two who make One."

"You see this in the Dream?"

"Yes."

"You're a Serpent?"

"No. I am the place where Dreams cross." His smile seemed to cast a glow into the gloomy interior.

"But...but Masked Owl. He is your Spirit Helper," she stammered, trying to understand. "And he *killed* your brother?"

"It is a battle for the souls of men. Just like the one being fought here. Between the clans. Power sways and rises, like mating copperheads, twining and spinning, Dancing, and pulling apart. Look at it! So very beautiful—and so deadly! We are all part of the One, forever split apart, lonely, yet united. I see now. I begin to understand."

He spread his arms wide. The buffalo robe unfolded like huge wings.

She gasped at the sight of his naked body. Lit from below, his thighs, the tip of his penis, his bony rib cage, and his jaw glowed orange. Shadows were cast across the hollows of his hips, over the twin arcs of his breasts. His eyes were hidden in blackness atop his lighted cheeks, his brow golden under a dark forehead. A man of fire and shadow, he stood before her, and she felt Power swelling within him.

"Salamander?" she asked timidly.

"Summer," he said suddenly. "I have until the solstice. They will move then."

"How can you fight them?" She shook her head. "Salamander, they are suspicious of me, but even I know that every clan is being turned against you. Deep Hunter is rabid, especially after Anhinga wounded and scarred Saw Back." She clenched her teeth. "The Speaker, my uncle, suspects you of murdering Eats Wood. The young man has disappeared, and no one knows where."

She was watching his face, searching for any reaction as she asked, "Did you have words with him? Did he threaten you?"

"I said nothing to him."

She heaved a sigh. "Snakes, I was worried."

His head tilted, the birdlike image ever sharper. "You may have to choose: Light or Dark. You may have to Dream with us."

She closed her eyes, souls dulling. *Blessed Sky Beings, what am I involved in here?* "Don't ask me to go against my clan, Salamander. Don't put me in that position."

"Would you chose the clan," he asked, "or the People?"

"I am nothing without the clan. Kinship is who we are. Without it, we are lost. Nothing. Faceless and nameless."

"Nothingness is all there is," he told her sadly. "It is the One. You can only understand when you Dance with it. The clans, this struggle to dominate, it is all empty, Pine Drop. In the end, it is as bitter as a green nightshade stem. Illusion, spinning around us like a waterspout."

"So you will just let them destroy you?"

"You stand at the center of the world, Pine Drop. When the time comes, you will reach out and pick a direction."

"What are you talking about?"

"The navel," he answered. "The place where life starts, and peoples are born. Something special is happening here. See it growing? Carried by the Trade, borne by the bonds we form. The future flows from within our ridges. Like that infant in your womb, Pine Drop, we have made the future. Sun Town is the starting point. The clans don't understand. They are bound, circumscribed by their mighty mounds."

"Is that bad?" she felt herself lost, adrift in the peculiar ideas spinning out of his Dream.

"When the time comes, you can reach out to them. Accept their canoes, and make the future."

"I can reach out to whom? What are you talking about?"

"I can Dream the future, Pine Drop. *You* have to *live* it!"

Blessed Owl, tell me he is not insane!

As the words formed in her souls, he threw back his head and laughed.

Sick! So very sick! Salamander curled on his side, eyes closed against the violence in his aching head. He kept one arm on his stomach, feeling the painful knots that had tied themselves in his guts. Between breaths, they pulled tight, only to twist and then loosen. The watery tickle of vomit hung behind his palate.

"Salamander?" Anhinga's voice came from far away. He barely felt her cool hand on his sweat-ridden forehead. "I went for help."

Anhinga? Where had she come from? Where was he? Floating. Floating above a dark pool of death.

"How are you feeling?" Pine Drop asked, also from a distance.

"Can't...dance..." he whispered, and in his fractured souls, the images of what he had experienced tried to form. Like bent and distorted memories, they wavered and refused to coalesce. As if part of his souls could just reach out. There. In the red-black haze beyond his consciousness.

"Drink this." The thick rim of a ceramic cup was placed to his lips.

He opened his eyes to slits. The misery of white light burned the backs of his eyeballs, searing his thoughts into charred meat. Cool liquid rolled around his tongue, only to make him gag as he tasted the bitterness. Nevertheless, he drank, each swallow knotted agony, until the cup was pulled away. He let his eyelids slide closed, accepting small relief in the hot acid darkness.

I am sick. Dying. The mushrooms are going to kill me, I wasn't strong enough. Help me! Help! By all the Beings in the Sky and Earth, Help me!

His calls echoed away like thunder over a distant and dark land.

He felt himself turning, ever so slowly as his body slipped away. His souls had begun to float, carried on the waves of fever, spasms, and chill. A burning sensation, like half-dead embers, lay heavily on his gut.

A dull glow—like a forest burning in the distance shone crimson in the darkness.

Dying.

The glow continued to grow, filling the horizons of his consciousness.

Help!

"Help you with what?" a crone's reedy voice asked.

Why are the mushrooms killing me this time?

"Because they want you to die."

He focused the eye of his Dream Soul, and saw her —a shadow behind the red glow.

Who are you?

"I have been called differently by different Dreamers. In the beginning I was *Spirit Woman* to some. *Witch* to others. Wolf Dreamer knew me by the name of old Heron. Other names have come and gone through the passing of ages."

What are you doing here?

"I heard you call, boy. It happens, with the ones who have Power."

I called you?

"Not by name," she told him.

He could see her now. She didn't look like the old woman her voice suggested, but beautiful, with gleaming black eyes that danced with internal light. Sharp cheekbones made soft angles over her full mouth and delicate chin. Hair, in a raven wealth, tumbled from her head and pooled around her shoulders before spilling down to her waist. Her high breasts and narrow waist were partially hidden by a white bear hide that she draped around her naked flanks.

You are beautiful!

"Not as beautiful as Broken Branch was." She

smiled, and he felt his souls soaring. "I can appear as I please. For the moment, it pleases me to appear as I was, before I tripped over love and fell face first into the Dream."

Are you one of the Sky Beings?

"Older." She stepped closer in a fluid grace. "I was there at the beginning. I have been here since, tied to Power. I came before First Woman, before First Man. I was there before Runs In Light Dreamed the Wolf. I have Sung the Sacred Bundles, and watched the world change. I have seen the final Dance of the mammoth, mastodon, sloth, and short-faced bear. I have loved and cursed the People, and tricked and beguiled the Dreamers as they came and went. I have Danced between the Hero Twins." She smiled, and the radiance of it melted his heart. "As you now Dance between them."

You mean Masked Owl and Many Colored Crow?

"They, too, have had many names." She cocked her head, exposing her perfect throat. "Who are you, boy?"

Salamander.

"You are aptly named." Her dark gaze sharpened like obsidian. "Powerful, boy. The golden haze of the mushrooms surrounds you. Dangerous things, mushrooms. They live off Death, grow out of rot and corruption. They are rebirth, Salamander. Treat them with respect. Never toy with them. The most Powerful Dreaming of all comes of Dancing with the mushrooms. Unless you become the One, they will kill you."

Sick. So sick. Pain is tying knots in my body. My bones and muscles ache. My souls...they are floating up into Death.

"Why did you wish to Dance with brother mushroom? What were you trying to do, Salamander?"

I wanted to Dream. To fly on Masked Owl's wings. I wanted a vision! To see the channels of the future. I must know why Masked Owl gave me such gifts—and killed my brother. Why did Many Colored Crow warn me? What does Power want of me? How can I do what is right when I don't know what Power wants?

She was so close now, he could almost reach out and touch her. He had never seen skin so beautiful, soft, and sleek. Her perfect round breasts rose and fell behind the white bear's hide. "Do you ask for yourself, for your own gain? Is it glory you seek? Fame? Authority or prestige?"

I just need to understand, Heron! That is all. I want to know what to do. What is right. For everyone.

"My poor young Dreamer, are you truly so naive? People are good and evil at the same time, in the same breath, in a single heartbeat. Justice for one is injustice for another."

Would you help me?

"What would you give for my help?" She gave him a predatory stare.

Fear stabbed through him. *Whatever you asked.*

"Would you give your life? Would you let me destroy you? What if I say I will help, and let brother mushroom take you here, now? Alone? Will you give me your souls here, in the darkness?"

How did he answer that? How could he do the right thing if he were dead? How could he make things better if he didn't understand? How could he find the One?

"Ah, the One? That is a different matter entirely." She laughed, the sound so musical his souls ached at the beauty. "You are not even close to finding the One, Salamander. You have a long, long way to go." Her expression saddened. "And no one among your people to teach you. Like me, you must find it on your own."

Grief stung him.

Heron's gleaming eyes ate through his souls, turning him inside out, seeing into the corners, behind his thoughts. Fear paralyzed him, and he cried out. In that instant, he felt himself vanishing, burning away under the heat of her blazing dark eyes.

She's eating me! She is devouring my souls. Terror, horrible engulfing terror, filled him as she violated every corner of his souls, eviscerated his memories and thoughts, and inspected his most private fantasies. Bit by bit she tore pieces out of him the way a fisherman plucked guts from a catfish's belly.

It seemed an eternity before she backed away, leaving him whimpering and weak like a wounded puppy. Her chin was down, brow furrowed. This time her eyes didn't violate him, but simply watched in a passive stare.

After an eternity, she said, "You are an unusual young man, Salamander." She paused. "You would have made a great Dreamer."

I won't be a Dreamer? Nothing had prepared him for the sense of loss that washed atop his fear.

She smiled then, an expression of pity on her perfect lips. "Nothing comes without a price."

A feeling of despair washed through him. How did he chose between Dreaming and helping his people? How did he know what was right. *It would be easier to let brother mushroom kill me.*

"It would." Her smile challenged him. "Is that your choice?"

No. I will live.

"Once upon a time, I, too, followed the path you have taken. Brother mushroom can show you a great many things, but unless you are trained, it is illusion. Not to be taken lightly."

I know.

"I will help you Dance with brother mushroom's Power. We will have to do this together, you, and I, and brother mushroom."

Thank you!

"Do not thank me, Salamander. My help will rouse jealousies. Wolf Dreamer and Raven Hunter rarely join forces, but my interference could be enough to ally them against you."

Who?

"You know them as Masked Owl and Many Colored Crow. They are the Hero Twins, the brothers of Light and Dark. Terrible things happen when opposites are crossed."

She reached out, her slim fingers tracing his cheek. Waves of cool relief washed through him. Had he ever felt such pleasure?

"You cannot escape brother mushroom by yourself, Salamander." She stepped closer, her ethereal body a hand's breadth from his. Her dark eyes sucked at his souls. "You do not know the way to the One. I will have to Dance it with you. In the process, you can see the channels of the future. I warn you now, it will come at a price, young Salamander. Will you pay it?"

Yes.

He was aware of the white bearhide as she wrapped it around them, pulling his souls against hers, locking them together. He opened his mouth to cry out.

And then...ecstasy!

Chapter Five

S ecrets! The whole world was filled with secrets! Night Rain fumed, but it did little good. She kept her own secrets, while the secrets of others remained hidden from her. She didn't want to be here, out in the cold gray day, pinned in place by her uncle. Alone, she had to bear that hard penetrating look in his eyes.

Mud Stalker clamped a hand on her shoulder. "You must have heard something about Eats Wood?"

"I can tell you honestly that I have never heard my husband or Anhinga mention Eats Wood. Not once."

Uncle's gaze pricked at her souls like a copper needle. "He vanished the last time that barbarian bitch left Sun Town, Niece." His eyes narrowed. "You and I, I thought we had a special relationship. Especially after our last little talk."

Like a fish in a weir, she could feel bars rising to catch her. "I would hope that we do, Uncle."

He shook his head, glancing around at the blustery brown day. "I raised you better. Think, woman, what could you possibly owe that barbarian bitch? And after what she did to you? The way she humiliated you?"

Night Rain bit her lip.

"What are you hiding?" Mud Stalker shifted, leaning back. "Don't trifle with me, woman. I've been at this game for so long I can smell deception."

"I swear to you on my souls that I haven't heard a single word about Eats Wood from anyone! Salamander hasn't mentioned him. Neither has Anhinga!"

"And your sister?"

"I can only tell you that she doesn't think Salamander had anything to do with his disappearance."

"What does Deep Hunter say?"

"I haven't seen him since I went home to my husband."

"And Saw Back?"

"I haven't seen him either, and I don't want to."

He watched her through narrowed eyes. "For the right reasons I could be tempted to support a divorce. Owl Clan couldn't deny us—and that silly Moccasin Leaf would agree to fly off to the moon if I asked her to. She is desperate to curry our favor."

"No, Uncle."

"What?"

She glared at him. "I will stay with Salamander." Assuming she could figure out who this new Salamander was. During his illness, something had changed. When he looked at her now, it was with a longing that melted her souls. She could feel it, a sensation of Power that spun around him. It was as if he could touch a winter-dry stem, and it would burst into bloom.

Uncle, his eyes narrowed, might have heard her

thoughts the way Pine Drop claimed that Salamander had heard hers. "What is it, Night Rain? Snakes and poison! I'm your uncle. You can tell me. What hold does he and that cunning barbarian witch have on you and Pine Drop? Is it witchcraft? Some spell he's cast on the two of you?"

"He is my husband," she replied softly. "I can't... well you wouldn't understand." Snakes! How did she explain to her hard-eyed uncle that no matter what happened in their bed, but for Salamander's goodwill she'd be a laughingstock throughout Sun Town? That in his arms, she was safe from the guffaws and jokes?

Mud Stalker studied her thoughtfully. "I saw him the day of the old Serpent's cleansing. He was hearing things, talking to the air. His eyes were vacant, as hollow as the Land of the Dead. Pine Drop was so frightened she dragged him away—and then he was out of sight for days, rumor said he was sick."

"He was." Night Rain swallowed hard. "He ate mushrooms. Something he found at the Serpent's after cleaning the bones. It did something to him."

"I see. Are you sure it wasn't poison? Something a witch would be involved in?"

"Salamander? A witch? No, Uncle, he's no witch." *But what is he?* That question had begun to preoccupy so many of her thoughts.

"You are protecting him! Why? What has he done to you?"

"Nothing!"

He grunted, lips pressed in thin anger.

"I have told you the truth." She could feel sweat beginning to warm her armpits, and the flush that rose in her face.

"Yes," he hissed. "I see. The truth." He paused, as if an idea had been born in his head. "A witch would have many ways to bend people to his will. And, what if..."

"What if what?" she demanded, a feeling of unease creeping through her.

Mud Stalker's smile took on a predatory look. "If I asked you to make a choice, would you choose to serve your clan, or Salamander?"

"The clan," she insisted doggedly.

He chuckled then, a coldness in his eyes. "Remember this day, Niece. I will hold you to your words."

She breathed a sigh of relief when he stalked off. But what had been behind that last hard look?

Salamander sat with his back to the clay-daubed wall and watched his mother as she worked at her loom. Her hair, once so dark and perfectly kept, now reminded him of dirty cottonwood seed, windblown and tumbled. Her face had sagged. He thought the tissue that had once held it to the bone had grown tired and no longer cared.

A yellow fire popped in the central hearth, sending sparks to dance up toward the rafters. Above him the packed thatch slumbered under a blanket of soot. Bags and netting hung from the high poles, preserving the last of the pecans and acorns against the coming of spring. The other bags he remembered from fall had disappeared over the winter.

His mother's bed, on the west side of the house, was

unkempt, as if she'd just thrown the buffalo robe to one side and gone about her work.

"I have come to understand something," Salamander said. "About you. I began to understand the night I watched the Serpent's souls rising. With the help of the mushrooms, I could hear his souls."

His mother slapped at her ear as if pestered by a mosquito.

"I think you tried so hard to talk to Uncle Cloud Heron that your Dream Soul slipped into the realm of the Dead. When White Bird died, he took the last of your world with him. I understand why you would want to send your souls after White Bird and Cloud Heron." He paused. "I have seen the different paths of the future, Mother. I have to make some terrible choices. It would be so easy just to let go. She tilted her head, her fingers using the shuttle to pass more of the white thread through the warp. If he listened intently, he could hear the soft hum of the Lotus Gathering Song coming from deep in her throat.

"I want you to know that I don't blame you." He looked down at his thin hands. "Since I Danced the One with brother mushroom and old Heron, I have been haunted by what is coming. There is a very good chance that I will lose everything: my wives, my children, my family and clan. How am I supposed to choose between my life and a Dream?"

She plucked a knot out of the weave, part of a pattern of interwoven flowers and swooping eagles.

"I caught a faint glimpse of myself in the future. Old, wise, and surrounded by my children and grandchildren. At that moment, I knew complete contentment. I was surrounded by love the way a person is bathed with golden morning sunshine in the spring. I had this knowledge that I had lived my life to the fullest. My souls were bursting, and my wives were smiling their love at me. It was so wonderful!"

He smiled at the glorious ache of happiness.

Wing Heart mouthed words, lips moving silently.

"Another part of the vision let me share the One. Old Heron Danced me through it. You cannot imagine! Mother, it is bliss. Like flying while weighing nothing. The purity of that brief instant makes a part of my souls crave it with a hunger you can't conceive." He shook his head. "No words will describe the silent thunder of its beauty. How can I give that up?"

She began to hum louder. He could see the thin muscles in her neck and imagine the brittle bones under that sagging skin.

"Another fragment of the vision showed me Sun Town, tens of tens of tens of years from now. All that was left was unbroken forest. The People were scattered, living in little villages among the trees. We no longer built our giant earthworks, no longer built monuments to the Creator and the Sky Beings. The Trade was dead. Each tiny band feared its neighbors. They lived in isolation." He shook his head. "They had lost their souls, Mother. Had lost that inner strength that told them who they were. I felt such emptiness."

He watched Mother's long fingers. Never had anyone seen such fabrics as those that came off of Wing Heart's loom after she lost her souls. The weave, so tightly packed, could hold water. The intricate designs she wove into the warp and weft were magical. The creatures she created looked real. Even the texture of feathers could be seen in the pattern of threads she used to make her birds. Veins filled the leaves and flowers. With a fingertip, one could trace the texture of bark on the stems she wove.

"I caught another flash of the future. Of all the bits and pieces of visions, this is in many ways the hardest to explain. The people were so different. They lived for one ruler, crushing all others under their feet for his glory. Imagine what the clans would be like if instead of obligation, they used force to achieve their ends. What makes that future enticing is the size of the cities, the splendor of the high mounds and great buildings. I see canoes so huge they carry tens of tens, and cross the oceans to the ends of the world. We could be so great." He shook his head. "Imagine your great-grandchildren raising mounds in the distant lands. Imagine them speaking your name in barbarian languages."

Wing Heart smiled despite her empty eyes. Her lips must have felt something the rest of her body did not.

"I don't understand how the visions are linked together yet. The choices I make will influence those futures. To make one come true, I must give up some- thing else. I just don't know how it all fits together." He leaned his head back, an emptiness in his breast. "I can see the coming trial. I know what they have in store for me. I have seen it, Mother. When I flew with Masked Owl, I caught glimpses, but only those that Masked Owl wanted me to see. When Heron and I Danced with brother mushroom, I saw the whole future unfolding like a magnolia flower in the morning."

She chuckled under her breath, hearing something in her imagination. The twitching of her lips slowed, humor in her eyes before it faded to blankness.

"I understand why you made the choice you did. I wish I could choose the past, too. It would be so easy." Salamander frowned down at his hands. "I could tell Heron that I wanted to Dance the One. She could take me away from all of this. How does a lone man make that decision? How can Power expect me to choose misery over paradise?"

Wing Heart gave him no answer.

"Oh, Mother, how I envy you."

Mud Stalker lay with his back pressed into the rounded stern of the canoe and peered out through the screen of cane and grass that had been tied around their craft. He fingered the hard knot of his bola with his good left hand. The weapon lay on his flat stomach. The bola was a series of three leather thongs the length of a man's arm, each tied with a round stone at the end. When thrown, it rotated through the air like a three-legged spider to ensnare whatever it encountered.

In the bow, Clay Fat lay with his bulk wedged between the gunwales. The Rattlesnake Clan Speaker made the bow float considerably lower in the muddy shallows than Mud Stalker's stern.

On the strengthening southern winds, the migratory fowl were riding their way northward toward spring. Sun Town lay at the southern end of the great flyway. This was just the beginning of the great migration. For days the flocks would blacken the sky, Vs of birds winging northward. From it the people harvested any number of ducks, geese, coots, cormorants, herons, and other species.

Mud Stalker's clan had used this old choked channel for many turnings of the seasons. Last night he and his kin had strung nets along three sides of the narrow cove. The netting was stretched from tree to tree, and propped on posts to overhang the brackish water.

The open end that emptied onto a sluggish channel had two screened blinds at the entrance: One that he and Clay Fat rested behind, and the other, opposite them, where Red Finger and Thumper waited, their canoe obscured with a similar willow, grass, and cane blind.

In the middle of the trap, duck decoys made of feathers, wood, and bundled reeds floated in a fair imitation of a flock.

Mud Stalker's party had been here, waiting for more than a hand of time. Two flocks had gone winging past, neither falling for the bait.

Red Finger clicked a warning that brought Mud Stalker alert.

He heard the rasping of wings before he spotted the ducks—mallards all—flying up the main channel. Immediately Thumper began his quacking and chattering. Of all the hunters in Snapping Turtle Clan, none was as talented when it came to calling ducks.

To Mud Stalker's delight, the flock turned, wheeled overhead, and came swooping in to land just past the decoys.

"Be ready!" Mud Stalker whispered as he loosened the cord that held their blind up. He would have to drop the blind, grab the knot of his bola, straighten, and cast as if in one motion.

"Ready!" Clay Fat said in a breathy exhale.

In heartbeats the ducks would detect the ruse. Mud Stalker, as hunt leader, watched the ducks as they splashed to a halt behind the decoys. Paddling, they turned to inspect the decoys. They couldn't have been more perfectly placed in the trap.

Thumper was continuing his calling, making the sounds ducks made by blowing air past his cheeks, onto the back of his hand, and clicking his tongue.

"Now!" Mud Stalker called, letting the blind fall and sitting upright. As he rose he grasped the center of his bola, whirling it around his head. The taut thongs hissed as they tore through the air.

The ducks began to bolt, reaching out with their wings as they turned away from the falling blinds.

Mud Stalker made his cast. From long practice, the whirling stones, bound by their leather thongs, sailed out, neatly wrapping around the nearest mallard, fouling her wings.

Clay Fat, too, cast—then capsized their canoe as he floundered out into the knee-deep water.

Mud Stalker clawed for balance, then closed his eyes as cold murky water rolled over him. He thrashed, twisted his way upright, and managed to get his feet under him. As he shot up out of the water, he flipped his head to clear his vision.

Clay Fat was howling, sloshing like a giant buffalo through the water. Mud churned in his wake. Across from them, Red Finger and Thumper were likewise charging forward, waving their arms and howling.

Retreat cut off, the panicked ducks flapped and paddled, taking off straight into the overhanging nets. As they entangled themselves, the net was pulled loose, dropping down over the frightened birds.

"YoooYaaah!" Clay Fat yelled, splashing from foot to foot in the waist-deep water. Mud Stalker ran his hand over his wet face. Next time the big oaf could wait in a blind onshore. He looked back at the capsized canoe, the gunwales just breaking water, then waded over and grabbed up his bola-entangled duck. He grasped the duck by the head, whirling it around and around until he broke the bird's neck. Then he unwound the leather thongs from the wings.

Ahead of them, the mallards thrashed in the net. In a line, the men waded forward, taking the ends of the netting and gathering it in.

"Where's your canoe?" Thumper asked as he floated his up to the catch.

"Underwater." Mud Stalker jabbed a thumb over his shoulder.

"There's a lot of me to get out of a canoe in a hurry," Clay Fat said with a wide grin. "It was faster just to turn it over."

"And drown me in the process," Mud Stalker growled, but he could see Clay Fat's delight. The Rattlesnake Clan Speaker was happy. Against that, a dunking in the water hardly mattered.

One by one they retrieved the terrified ducks from the netting, breaking their necks and tossing their spasming carcasses into Thumper's canoe. In the end, they had trapped three tens and eight, a nice morning's work. The feathered mound in the middle of Thumper's canoe gleamed cream, brown, and greenish blue in the light. In the pile of ruffled wings he could see orange-webbed feet, yellow bills agape, and the green-headed males, their eyes dimming and half-lidded in death.

Feathers from the spring molt drifted in the calm air and dotted the roiled water.

"Come," Clay Fat called to Mud Stalker as Thumper and Red Finger began drawing in the net, neatly folding it between them. "Let us right your canoe. They can take the catch, we'll carry the net."

"If you don't sink us again."

It took but a moment to lift one end, shipping the water out. The knuckle's worth that sloshed in the bottom didn't seem to bother Clay Fat as he carefully climbed aboard. Their paddles were recovered from where they floated under the crushed blind.

Slipping over the stern, Mud Stalker seated himself and tucked his paddle under his right arm, using his left awkwardly to maneuver the craft around. They paddled up to where Red Finger and Thumper waited. The two men carefully lifted the wet net and settled it amidships.

"Don't lose Clay Fat's ducks on the way back to Sun Town," Mud Stalker warned. "The Speaker will sink your canoe next time."

That brought a round of good-humored laughter from everyone.

"Are you sure you want to give me all of those ducks?" Clay Fat asked, as they paddled out to the main channel.

"You seemed to take the greatest pleasure in the hunt. I still have ducks from last fall. Snakes, my sister keeps insisting on boiling one every ten days. I'm tired of duck meat."

"But these are fresh. Not dried and covered with soot. They won't taste like smoke and mold."

Mud Stalker laughed, making his irregular strokes

with his paddle. "Enjoy them. It is a gift from Snapping Turtle Clan to you, Speaker."

"We are obligated."

"Can I ask you a question?"

"Of course."

"Clay Fat, were you and Wing Heart ever lovers?"

"No." A cautious pause. "Why do you ask?"

He jerked his head back, indicating Thumper's canoe where it followed a couple of lengths behind them. "My cousin back there was married to her for a while. In a fit, one night, she divorced him. I think she was mad at me and took it out on Thumper. It hurt him more than he ever admits. I think he really loved her."

"We were never lovers." Clay Fat sounded sad.

"Just...what? Friends?"

"Yes. I always admired her. I enjoyed just sitting, talking to her. Some of those times were the best in my life. I can remember the dark sparkle in her eyes, the way her throat looked when she laughed. In all of my Dreams I would never have thought she'd have lost her souls like she did. She was so strong. I thought she was the smartest Clan Elder I'd ever met."

"From your voice, I can tell you liked her." He made a face. "She and I fought like weasels."

"She always enjoyed beating you."

"I'm sure. That's why, in the end, I let her win."

"Indeed?" Clay Fat's tone was neutral.

"What do you mean, *indeed*? How could any of us have stood against White Bird? The youth would have made one of the greatest Speakers ever."

"He didn't last very long if you will recall."

"You needn't remind me. I grouse every time I remember that I married my favorite nieces to him.

Who would have thought they would have gone to that
skinny little scorpion?"

"I'm not sure I'd use that word to describe him."

"How well do you know Salamander?"

"I saw him a lot at Wing Heart's."

"Was he always into sorcery?"

Clay Fat was silent.

"My nieces are married to him. They haven't been
the same since they went to his bed."

After a while longer, Clay Fat asked, "Don't you
think sorcery is a harsh word? Are you sure it isn't just
jealousy? Perhaps they like him?"

"Do you think my girls would like that Swamp
Panther bitch, too? No, I tell you, there's something
going on there. I tried to get Night Rain to tell me the
other night. She insists on hiding something." Mud
Stalker paused, then cast his gaming pieces. "Tell me,
what did you hear him say the other day at the
Serpent's cleansing?"

"He was talking to his dead friend." But Clay Fat
didn't sound too certain.

"Did you see how quickly Pine Drop dragged him
away? Did you see the expression on his face? The way
his eyes looked? That wasn't a man in grief, my friend."

"Now that you mention it, he looked almost
euphoric. As if he were seeing something wonderful
instead of the freeing of a dead Serpent's souls."

"What did he ever get from the Serpent, anyway?"

"The old man liked him."

"They processed bodies together. Salamander spent
a great deal of time with the old man. I'm not sure he
wasn't learning other things."

"Such as?"

"Poisons. The dark uses of Power. Is Salamander truly an idiot, or is that just what we are supposed to think?"

Silence.

"I want you to remember that, Clay Fat. I want you to keep an open mind. You owe me nothing for the ducks but your promise that you will keep an eye on Salamander. And consider him anew."

"I will, Speaker. But what are you really thinking? That Salamander is a sorcerer?"

"Do you remember the night of his initiation? He talked to spirits! He laughed, Speaker. When has any young man laughed? And do you remember how the Serpent stalked off into the night? Had you ever seen him do that before? I hadn't. Let me add one last thing: Salamander's enemies never seem to last long."

"I don't understand."

"His uncle, Cloud Heron, lingered in death for many moons. Curious, wasn't it, that he didn't die until White Bird had returned from the north?"

"You can't blame that on Salamander."

"Who stood between him and the Speakership?"

"White Bird."

"He is dead."

"Salamander can't throw lightning, Speaker."

"What did Wing Heart think of her youngest son? Did she like him? Was she proud of him?"

"No." Clay Fat didn't sound so sure of himself anymore.

"And what happened to your old friend, Wing Heart? What kind of person can drive his own mother's souls away?"

"I can't believe that Salamander is a witch! He

doesn't look like one, doesn't act like one. He's not that smart."

"Perhaps he isn't," Mud Stalker said offhandedly, knowing full well the seed had been planted. "What about his Swamp Panther wife? Eats Wood had been spying on Anhinga. He came to me, telling me that he suspected she was here to harm us. Do you remember that she went away every moon, even when her belly was swollen with Salamander's child?"

"Yes."

"She was meeting with Jaguar Hide. Eats Wood was sure."

"Did he ever see her meet with him?"

"He did. From a distance. The thing is, the last time he left to spy on her, he never came back. I have no proof, but as I said before, I just want you to think about these things. Especially about what happens to people who are close to Salamander."

"You have two nieces married to him. What do they say?" Clay Fat's voice had taken on a pensive tone.

"They say nothing, Speaker. If you were married to a witch, to someone who could drive his own mother's souls away, would you say anything?"

A deep frown lined Clay Fat's forehead.

"Oh, forget it. It's probably nothing." Mud Stalker smiled.

Pine Drop rinsed her cloth in a bowlful of water before she bent over and sponged Anhinga's brow. Outside a wind whispered and moaned, driven by a spring storm. Had she ever known such a wet winter and spring? No sooner did one storm blow itself out than another rolled in.

Anhinga lay on a bison hide that padded the dirt floor. To her side the fire crackled and popped, its flame illuminating the inside of Salamander's house. Over the winter, soot had blacked the roof and laid velvet fingers on the hanging bags of squash, smoked fish, jerked venison, and the desiccated carcasses of geese, ducks, and turkeys that hung from the rafters.

Anhinga gasped as another contraction tightened in her belly. Pine Drop smiled down at her in reassurance and took one of her hands, squeezing it. She glanced at Water Petal. Steady as a stone, Salamander's cousin had seen them through the long watch.

"Aiiahhh!" the cry broke through Anhinga's clenched teeth. Her pretty face contorted, and water beaded on her skin before trickling down the lines of pain.

"You must push now," Water Petal said as she squatted between Anhinga's bent knees.

Night Rain watched from the side, a wad of dried hanging moss in her hands ready to soak up fluids. She had sponged up the Swamp Panther woman's water several hands of time ago.

Pine Drop continued to hold Anhinga's hand, squeezing firmly. "Don't fight it. When the time is right, when your womb is ready, the little one will come."

Anhinga's expression relaxed, and she gasped for air. "By the Panther's Bones, nothing prepared me for this."

"It is a first child," Water Petal reminded. "Your body has never done this before. That infant has to push your hipbones apart."

"Crack them in two, you mean." Anhinga gasped as another contraction tightened inside of her.

"Push," Pine Drop told her. "Push."

The realization that she herself was only two moons from this same ordeal brought a trickle of fear into Pine Drop's guts. She absently reached down with her free hand to feel the swell of her pregnancy.

"I'm...ah..." Anhinga didn't finish but gasped a full breath, chest swelling, her heavy breasts taut as she bit down hard and grimaced with the effort.

Water Petal looked up, met Pine Drop's eyes, and said, "It is soon. She is opening."

"By Panther's blood!" Anhinga gasped, her head flopping weakly to the side as she gulped breath. "My insides are tearing apart!"

"If they were, I would be seeing a lot of blood," Water Petal answered matter-of-factly. She patted one of Anhinga's brown knees, her critical eyes monitoring.

"And there isn't?" Anhinga asked.

"A bit. Watery. Just what's normal."

The next contraction brought Anhinga's head up. Strong thigh muscles slid under her smooth brown skin as she strained. Her hand tightened on Pine Drop's in a grip the likes of which would slip the skin from her finger bones.

"Aaiiiahhh!" she cried. Her legs were trembling.

Pine Drop saw the change, the difference in the swell of Anhinga's belly as the infant moved lower.

"Soon, now." Water Petal smiled. "The tissue down here is swollen. Night Rain, be ready to hand me that moss."

Anhinga's jaw worked like a beached fish's. She

kept blinking against the sweat as Pine Drop wiped her brow with the damp cloth.

"Deep breath. Push!" Water Petal ordered, as Anhinga contorted with another contraction. "Hold it! Keep pushing!"

Pine Drop bent to one side in time to see Anhinga's red vaginal lips peel out and part as the blood-streaked globe appeared. "Push!" she cried. "The head's almost out!"

"Arghhh!" Anhinga gasped a lungful of air, curled up, and tightened her muscles. Her eyes were wide, staring, as the mound of her belly deflated.

Water Petal smiled in delight as the infant slid into her hands. Pine Drop could only stare at the wet thing, splotched in red, its unsightly blue color picking the odd memory of fish guts from her memory.

Night Rain thrust handfuls of hanging moss out, looking oddly cowed by the sight of the squirming infant, slick with fluid, its thick umbilical trailing back into Anhinga's vagina.

With practiced hands, Water Petal wiped the mouth clean. She turned the infant facedown, lifting the hips and massaging the lungs. Fluid dribbled from the mouth, and Pine Drop watched the baby take its first breath. It coughed, expelled more fluid, then drew its lungs full and squalled.

"A girl," Water Petal told the exhausted Anhinga. "Your lineage has an heir."

Anhinga lay panting, her hands knotted into fists. She had fixed her eyes on something beyond the dark roof. A weak shudder ran through her.

Water Petal used a white chert flake to sever the umbilical. She tied it off with calloused fingers. Mindless of the infant's squalls, she continued to wipe the now-pinking flesh dry. "There, there, little one. You are safe among us. We want you to know that you are welcome here, and we hope that good souls come to fill your body."

Pine Drop sat back, one hand on her belly. "I pray that it will be that easy for me."

"Easy?" Anhinga rasped. "My guts are pulled in two."

It was Night Rain who said, "I don't know about the rest of you, but I don't think I'm going to let Salamander's manhood ride in my canoe again. It isn't worth it. I can find my pleasure in some other way than with a man."

"You'll take Salamander back to your bed." Water Petal chuckled dryly. "Having been through this, I can tell you that the body forgets the pain, remembering only the pleasure." She arched an eyebrow. "Night Rain? Could you go find Salamander? He's atop the Bird's Head, praying. Tell him he has a daughter, and that his wife is healthy, too."

"I'll be right back." Night Rain ducked out the door into the windy evening.

Pine Drop sighed, smiling down at Anhinga. "How do you feel? The afterbirth still has to come out."

"In its own time." Anhinga raised her arms to take the tiny infant to her breast. As the little pink mouth found the nipple, Anhinga closed her eyes. "By the Panther's blood, that feels good."

"Is she sucking?" Water Petal asked. "Are you making milk?"

Anhinga nodded, and Pine Drop noticed the wetness around the baby's mouth. "She's doing fine."

Water Petal grinned. "Well, women, that's that. No complications. We're off to a good start." She reached up, massaging her own breast. "It brings a tenderness to me."

"You will have more children," Pine Drop said evenly. "We pray for you."

Anhinga's breathing turned shallow. She blinked, tears hidden behind her eyes as she said, "Thank you. Thank you all for staying with me."

"We are a household," Pine Drop said, speaking for all of them. "You would have been there for us."

"If I survive this"—a faint smile crossed her lips— "I'll look forward to watching your expression as I repeat all the things you told me."

Pine Drop laughed as she handed Water Petal the damp rag to clean her hands. *So, somehow, in the face of looming disaster, we have become a household. What a delight it would be if forces were not gathering to destroy us all.*

Chapter Six

S alamander crouched in the darkness, his bone stiletto driving into the dark soil. He laid it to the side and used his fingers to pull the loosened earth from the hole. In his other hand, he held the baked silt effigy recovered from under Anhinga's bed. The hard part had been wiping the fetish with the afterbirth. It had taken all of his wits to accomplish that before Water Petal took it out beyond the rings for a proper burial.

He looked up at the night sky, so incredibly clear on this moonless equinox night. The stars wove patterns of white across the blackness. Bird Man's trail looked like fog running from north to south.

"Are you watching, old friend?" Salamander stared up into the darkness. "My wife's baby was born healthy. I am here, as you told me to be. I remember what you instructed me to do."

He reached down and grasped the little figurine around the head with one hand and the body with the other. Twisting, he snapped the neck cleanly. Then, laying the pieces in the hole, he covered them with the dark earth. "Thank you, Elder. I ask your souls to look over us, to watch out for this little infant girl who has joined our lives. Anhinga has enemies here who would harm her and her child. Guard us from all manner of evil."

He picked up his stiletto and stood in the darkened ring of the Serpent's burned house. His old friend's flat face smiled at him from the firelit warmth of his memories. Did he feel that warm soul drifting around him now?

Bobcat's cleansing on the Turtle's Back was almost complete. He would come here with the full moon and begin construction of a new Serpent's house on the foundation of the old one. It had always been thus, one Serpent after another living on this spot on the third ridge in the center of Owl Clan's territory.

In that instant, he could feel Power washing around him. Unseen eyes peered at him out of the darkness. Just how many of those little figurines were lying buried around here? How many of the Dead pressed around him, stroking his skin with their fingers? The thought of it brought a shiver to his cool flesh, and he turned his steps for home.

A couple of dogs barked at him, but no one would be out this late at night. He walked alone, accompanied only by the Dream Souls of the Dead.

He ducked into his doorway and crossed to Anhinga's bed before lifting the buffalo hide and slipping next to his wife's warm body.

"What was that?" Anhinga asked, catching him by surprise.

"What was what?"

She shifted, and he could feel her eyes with the same intensity that he had those of the ghosts. "That thing you dug up from under my bed?"

He took a deep breath. "I thought you were asleep."

"The infant was sucking. I watched you dig something out from under the bed."

"A charm," he told her. "Something the Serpent gave me before he died to ensure that your pregnancy was healthy. Now that you and the little girl are all right, I had to care for it properly."

"That is all it was?"

He could hear suspicion in her voice and slipped his cold arm around her, careful not to disturb the infant sleeping between them. "It was enough. You and the baby are fine."

"Are you witching me?"

"Why would I be witching you?"

"To make me like you."

He laughed. "Too bad I didn't think of that earlier. I might have tried it. Instead, you have only me, as I am, with no witching."

She shifted again, snuggling the infant into the hollow of her hips. "Why did you follow me to the island that day, Salamander? What am I to you? Why did you care if I was safe? Is it just the sandstone?"

"You are my wife."

"Is it that easy for you, Salamander? No questions about what truly lies in my souls?"

"I know who you are." He smiled sadly in the darkness. "And I know that in the end, you will do what you must."

She lay silent in the darkness, and after a moment, he heard soft sobbing.

Chapter Seven

Pine Drop climbed the long slope, stopping on occasion to catch her breath. She was tired of pregnancy. Tired of the discomfort of having to rise every so often in the night to waddle out and urinate. The shifting of her daughter—for she assumed Salamander had been right about that—disrupted what little sleep she managed.

Above her, the Bird's Head loomed out of the graying dawn. The last of the stars were fading. A warm misty breeze blew up from the south, carrying with it the scent of greening grass, the perfume of dogwood, redbud, elder, and locust blossoms.

Spring had warmed the land, stirring the life that had lain dormant in memory of Mother Sun's flight to the south. As she climbed she could hear the high piping of one of the last flocks of blue herons heading northward on the gulf wind.

The grass, thick and lush, fed by the winter rains, curled around her feet when she wandered off the path. A vole rustled away from her passage.

When she looked up, she could see the ramada, and there, on the palmetto-thatched poles of the cane roof, she made out the solitary shape of an owl. In the twilight, it watched her, huge, the largest barred owl she had ever seen. Black eyes studied her from within the twin circles of the facial disks.

She froze, a prickle running through her as their eyes met. Her souls began to tingle. She could swear that she could not only feel her own heartbeat, but that of her daughter deep in her womb.

Time seemed to swoon, silvering and shifting around her like vision through clear, moving water.

She sensed rather than saw the owl spread its wings. The giant bird drifted down, silent, its wings enlarging until they filled the sky. To the last moment, she stared into the liquid depths of those huge brown eyes, and then, as if with a snap, the owl was gone. Vanished.

She spun on her feet, staring behind her—and saw nothing. The clear gray air was empty.

Snakes! Where did it go? How could such a big bird have just disappeared into the air? Her throat tightened. She could feel her blood bursting through her with each pounding of her heart.

Resuming the climb took every resource and all of the courage she could muster. She laid a hand on one of the ramada poles, panting for breath, and looked up at the great mound's peak.

She could see him sitting there, legs crossed on the summit, his head back, eyes closed. His hands rested, palms up, on his bent knees. Morning dew had settled on his black hair, turning it silver.

The expression on his face stopped her. He had a

beatific look, a lax smile on his lips. He might have been savoring some taste, perhaps a sweet squash flavored with honeysuckle that lay so delicately on the tongue.

Filling her lungs, she forced her weary legs up the last slope and lowered herself quietly to sit beside him. Every muscle in her body vibrated like a stretched cord. An electric sensation, like that from rubbed fur, crackled along her nerves.

She swallowed hard and studied him. *What sort of man are you, Husband? Does Power flow through you like sap, or is it a madness?*

Salamander seemed oblivious, so locked away in his visions that nothing else existed in the world.

She waited, turning her eyes to the eastern horizon and the reddening beyond the distant tree line. The bulge of the sun slowly emerged from behind the forest's bulk. She sighed, unconsciously reaching out for Mother Sun's light, as if she could grab hold of those first glorious rays and scrub the darkness from her souls.

"It is glorious, isn't it?" Salamander barely spoke above a whisper.

She spared him a glance. His eyes remained closed, the blissful look on his face.

"Yes." She took a breath to still her souls. "Look how far north it has moved since the solstice. We are forest people, Husband. Knowing that Mother Sun moves across the sky is one thing, actually seeing it makes the stories about her come true."

He remained as calm as a rock, unmoving, his hands still on his knees as though supporting something in the air.

"I saw Masked Owl," she told him nervously. "I think I sacred him away."

"You did not scare him."

She shifted, pulling her kirtle around so that it didn't chafe her pendulous belly. "Does he always come when you call him?"

"No. He came to see me. He is worried."

"About what?"

"About my new Spirit Helper. She has changed the balance between Masked Owl and Many Colored Crow. The future is no longer certain, Pine Drop. They don't know what I am going to choose."

"I don't understand. What do you mean, choose?"

His smile was sad. "Nothing comes without a price."

She ground her teeth for a moment, then asked, "Husband? I must ask you something. It is very important to me."

"I am not a witch. Masked Owl is not evil. I seek to harm no one."

A flood of relief washed through her. "Then you have heard the talk?"

"No. You are the first to mention it to me."

She flinched, unsettled. "You are becoming ever more strange, Salamander. Power is growing in you, and it frightens me."

"You are a wise woman."

"I don't feel very wise these days, Husband. Things are happening. A trap is being built for you, and I can sense the cords that ran to the deadfall trigger. I can feel people tugging on them. If they pull the trigger loose, the weight is going to fall and crush you."

"I Dance on such a thin edge," he whispered. Sunlight flooded his face, washing his delicate skin in red. He looked so young and fragile. "I'm scared, Pine

Drop. If I slip and fall, it will be into a horrible nightmare. The worst thing is, it isn't just me. It is you and Night Rain and Anhinga and Water Petal. One misstep on my part can destroy you all."

She clenched her fists. "The clans are moving against you."

"Wife, it would be so sweet if my only concern was the clans. Masked Owl would have me believe that the One and the Dance are all that matter. The One is so Powerful. It calls to me. It would be so easy to give in. To find happiness like Mother did. The only thing that calls me back is you, Pine Drop. My wives and my daughters. They need me. The People need me."

"Of course we do."

A great sadness filled his voice. "Wolf Dreamer said that a man couldn't love and Dream. I want to do both. If only I could tear myself in two, send my Dream Soul to spin with the One, and my Life Soul to embrace you and watch my daughters grow."

"Half the time, I have no idea what you are saying."

He smiled sadly. "Someday you will. You are the future."

"Forget that for a moment *and listen to me!*" She took a breath. "Uncle is working in secret, building an alliance to have you declared a witch." There, she'd done it. Betrayed her clan as surely as Night Rain had done. A sick feeling stirred in her gut.

"They can't destroy what they do not comprehend."

"They can smack you in the back of the head with an axe," she declared. "If the Council decides to brand you as a witch, they won't give you any warning. They will act by surprise, and you won't know until you feel your skull split open."

For a long time he sat there, eyes flickering under the closed lids. "Why do you care, Pine Drop?"

She looked down miserably where she picked at her fingers. "I have come to love you."

"There is no greater gift and no greater curse."

"Curse? What do you mean?"

"You draw me back from the edge."

She squinted in disbelief. "You really want to fall off that edge you were talking about?"

"More than anything you can imagine, Wife." A faint smile bent his lips. "But for you, all of you, I would be drawn like a bee to a pitcher plant. I would lick desperately at the sweetness as I fell into the depths."

"By the Sky Beings, why?"

"Because the other way would be too painful."

"What are you talking about?"

"I'm talking about what I will have to give up for the future, Pine Drop. I just don't know if I am strong enough to see it through. I am so tempted to choose a long and happy life."

"Then choose it! Help me stop this witchcraft story before it starts."

He smiled, as if amused by her worry.

"I need to know something, Salamander. Did Anhinga kill my cousin, Eats Wood?" There, she had asked. Now, waiting for his reply, her souls twisted in anticipation. In response, he just sat there, legs crossed, eyes closed, holding his hands palm up. "Salamander?"

"No, she did not." He raised his hands, inspecting them intently as he worked his fingers back and forth. He blinked, clenched his fists, and stiffened his back as if stung.

"Salamander? Did you kill him?"

"I think it would have taken someone with a warrior's courage to kill your cousin." He shot her an innocent smile. "I've been meaning to give you something."

She frowned, unsure what had just happened between them.

He reached into the tuck of his breechcloth and pulled out a sinew-wrapped square. With careful fingers he unwound the thread, revealing two pieces of flat bark. This he handed to her.

The wood felt warm to her fingers, as though they had been baking in the sun. She separated the pieces finding five blue jay feathers that had been resting there, perfectly pressed by the soft bark.

"What?" she asked, lifting the delicate feathers.

"You left them the morning you took the little carved owl. I am returning them. You didn't have to leave anything in payment. That owl was for you. I just hadn't finished it yet. I would rather see those feathers sewn into the bare patch on your cloak."

Tears caught her by surprise and blurred her vision with silver. "What is happening to you, Husband? What are you becoming?"

"The future."

Pine Drop's daughter had been born in the middle of the night while a misty spring rain fell. They had run low on wood, having to send Night Rain to borrow from one of her cousins. Anhinga wrung out a cloth as she cleaned the blood-streaked infant. Curious, wasn't it, that caring for a newborn could become such second nature in so short a time?

She glanced at her own daughter, asleep in a cane-framed cradleboard. The child's wispy black hair was visible above the cloth bundle, her skull like a delicate gourd. Looking closer, Anhinga could see that her eyes were closed, the tiny mouth open to expose pink gums and a curl of tongue.

"It was easier this time," Night Rain said as she held Pine Drop's hand.

"Easier for you," Pine Drop answered wearily as she lay gulping air like a dying fish. Sweat beaded on her brown skin, pooling in the stretch marks around her navel.

"I thought it was enjoyable," Anhinga said, eyes flashing. "I enjoyed repeating those things you told me."

"Next time," Pine Drop mumbled, "you can deliver your own child."

Night Rain used hanging moss to wipe up the last of the blood from the matting that lay between Pine Drop's legs. She pressed it into a bundle, and before Anhinga could draw breath to stop her, tossed the moss into the smoldering fire. Flames licked around it before climbing through the moss. The wet blood and tissue steamed and hissed as it burned. The air filled with a pungent odor.

"I would have burned it outside," Anhinga said, scrunching her nose.

"I didn't think of that," Night Rain replied sheepishly.

Anhinga finished her cleaning before dropping to her knees beside Pine Drop. The newborn hung on Pine Drop's right breast. The woman's tired arms

W. Michael Gear & Kathleen O'Neal Gear

cradled the infant. Anhinga watched from half-lowered eyes as the tiny mouth worked the nipple.

She thought it curious that Salamander had arrived bearing a fiber-tempered bowl and offered to carry the afterbirth out beyond the clan grounds for burial. Shifting, she noticed the turned earth under Pine Drop's bed, as if something had been recently dug from there. A slow smile crossed her lips.

"Snakes," Pine Drop whispered. "I could sleep for a solid moon."

Anhinga sighed, throwing her head back and feeling her dark hair spill down her back. Panther's blood, she was tired. "I, too, am ready to fall over. If you need me, you'll find me at Salamander's. Sleeping."

"I can call on kin," Night Rain told her. "Thank you, Anhinga. We didn't think it would take so long."

"Mine did," she replied as she reached for her daughter. Wrapping the fabric to protect the baby's face from mosquitoes, she took a last look around, nodded, and ducked out into the night.

The faintest of breezes played with the heavy night air. She could feel the promise of summer's coming warmth. A cloudless sky was painted with stars, while a sliver of moon hung just above the eastern horizon. A whippoorwill called plaintively from beyond the house-topped ridges. Crickets and frogs added their voices to the night. Wood-smoke hung in the air, mixing with the cloying odor of rotting trash and the tang of human waste.

She tucked her daughter close to her shoulder and walked down the ridge before turning north along the edge of the bluff. The ridges here, she was told, had been built atop an old gully. One the Sun People had

86

filled before plotting out the Snapping Turtle Clan ground.

Below her the tree-filled bottom land south of the lake lay in dark shadow. She could smell cooler air, the pungent scent of the swamp carrying to her position.

She passed the edge of the ridges and glanced uneasily at the dark houses. The last one belonged to Mud Stalker. She stopped, staring at it.

A wicker door blocked the entrance. She cocked her head, stretching down with her free hand to reach into her pouch. Her fingers caressed the stone-tipped knife that lay there. Salamander had sharpened it, using an antler tip to pressure flake an edge keen enough to slice hair.

It would be so easy. She need only slip that doorway aside, step in, and one quick slash would leave his throat severed from side to side. Before he could fully call his souls to wakefulness, he would be choking on his bubbling blood, tasting it as it rushed up in his mouth and nostrils.

She snorted to herself and hurried on. Pus and blood, what was happening to her? Uncle hadn't been right, had he? She wasn't beginning to see these people as her own?

Disgusted with herself, she strode purposefully on her way, passing the head of the narrow ditch that drained Snapping Turtle Clan when she stopped short. Her path had taken her to the plaza where the Men's House stood on its double-humped mound.

She stared at the structure, its thatched roof inky against the sky. The carvings atop the ridgepole guarded the building—black silhouettes against the night.

She swallowed hard, taking careful steps to the pole where she had been tied. Reaching down, she touched the grass-covered earth. The dirt was cool, damp on her fingertips.

She tucked her chin, smelling her baby daughter's delicate scent as it rose from the cradleboard. How many things had changed since she had been bound and helpless here?

In the eye of her soul, she relived that terrible day. Remembered how they had cut Cooter's liver out of his body. How they had laughed as they bent down to defecate into Mist Finger's empty eye sockets. Once again the camp dogs slung silver drool as they snapped up bits of raw flesh cut from her friends. She could see the stripped rib cage, all that was left of who? Slit Nose? Spider Fire?

So much hatred. So much death.

What brought me here?

A fist tightened around her heart. Was that the price she had paid by waiting for so long? That her memories would begin to weaken, that the pain of that day, the humiliation to their spirits and memories, would begin to fade?

She could feel Bowfin and her dead friends, watching her from the darkness, their eyes burning as they studied her. She could sense their frustration and swelling anger.

Will you act? The words seemed to linger on the night.

She steeled herself and stood. To her surprise her fingers hurt, and something firm filled her palm. She opened her hand, wondering when she had clawed the soil from the ground.

He sat in the doorway of the Men's House, his form obscured by the deep shadow. He had barely seen her coming as she walked across the plaza. Hadn't recognized her until she stopped at the pole and bent down to feel the ground.

Now he watched as she hurried away, her gait halfway between a run and a walk.

Saw Back reached up and fingered the side of his crushed face. It would have been so easy. He could have sneaked up on the balls of his feet. She'd have never known he was there until the snapping of her skull as he drove his axe through it.

"Someday, woman."

It would not be in the darkness. Not in the quiet night. No, he wanted her to know he was going to kill her. He wanted to look into her eyes, see her fear, as he choked the life out of her body.

Chapter Eight

Salamander had spent the last week since the birth of Pine Drop's daughter alternating back and forth between his two houses. On this night he lay in Night Rain's arms. Their coupling had been like an intimate dance that led to a pulsing ecstasy that Night Rain shared as she absorbed his seed. Wrapped in each other's arms they had fallen into an exhausted sleep.

Salamander didn't hear the rasp of black feathers in the night. Above the house, midnight spirit wings enfolded his Dream Soul in downy softness.

The Dream, so vivid, captivated him: He was climbing the Bird's Head. The day was one of those that came in late spring: bright, sunny, with a scattering of clouds in a light blue sky. Humidity had softened the air, its moist touch on the verdant growth.

Grass waved at his feet as Salamander climbed. Around him, the world seemed to glow with an emerald heartbeat. He could feel the earth, alive, breathing. Even the air seemed to swell in his nose and lungs.

His climb was effortless. He almost floated upward
—a leaf borne upon the breeze.

At the top, a lone figure made a dark silhouette
against the sky.

Salamander squinted against the glorious light,
trying to identify the person. But no, not a person at all.
Rather, it looked more birdlike, or was that just a black-
feathered cape that hung from the figure's shoulders?
The head, when it turned, was indeed a giant bird's. A
straight black beak protruded, shining like polished jet.

Salamander slowed, suddenly uncertain.

"Come, my friend!" the being called, waving a
feather-laced arm. "It is time that we finally talked."

Salamander trod the last couple of body lengths,
studying the apparition. Long black feathers hung
down from a cloak that covered the man's arms. From
behind a raven's mask, two sharp brown eyes could be
seen. A short tunic made of snakeskin ran down
between the man's legs to end in a rattlesnake's tail.

"Bird Man?" Salamander gasped.

"I have come to see you, Salamander. Come to see
who and what you are. There are things you have not
been told. It wasn't easy to reach you as it is. Masked
Owl guards you well."

"Why? What is he afraid of?"

"He fears that you might find all the pieces of your
scattered visions. He fears that when you fit them
together, you may choose a different path than the one
he has been so carefully planning for you."

"I don't want to be in the middle of this!"

Bird Man extended a feathered finger to indicate
the cross-shaped scar on his chest. "You have been
marked with it, young Dreamer. Whatever you wished,

Power has found itself at the center of those intersecting lines over your heart. Do you feel it?"

When Salamander lifted his fingers he detected the throbbing under the hard knot of scar tissue. Looking down, he could see a yellow glow at the center of his breastbone.

"Yes, there," the gentle voice told him. "What an unlikely sort of hero you are. I can understand Masked Owl's interest in you. He always seems drawn to the odd ones, to the deformed, or the naive."

"I don't understand."

"Neither do I. He seems taken with that silly notion of looking for strength in weakness. You are his type, but what I really don't understand is how you could have managed to involve the old woman. Mostly she huddles in her cave like an infant wrapped tight in the womb. She seems content to watch from afar."

"What old woman? Do you mean one of the Clan Elders? Cane Frog, or..."

"No, young fool. I mean Old Heron. For some reason—and it's beyond me—she has taken a liking to you. It upsets things, you know. Any hint of predictability vanished the moment she saved you from dying from your stupidity."

"Stupidity?"

"Taking those mushrooms you found in the Serpent's lodge. That first time, the old man gave you just a taste. Only enough to allow your souls to drift up and glance the Spirit World. The second time, you ate too much. I thought all of our problems were over—and by your own hand, too."

"Problems?"

"What did the old woman promise you? That you

would become a great Dreamer? Is that what you intend to do? Just when everyone needs you the most, you are going to bundle yourself into a canoe, paddle off to some secluded isle, and Dream for the rest of your life?"

Salamander frowned. "The One calls to me."

"It calls to everyone," Bird Man said irritably. "Just because it has a certain lure, you're set to abandon all of your responsibilities to your wives, your children, Water Petal and Yellow Spider, your lineage, and Owl Clan. How noble of you. You will spend the rest of your life eating bugs and leaves, trying to escape yourself in an attempt to find nothingness."

"But to Dance with the One—"

"Means disappointing people who love you and depend on you."

"Then why is it there?"

"An accident of the Creation. You answered your Serpent's question, didn't you? When the sky was separated from the land it was to create duality, otherness. Opposites, if you will. Do you really think a young man like you can Dream them back together? What you feel, fool, is the hole that was left, and it's trying to pull you in."

"It is?"

Bird Man cocked his head. "Think about it, Salamander. I remember my idiot brother trying to tell me once, long ago, that I was unschooled, but that I could still find a way to the Dream." His lips quirked behind the mask. "Now, having been part of the Spirit World for so long, I can tell you that the One isn't all that there is."

"It's not?"

W. Michael Gear & Kathleen O'Neal Gear

Bird Man spread his feather-clad arm to take in the huge vista of Sun Town. "Look down there, Salamander. Do you realize the majesty of this place? Nothing else like it exists in our world. It is from here that the vision will spread. You and your brother have spurred it. Hazel Fire and his companions have taken the bait! So, too, have so many of the others. You have set fire to their imaginations, like blowing on a dying coal. Even Striped Dart is beguiled. Your impulses are correct, Salamander. You can grasp the future!"

"As my brother did with his seeds?"

"Yes, my friend." A thoughtful brown eye studied him. "I could do nothing to save him."

"Masked Owl killed him." Salamander frowned. "I don't understand it. White Bird would have made a brilliant Speaker, the greatest ever."

"You are wrong."

"I am?"

"You could make an even greater Speaker, Salamander." Those piercing brown eyes were taking his measure. "That is one of the things Masked Owl doesn't want you to know. As Speaker you can change the People forever. You can start them on a path of greatness that will rival anything in the world."

Bird Man smiled at Salamander's surprise, and said, "Salamander, you have been agonizing over your visions of the future. You caught glimpses, but not a full picture. You saw the grand ruler, high above the river. Do you remember?"

"Yes."

With a swirl of his feathers, Bird Man outlined a burning circle against the sky. Within its ring Salamander could see pointed pyramids of stone, people beyond count laboring in fertile fields alongside a winding brown river. Giant stone buildings stood above the sun-baked shores. Square stone spears thrust into the sky like giant awls.

"They are already building marvels over there," Bird Man whispered.

"Where is that?" Salamander gasped, trying to understand the scale of the buildings and pyramids. Was it his imagination, or did they dwarf Sun Town?

"In another world, my friend. Far to the east, across a huge ocean of water." Bird Man shrugged.

"We could do that? Here?" Salamander marveled. "We don't have the stone!"

Bird Man laughed again. "Just because you live on a low ridge of windblown silt, do not worry about stone. I can teach you to think in grander terms. I can help you to break the petty politics of the clans. Smash them once and for all. You can begin the process of molding the People into a new direction. You can do it the same way you shape your little red owls. It won't be easy, it won't be painless. But *you* could do it! You could sit atop this mound and control this entire river! Generations of your descendants will speak your name with awe as they rule from on high."

Salamander shook his head in disbelief, thunderstruck by the images that formed within Bird Man's fiery circle: Scenes of people in huge canoes that crested tremendous ocean waves. Cities of stone and wood. A literal flood of people tending fields where plants grew. Others, warriors bedecked with plumes of colored feathers, marched in thick rows and carried weapons of shining silver metal.

"It is illusion!" Salamander cried.

"A possible future," Bird Man corrected. "A shining vision of what could be. Provided, of course, that you have the courage and commitment to see it come true. That, or we can fulfill my brother's vision. You could turn the People into nothing more than scattered bands of Dreamers, lost in the mystical, empty-eyed and wandering the forests, ever tied to the One."

"I could make that kind of difference?"

Bird Man smiled in a beguiling way. "Somehow, my young friend, it has come down to you. Sun Town, at this time and place, can change the future of the People. Choose one way, and you, and this place, will be remembered forever. Choose another, and you, and the greatness that is Sun Town, will vanish from the People's memory."

"I would have to give up the One?"

"It would seem a small sacrifice, Salamander. In return you get to live your life, watch your children grow. You saw yourself in old age, surrounded by your wives and basking in contentment from having *served* your people. In doing so, new earthworks will rise. Trade will expand from ocean to ocean. In your lifetime you will see cities founded across your world. *You* will make the Dream live."

"And if I choose Masked Owl's way?"

"Mud Stalker and Deep Hunter will destroy the magic of Sun Town. The clans will be at war within a turning of the seasons." Bird Man flashed his feathered arm in a circle, and Sun Town appeared. Houses were blackened and burned. Wreckage lay scattered about. Among the weeds and seedling trees growing along the ridges lay the rotting bodies of dead people. "Masked Owl didn't show you that, did he?"

Salamander stared at the half-rotted corpses. "Mud Stalker and Deep Hunter will cause this?"

"Along with the allies they convince to side with them. Despite public appearances, in their hearts they hate each other. They will do anything to place their respective clans in the void left by Wing Heart's madness. In their rush to rid themselves of you, they will set in motion the seeds of their destruction. Lies will lead to betrayal and murder. Yours first, and then Thunder Tail's, and Clay Fat's and Half Thorn's. They have already forgotten their obligations. Honor will be next. Their actions will split the People down the middle. You and I, however, can prevent this."

"This is the result of my choice?"

"You must choose the future, Salamander." He added softly, "Choose well."

With that, Bird Man spread his arms and leaped into the sunlit sky. His cloaked arms flattened, becoming black wings that shone in the sunlight. With each changing position they blazed in blue, red, orange, and green.

Salamander jerked upright in his bed, stunned. *"Many Colored Crow!"*

Night Rain cried, "Ouch! You smacked me with your elbow!"

Salamander blinked in the darkness of Pine Drop's house. A faint glow marked the fire pit. Coals still smoldered among the branches of green wood they had left to smudge the mosquitoes.

"A Dream," he murmured. "A Dream unlike any other."

"What are you talking about?" Night Rain repositioned herself, one hand on his shoulder.

"The future, Night Rain. Giant cities like Sun Town up and down the river. Warriors beyond count, marching in lines. Huge canoes that can cross oceans of salt water."

"You saw this?" she asked.

"That, and war between the clans. Sun Town deserted and burned. Many Colored Crow showed me. He was dressed as Bird Man. He said I could save Sun Town. All I had to do was choose it."

"You will do this thing, won't you?" Night Rain's voice pinched with excitement.

"I don't know."

"What do you mean, you don't know? You could be the greatest Speaker ever! You would have Many Colored Crow as a Spirit Helper! No one could stand against you."

Then Heron's words echoed in his memory. *"Everything comes at a price."*

The day had turned out clear but humid. Sunlight touched the leaves with a green that almost wounded the eyes. Brightly colored birds flitted among the trees. Thick curls of vines bloomed, the colored flowers at odds with the tiny green blossoms on the tupelo.

"I just can't believe Deep Hunter and Mud Stalker would start a war between the clans! Would they really stoop to murdering their rivals?" Salamander cried as he helped Anhinga bait and drop one of the fish traps into the current. He played out the thin cord that tied it to a wooden float with its identifying owl carved in the weathered wood.

Their canoe sat in the middle of one of the winding channels, riding on smooth chocolate waters. The spring flood was marching across the bottoms, carrying silt and water into the backswamps. With it came fish, eager to feed in the newly created shallows, to breed and lay their eggs. Life was coming to the bottomland swamp.

In the rear of the canoe, Water Petal watched him with uneasy eyes. "There are stories of witchcraft circulating about you, Cousin. If they will lie to get you murdered, why not someone else?" When she used the paddle to drive them forward, smooth muscles made her greased skin shine.

"He is no witch!" Anhinga declared, then glanced suspiciously at Salamander. "Are you?"

"No."

"Did you bury one of those little statues under Pine Drop's bed?" Anhinga was watching him with hard eyes. "I saw where the dirt had been disturbed."

"Yes."

"Did you dispose of it?" She glanced thoughtfully back at her baby where it rode in the cane cradleboard.

"I did. Just as the Serpent told me to."

"What is this?" Water Petal asked.

"I wanted my wives to have healthy deliveries. Relax, Cousin. It was the Serpent's charm, not something from the dark side of Power."

"You worry me," Water Petal told him.

He chuckled uncomfortably. "You have no idea

what worry is. One night I Dream and I fly with Masked Owl, knowing he drove a lightning bolt through White Bird. The next, it is Many Colored Crow who comes to talk to me in my sleep. Each wants me to choose his way." He dared not mention Heron. She was the most enigmatic of all. "I just don't know what the right choice is. Everything is coming together here, and I am right in the middle of it."

"That is an understatement." Water Petal sent them deeper into the channel, her face marked with unhappiness.

Salamander took the moment to study Anhinga. She, too, looked uneasy. A tension lay behind her pretty face. Something smoldered behind her eyes. With the sunlight glistening in her raven black hair, she looked dangerous yet vulnerable. An irresistible combination. He stifled the sudden urge to reach out and run his fingers down her muscular thigh. Since giving birth, both she and Pine Drop seemed oblivious to his sexual desires. Water Petal had told him that would pass with time.

"I feel trapped," he said. "Whatever decision I make, I will offend one or the other."

"I'd keep an eye on the clans, Cousin," Water Petal retorted. "Within a moon, they will act to remove you from the Council. You know that threat is coming. What about the ones that are being planned in secret? Who can tell when someone might call you a witch and use that excuse to sneak up behind you and smack your skull in two!"

He gave her a wry smile. "I should be worried about a simple smack from behind when a lightning bolt might explode my head the way it did White Bird's?

Somehow, upsetting Masked Owl or Many Colored Crow is a little different than worrying about Mud Stalker and Deep Hunter."

"You could leave," Anhinga told him. Her dark eyes bumed. "You don't have to stay here. You could come with me. We could go to the Panther's Bones, and you could leave these people who do not appreciate you."

He reached out and took her hand, beguiled by her desperation. "I thank you for that, Wife. Your offer means more to me than I can ever tell you. As much as I would like to have that freedom, it wouldn't solve my trouble here."

"It would take you away from Sun People who want to murder you!"

"Masked Owl could drop a tree on me down at the Panther's Bones just as well as he could here. Spirit Helpers aren't bound by human territories."

"As you described it, Many Colored Crow would make us great," Water Petal said thoughtfully. "Our clan would become preeminent. No one could challenge us. Imagine that, Salamander. Owl Clan would be forever. Everyone else would be obliged to us. The uncertainty would be gone. We would lead the Council."

"At a price, Cousin." He reached for another piece of bait and dropped it into the next fish trap. "Power doesn't promise these things freely. You speak of obligation? What would we owe Many Colored Crow?" He shook his head. "The Hero Twins are just like us—like our clans. If you just choose one, the balance will be ruined. The harmony that we have tried so hard to maintain will be broken."

Anhinga was weighing his words, a frown on her

smooth face as she played out the cord while the trap sank in the murky water.

"Did we do so badly?" Water Petal asked. "Has Thunder Tail been a better leader in the Council than Wing Heart? What of Mud Stalker if he is chosen for the leadership? Would Deep Hunter have been better than Cloud Heron over the turnings of the seasons? Or, Snakes help us, Cane Frog? Could she have done the things your mother and uncle did? Our lineage has been good for Sun Town, Salamander. Look at the building we have done! The ridges are finished. People live in constant protection from the forces of the North and West. We are Trading with peoples we have never heard of before. Life is good."

He nodded, unable to argue with her. "That might have been luck."

"Luck?" Water Petal asked.

Anhinga raised a questioning eyebrow.

"What if Mother hadn't been chosen to follow Grandmother? What if Moccasin Leaf had been chosen Clan Elder instead? Would life still be good?"

Water Petal's eyes hardened.

"This talk is helpful, but it doesn't dig down under the guts where the real question lies." He dropped a square of fish meat into the next trap and with Anhinga's help, lowered it over the side. The marker float bobbed in the current as Water Petal steered them down the channel.

"And just what do you think lies under the guts?" Anhinga asked.

"Doing what is right," he answered. "Not just for us, not just for Sun Town, but for everyone."

"Right? By the Panther's blood, what is right?"

Anhinga's frown deepened. "What is right for Sun Town will not be right for my people. Even your own clans have different ideas about what is right."

"That, Anhinga, is my problem," he told her. "How I can choose what is best for everyone?"

Water Petal cocked her head. "Salamander, why should you have to?"

"What?"

"Why should *you* have to do this? Why not someone else? Why did Power choose *you*?"

He shook his head sadly. "I don't know, Cousin. All I can tell you is that if I don't choose correctly, I just know something bad is going to happen."

A shaft of ocher light bored through the Dream, as though barely penetrating a midnight gloom. Anhinga stood passively—partially hidden. She could barely discern the grim surroundings. Darkness swirled at the edges, as if smoke choked the air and devoured the reddish light that illuminated the place. Dark shadows, beings of some sort, flickered and twisted at the sides of her vision. She could faintly make them out—only that they were whip-thin, quick, and dangerous. In the center, the bloody light bathed five somber young men.

Mist Finger stood at the head of the group. His arms were raised high, like a bird preparing to leap into flight. Behind him Cooter, Spider Fire, Right Talon, and Slit Nose followed his lead, lifting their arms at angles. About them, the eerie figures detached from the darkness, lunged, struck, and withdrew. The attackers were menacing, vaguely human, thin as whips, and so incredibly fast. They struck with blurred movement, and each touch of their sharp arms sliced skin on one of the youths. Each feint, each stroke, came with the rapidity of a snake's lightning tongue.

Anhinga watched in horror as her friends' bodies writhed in pain. Their faces twisted in terror. Why didn't they run? Why didn't they act to protect themselves? She found her voice, calling out, "Mist Finger?"

He turned terror-bright eyes on hers, his face contorted, the black hole of his mouth open in agony. "Dead," she heard him say.

"Get away!" she cried. "All of you, flee! Run! Escape!"

Yet they stood, arms lifted, heads rolling as they flinched from each blow given them by the darting wraiths. Their bodies shone red as blood slicked their quivering skin in sheets. Each gaping cut hung open, and beneath the cleanly sliced skin she could see exposed muscles straining and jumping like knotted ropes.

The darting manlike shadows continued their dance, flitting, slashing with pointed hands. Anhinga stifled a cry as patches of skin began to hang, draping like soggy cloth. Her friends opened their mouths and shrieked—but she heard only silence.

"Run!" she pleaded, clasping her hands in front of her as she sank to her knees. "In Panther's name, run!"

Cold stone ate into her knees as tears streaked down her cheeks.

The shadowy apparitions ducked, whirled, and lanced out with greater frenzy.

Anhinga saw sections of muscle sliced away, bloody bone exposed here, entrails dropping out of gut cavities there. And still the screams her ears could not hear shattered her souls.

Bit by bit their guts came tumbling out, falling past their savaged crotches to puddle in a slippery mess at their feet. It didn't end as bits of their bodies were flayed away. It didn't even end when only crimson skeletons stood teetering in the gaudy light, bits of sinew hanging like web from the brutalized bone.

The darting wraiths continued to collect in the smoky shadows only to strike repeatedly. Now each flashing stab of arm or leg neatly severed a bone from the wavering remains.

One last strike snapped Mist Finger's blood-matted skull from his neck, sending it tumbling down. Like a gourd, it spattered into the steaming viscera, and rolled down to rock on its side no more than an arm's length before Anhinga's face.

Wide-eyed, she stared into that grisly visage. Where once Mist Finger's dark brown eyes had rested, now raw hollows rimmed with torn tissue gaped. Blood caked the skull's teeth as it gave her a thin grin.

"What can I do, Mist Finger?" she wailed, sagging further toward the cold stone floor.

The voice, lonely, as dismembered as the corpse before her, hissed, *"Kill them, Anhinga. Kill them for all of us. It is time! Send our souls some relief. Make them pay...for us."*

Jerking awake, she bolted upright, surprised at the vividness of the Dream. Cool air washed over her sweat-slick skin. Her daughter was crying in the darkness, disturbed by her thrashing.

A Dream! Blessed Panther, only a Dream. She closed her eyes, seeing that blood-smeared skull staring back from her memory. So real, as if Mist Finger's Dream Soul had been wrapped around hers.

She rubbed a nervous hand over her damp face. Tangles of hair clung to her clammy cheeks.

"It is time, Anhinga," she whispered to herself. "It is time to do what you came here to do."

She reached out, feeling the bed where Salamander usually lay. Empty. He was at Pine Drop's on this night.

Her fingers caressed his bedding, tracing the memory of his face. She could see his worried eyes, sense the tension in the set of his lips. If she tried, she could imagine the beating of his heart.

Chapter Nine

"I think you should be fasting," Bobcat said to Salamander as he leaned forward and lit the end of his stone pipe with a twig from the fire. The mixture of sumac, sweetgum, and wild cherry leaves left an acrid tang in the air.

The Serpent's house was new, but the poles, saplings, and vines that supported the roof already had stained to a dark amber color. The place smelled new, having yet to develop that characteristic smoke-flavored stuffiness of an old house. The plaster hadn't been smudged by greased bodies.

Bobcat leaned back, puffing contentedly, and raised his eyebrows as he studied Salamander. "I don't know what more to tell you, my friend. Perhaps if the old Serpent had lived? Who knows? He might have known what you could do to prepare yourself."

Salamander squirmed as he leaned forward on the pole bench. He propped his elbows on his knees and blew through his fingers before saying, "Fasting would do little good."

107

"Purification always helps when it comes to the ways of Power."

"In my case, I don't need to find a vision. It seems like every time I close my eyes some Spirit Helper is chasing down my Dream Soul to impart advice. Masked Owl wants to lead me away to bliss as I Dance with the One. Many Colored Crow will give me the authority and prestige to save Sun Town from clan violence. He will make us great. That is the choice that looms before me. Enlightenment or fame and glory."

"Given my calling, Salamander, I would have to choose enlightenment. I can only imagine what the One must be like." Bobcat shook his head. "Truly, friend. I wonder sometimes if I am not fooling myself and everyone around me by becoming the Serpent."

"You know how to Sing the cures. You know the plants, Bobcat, and how to conjure their spirits to heal. I've been thrilled at the sound of your voice as you Sing the ceremonies." Salamander paused. "I think being the Serpent is more than losing your souls in the search for the One. Many Colored Crow is right about that. You have a duty here, to do your best for the People." He chuckled hollowly. "That is the trap, my friend. Do you save yourself? Or do you save others?"

"How can you save others if you do not save yourself first?" Bobcat asked.

"For that, I have no answer." Salamander rubbed his face. "But if you fall into the One, you will not want to leave it. I've touched it, felt its caress at the edges of my soul. It's..."

"Yes?"

"More wonderful than I can ever tell you."

Bobcat frowned at the wistful tone in Salamander's

voice. He puffed and exhaled a cloud of blue, thoughtful brown eyes watching the smoke rise. "I would give anything to have even that. Why don't you just give in to the Dream? Let the rest of us sort this out on our own."

"I have obligations."

"Ah, yes, obligations."

"They are what make us the Sun People, Bobcat. Obligations and responsibilities are what separate us from the animals." Salamander pulled his hands back, studying the lines in his palms. "Snakes, I recall Mother giving me that lecture the night she sent me up the Bird's Head. What I would give to be that simple boy again."

"You could go away, Salamander. Take your wives and travel off to the Twin Circles Camp on the gulf. Or perhaps over to Yellow Mud Camp. We have camps and villages throughout the land for five days' journey in any direction."

"That might solve my problems here, but what about Many Colored Crow's vision? Do you really think Deep Hunter and Mud Stalker could end up fighting? Could they really cause a war?"

Bobcat nodded seriously. "Yes, my friend. I believe it. They are driven men who see an opportunity. Owl Clan's very success has led them to desperation."

"If I choose one, how does the other react? If I choose Many Colored Crow, is my head split by a lightning bolt the next day?"

"If you leave, you are no longer at the center. Maybe they will lose interest in you."

"And maybe they will torment me and my wives for having disappointed them!"

"Well, you never can tell about Spirit Helpers."

"Thanks."

"I don't feel like I'm doing you much good."

"What would the Serpent have said?" Salamander mused. "What do you think he would have told me to do?"

Bobcat squinted one eye as he inspected the sooty end of his tubular stone pipe. "I think he would have told you to listen to your souls and to follow their bidding."

"My souls are full of questions and troubles, Serpent. They have no answers." Salamander rubbed his hands together as he watched the smoking fire pit. The pattern in the coals eluded him. "I know things about the future. I have seen Sun Town burned and abandoned. I have seen it strong and invincible. I have seen myself dead in one vision, and old and joyous in another."

"You have?"

Salamander nodded. "I've heard voices whispering on the future's wind as it blows to the past. I've caught flashes of things. Things I don't understand. Tens of tens of canoes paddling to Sun Town in some visions. And great evil like a foul cloud settling onto us in others."

"Is this some evil I can fight?"

"No, my friend. Not unless you have a salve for the souls of men."

"In that realm, I am lost, Salamander."

"So am I."

The day was mild, the hazy sky filled with occasional patches of white cloud that sailed northward on the endless breeze. Salamander sat at the edge of the ramada, drilling holes in bison bone while Wing Heart sat at her loom, humming and talking to the ghosts, her gray head nodding back and forth.

In the northern half of the plaza, the moiety's solstice team practiced pitching. They used sticks as long as a person's leg, flattened at the far end to cup and sling a deerhide ball. Made up of young men and a few women from the Northern clans, the team would defend the moiety at the conclusion of the summer solstice ceremonies. In the game the teams represented the struggle of the Powers of the North and South. It was thought that the winning side would be favored by luck and the Spirit Beings during the coming turning of the seasons.

If only it could be so easy. Salamander watched the sleek bodies, greased and streaked with sweat. Yellow Spider ran in the fore, gracefully dipping his stick, flipping the ball up, and while still hanging in the air, batting it with the flat to send it flying forward.

But no game would settle Salamander's dilemma. He rubbed his hands together and picked up his bow drill. With the device, he could drill holes in beads with dispatch. The hardwood drill stem was pointed by a red chert perforator, essentially a stone needle crafted from a flake. He would twist the stem around his small bowstring, place the tip into the dimple in the end of the bead, and using a wooden block to guide the stem, saw the bow back and forth to spin the drill. A drop of saliva eased the tip as it cut through the soft bone in the bison scapula.

Drilling the hole was only the start of the process. Short sections of cane, essentially hollow tubes of different diameters, lay ready for use. Beside them on the palmetto matting sat two bowls, one filled with sand, the other with water. Sun Town, lying as it did on fine silt, had no sand deposits. Sand, like so many things, was imported from afar. Salamander's had been sifted through fabric to obtain the correct grit, and then shipped in by canoe. He had Traded some of the buffalo hide for it that he had in turn obtained from Green Crane and Always Fat the summer before.

Once he had finished the line of holes, he removed his drill and selected one of the sections of cane, studying the size of the hole it would bore. He wet the end, dipped it in the bowl of sand, and fitted it to his bow. In the bead-making process, this final step was the most important. It took great concentration to start the cut so that the sand-tipped cane would grind a precisely round groove around the center hole in the bead. If he were not perfect, the bead would be off-center.

Salamander didn't realize his tongue hung out the side of his mouth as he fitted the cane over the first of the holes in the bison scapula.

"Have you ever thought of drilling the hole afterward?" Mud Stalker asked, his shadow blotting the sunlight.

Salamander looked up. "It's harder to hold a small bead and drill the center than it is to do it this way." He cocked his head. "We always make beads this way. Even when we're making them of stone."

Mud Stalker smiled, the lines in his face deepening. "Yes, but you like to do things differently than most people, Speaker." Knees crackled as he squatted, his ruined arm cradled in his lap. A faint smile bent his sun-creased lips as he looked at Wing Heart. The old woman's fingers plucked at the fabric on her loom. He raised his voice. "Good Morning, Wing Heart!"

Salamander's mother remained oblivious, her lips moving as she talked soundlessly to her lost souls.

"Can I be of help, Speaker?" Salamander asked.

Mud Stalker turned flinty eyes on him. "I thought perhaps we could have a little discussion, you and I."

"Speak." Salamander eyed his drill, positioned it just so, and began rotating the sand-encrusted cane. To his satisfaction it didn't slip to one side or the other.

"I made you."

"What?"

"I made you what you are, Salamander. Without me you would have had nothing. On White Bird's death, the Speakership would have gone to Half Thorn."

"I suppose."

"Good. I'm glad that you have enough sense to understand that." His eyes hardened. "You are in a great deal of danger, Salamander."

He couldn't stop the faint smile. "If only you knew, Speaker. But I think you are more worried about Pine Drop and Night Rain than any predicament I might find myself in."

"I would like you to divorce my nieces."

Salamander sawed back and forth on the bow as the drill ate its way through the bone. Only when the sand-tipped cane cut a clean round hole through the bone, did he look up. "Have you discussed this with Pine Drop?"

Mud Stalker's gaze hardened. "She has decided

that she will stay with you. I am hoping that you—obliged as you are to me—will be a little smarter than she is." His smile widened. "I would not like anything to happen to you."

Salamander carefully positioned his drill over the next of the holes. Using his block to bear down, he rotated the tip carefully to create a guide. "Speaker, let us make one thing clear, shall we?"

"Indeed, Salamander."

"I admit that you had a hand in making me Speaker. You were responsible for my initiation at the Men's House, and for all of that, odd as it may sound, I thank you."

"Why would that sound odd?"

"Because each of the things you did for me was for your own personal gain. You wanted me as Owl Clan Speaker precisely so that you could destroy me. Through me, you could strike at Mother and at Owl Clan. Given that fact, I have no obligation to you. That is the thing I would like made clear."

Mud Stalker reached up with his left hand to stroke his chin. "Others might not see it that way, Salamander."

"But I do, Mud Stalker. So does Pine Drop." He smiled. "Night Rain is pregnant."

"She hasn't missed her moon yet!"

Salamander enjoyed the rasping sound of his drill as it ground through the bone. "Shall we dispense with the rest of our pleasantries? Stated as briefly as possible: I owe you nothing. You and I have no obligation between us. In fact, if memory serves, Snapping Turtle Clan still has obligations to Owl Clan in return for the many gifts that my brother, White Bird, bestowed upon you when he returned from the north." With his chin, Salamander indicated the copper turtle hanging on Mud Stalker's necklace.

The Speaker's eyes narrowed to slits. "Do not attempt to remind me of my obligations."

"It is the food that nourishes the clans, Speaker." Salamander shot him a measuring glance. "Without obligation, we are nothing. Harmony disappears, and we end up at each other's throats. Depending on what happens, will you remember that in your dealings with Deep Hunter?"

"I have the ability to destroy you."

"By branding me a witch?"

Mud Stalker made a forgiving gesture. "All right, perhaps you are not obligated to me. I grant you that, but if you work with me, help me to unseat Thunder Tail and put Sweet Root in his place, I might be persuaded to save your life. Allow you to remain married to Pine Drop, at least."

Salamander chuckled softly. "As if that was my only worry? Oh, Speaker, if you only knew the choices that lie before me."

"Then I take it we cannot come to an accommodation?"

"Not this way, Speaker."

"This is your last chance."

"You railed when Night Rain acted in concert with Deep Hunter. Don't you think it difficult to blame her when you would use me, meddle with my clan's affairs?"

He didn't answer that, only saying. "I must destroy you, then."

"It is what you have wished from the beginning."

Mud Stalker jerked a nod, his eyes on the ballplayers across the barrow pit. "They're going to lose, you know. And so will you."

Salamander said nothing as the Speaker stood, shot a piteous look at Wing Heart, and walked around the borrow pit before heading south to his clan grounds.

Chapter Ten

Anhinga filled her lungs with the damp odor of the swamp. Her canoe drifted the final lengths to slide onto the muddy beach of the island. She could see the blue haze of smoke from the fire. The tall figure of Jaguar Hide reassured her. Her uncle stood with his hands on his hips, his gray hair spilling around his muscular shoulders. A keen wariness lay behind his eyes.

Lifting herself above the gunwales, Anhinga swung out of the canoe and pushed it up onto the bank. From within she lifted the cradleboard that held her sleeping daughter. The infant was wrapped against the mosquitoes and flies, her face greased, while beads of pinesap added further discouragement to the pests.

"Niece! Let me see my heir!" Jaguar Hide came striding down the slope, his arms out.

She charged up to him, a desperate sense of relief bursting her breast. Her daughter began to cry, jounced as she was by Anhinga's run.

After a crushing hug, she handed the cradleboard

over to Jaguar Hide. He inspected the little round face. The baby girl had her eyes closed, her mouth open as she squalled her displeasure to the world.

"Yes, that's it, my little joy, you tell the world that you are here. Bellow your presence out like the thunder itself so all may know that Jaguar Hide's lineage goes on."

"She needs changing and feeding," Anhinga said, unwilling to take her daughter back from the fawning Jaguar Hide.

"At this age, they usually do." Jaguar Hide was smiling, wiggling his finger like a worm in front of a catfish. "Here, little one, open your eyes. Yes, that's it. Let me look inside you. Are you there yet, my little niece? Have souls fastened themselves to your little body?"

"We don't know yet," Anhinga replied. "She is still so young. The Sun People don't believe that the Dream Soul fastens itself to a body until a child speaks. They claim that is the first actual proof that a soul is there."

"That's silly drivel," Jaguar Hide insisted as he played with the crying infant. "You've been among them too long. The Life Soul comes with the first breath. That's when the infant sucks it in." To the little girl, he asked, "How could you live otherwise?"

Anhinga reached out and half wrestled the cradle-board from her uncle. "I take it that we are safe?"

His smile faded, and he nodded. "I got your message. Warriors are out and about. There will be no surprises. What has happened? We haven't talked for moons."

"Striped Dart didn't tell you?"

Jaguar Hide shook his head, frowning. "Tell me what?"

Anhinga walked up to the fire, glancing uneasily toward the place where Eats Wood had been killed. Was his ghost still lurking here, prowling among the patches of hanging moss?

"Salamander killed a man who followed me. We swore Striped Dart to secrecy. Apparently, Uncle, my brother has taken such responsibilities to his heart."

"A man followed you? And Striped Dart didn't tell me? I'll pull his arms out of his sockets!"

"No, you will not. He gave Salamander and me his word."

Jaguar Hide narrowed his eyes. "You had better start at the beginning."

She related the story as she unwrapped the baby from the cradleboard and changed the fouled moss with fresh. Then she raised her daughter to her nipple. "But for Salamander's timely arrival, I would have been dead and Striped Dart ambushed," she finished.

Jaguar Hide frowned pensively at the fire. "I should have thought of guards in the beginning."

"We were being clever, remember? The fewer the people who knew, the better?"

"And this time?" He shrugged. "How do we know that you will not be ambushed when you return?"

"Yellow Spider will meet me. He has gone for sandstone at the quarry."

"I have been wondering about the fabrics that were left there. Striped Dart said little about them, only that he had bartered with the stone boat."

"I am starting to think he will make a good leader, Uncle."

"Bah! He's soft. Willing to take the easy way for less when the hard path will give him more."

119

"Is that so bad?" She studied the little mouth working so desperately at her breast.

She looked up at his silence, startled to find his expression hard, an unforgiving glint in his eyes. "Are you giving up on me, Niece? Is that what you are trying to tell me? That now that you have a husband who fought for you, and planted that child within you, that your heart has lost the fire of revenge?"

She gave him a grim smile. "No, Uncle. I came here to tell you that the time has come to strike."

He settled back, exhaling as he closed his eyes. "I cannot tell you how I worried. First Striped Dart returns, obviously bearing secrets. Then moons pass without word from you, and finally, when you do come, it is with the warning that we must be guarded here. What was I supposed to think?"

"Perhaps you should have thought less and looked deeper into my heart."

"So, you want to strike now? Why?"

"We are running out of time. The clans are gathering against Salamander." She frowned at that, surprised it hurt to admit that in front of her uncle.

"You fear for your life if they move against him?"

She shrugged. "It's not that. I will have warning enough to get away. He's a good man, that's all. And the odd thing is, he's a Powerful one. Uncle, he knows what is coming, but does nothing to avoid it."

"How is that?"

"He knows that the clans are poised to strike him down, but he goes about his life searching for the proper actions to save not himself, but everyone else."

"Sounds like the ways of a fool, if you ask me."

She gave him a bitter smile. "Never think him a fool, Uncle."

"A man with Power against him—not to mention so many people—isn't smart."

"My husband is a very smart man, Uncle." She gave him a half-lidded stare. "Smart in ways that I don't think you can understand, but we're straying from my reason for meeting you." She met his eyes. "The Dead have been coming to me, pleading with me. I have to act, Uncle, or they will lose their patience with me."

"How do you intend to do this?"

She gestured over her shoulder. "Do you remember the hemlock that grows on the far side of the island?"

A slow smile spread on his lips. "Ah, and then?"

"The next time I paddle south, Uncle, will be for the last time."

Chapter Eleven

F irelight illuminated the interior of the Men's House—it flashed on the masks and danced over cane walls decorated with the hanging trophies, war clubs, sets of antlers, and grinning human skulls. Beyond the east-facing windows, the night was black, veiled with thick clouds that promised rain. But for the crackle of the fire, only the sounds of the night insects broke the silence.

Mud Stalker reached for a section of broken oak and tossed it into the fire. Sparks crackled and whirled, dancing in the air. He stroked his chin, dark eyes watching the licking flames.

"Speaker?" Water Stinger called from the door. "Speaker Deep Hunter is coming."

"Is he alone?"

"Yes, Speaker."

"Please see that we are not bothered. And make doubly sure that no one is lurking around the windows or pressing their ears to the walls."

Water Stinger's lips twitched. "Yes, Speaker, I understand."

"Also..."

"Yes, Speaker?"

"Stick your fingers in your ears. You don't need to hear this either."

Water Stinger smiled, nodding. "Yes, Speaker. I understand." He ducked out the door and into the night. Several heartbeats later Mud Stalker heard soft voices, then Deep Hunter stepped in.

The Speaker wore a bobcat pelt over his shoulder—a dark brown breechcloth with interlocked alligators on the flap hung down the front. He raised an eyebrow as he stopped short and studied Mud Stalker. Then his eyes made a quick survey of the room, a question reflected in the set of his mouth.

"There is no one else here. Thank you for coming." Mud Stalker gestured at the mat across the fire from him.

"Just the two of us?" Deep Hunter asked. "In the middle of the night?"

"Just the two of us. My young hunter will ensure that we are not interrupted and can speak our minds without having it carried to every hungry ear and flapping set of jaws among the clans."

Deep Hunter shrugged and walked across to ease himself down onto the matting. His bones cracked as he settled himself and removed the bobcat hide from around his shoulders. With careful fingers he folded it and laid it neatly to one side.

Mud Stalker indicated a small steaming bowl that rested at the side of the fire. "I have provided us with fresh black drink."

Deep Hunter's hard eyes never wavered. "If I drink any of that, I won't sleep. It's already late."

"So? Do you have a busy day tomorrow?"

A faint smile curled Deep Hunter's lips. "No, I suppose not." He lifted the bowl, tilting it to sip at the hot liquid. When he set it down Mud Stalker reached out with his good hand and grasped it, lifting it to his lips to drink some of the dark bitter liquid. It almost scalded his tongue.

"You brewed it strong."

Mud Stalker set the bowl down and wiped his lips. "Something about black drink. It makes the thoughts clearer and races the blood."

Deep Hunter's eyes had narrowed. "I would assume, however, that you didn't call me here in the middle of the night just to share a pleasant drink and make a little companionable conversation."

"We have a problem."

Deep Hunter cocked his head. "We have a lot of problems, you and I."

"What are we going to do about Owl Clan?"

"What are *we* going to do? Why should anything my clan decides interest you?"

"Because no matter what is between us, you and I must work together on this."

"Why?"

"I think you know. You are waiting, planning on striking at Jaguar Hide. You would have done it sooner, but Owl Clan has an agreement with the old rascal. If you take action on your own, it could cause a stir in the Council. Thunder Tail, Cane Frog, Clay Fat, and Salamander could vote to condemn Alligator Clan. I might be tempted to side with them against you."

"You are assuming that the Council would take an interest in the Swamp Panthers' response to a *peaceful Trading expedition* that went wrong." He smiled warily. "You just can't tell about those people down there."

"That might work. And again, it might not. Someone could make the plausible argument that your warriors took that action as a provocation. That you were jealous of Owl Clan's domination of the sandstone Trade." Mud Stalker massaged the elbow on his ruined arm. "Or, Snakes take us, worse, that it was personally motivated, a backhanded way to repay Anhinga for what she did to young Saw Back."

After a pause, Deep Hunter asked, "What did you have in mind?"

"There might be a way that you could attain your ends, and I might attain mine."

"Your ends and mine have nothing in common." Deep Hunter's smoldering eyes took Mud Stalker's measure, his jaw muscles tight.

Mud Stalker made a pacifying gesture. "Let us lay our gaming pieces in the open. You and I have been adversaries for a long time. I know how you used Night Rain against me. Perhaps I deserved that. I shouldn't have placed such a naive young girl in that position in the first place." He chuckled at himself. "Knowing where we stand with each other, I propose that we work together."

"Why should we?"

"Because I think young Salamander has too much of his mother and uncle in him. If he has done the things he has as a fresh-made man, what will he be like in another ten summers?"

Deep Hunter digested that for a moment, his

expression pensive. "We thought him pretty foolish for the way he stripped his clan for Trade with those Wash'ta Traders. But look how well he did this last winter, giving out those hides. Who would have thought the weather was going to be so miserable?"

"Even a fool pulls in a full net on occasion, but this is something more."

"I would hesitate to mention that it was your insistence that put him in such a position of authority to start with." He gave Mud Stalker an ironic smile. "Let me guess. When White Bird was killed, you thought luck had dropped control of Owl Clan into your lap, didn't you?"

Mud Stalker shrugged. "I wanted to see Wing Heart's authority compromised."

"What prompted you? Everyone thought you were crazy when you married those girls to that boy."

Mud Stalker chewed his lip, hesitating.

"You said we should speak freely."

"A Dream," Mud Stalker admitted. "A Power Dream. Now, I cannot be sure if it was for good or evil."

"Which, I suppose, is the real reason you brought me here. What did you want to offer me?"

"An alliance. At least until we can fix our current problem. You have Thunder Tail's obligation. Cunningly done, I might add, through information provided by Night Rain. I have influence with Clay Fat. Rattlesnake Clan is obliged to me for the moment."

"What are you planning?"

Mud Stalker lifted the bowl and sipped black drink. Handing it to Deep Hunter, he said, "Salamander doesn't behave the way a young man of his age should, don't you agree?"

Deep Hunter drank, wiped his lips, and shrugged. "How should he behave?"

"A normal young man doesn't work with the Dead. He doesn't spend every morning atop the Bird's Head where he can look out into the Land of the Dead. He doesn't ally himself with Jaguar Hide for purposes that we can only guess at. And, most of all, have you noticed how those who stand in his way have been removed?"

"What?"

"You saw him when the Serpent's house was burned."

Deep Hunter gave a thoughtful nod. "Do you have any real proof that he's a witch?"

"We need only the accusation. People will do the rest. He has only a handful of allies."

"If I support the accusation of witchcraft, what do I get in return?"

"Warriors from Snapping Turtle Clan, and perhaps even Rattlesnake Clan, will accompany yours on the raid against the Swamp Panthers. We will break Owl Clan's peace and destroy their access to sandstone. Who knows, if we use Anhinga as bait, perhaps you might finally manage to lure Jaguar Hide into your reach. Whether you do or not, with Snapping Turtle Clan involved, no one in the Council will vote against you."

Deep Hunter sat silently, lost in thought. Then he nodded. "I agree, as long as I can kill Jaguar Hide, and Saw Back gets Anhinga—at least for a while."

"I think we can arrange that."

"What about afterward?"

"Owl Clan is discredited for as long as either of us is alive. Then you and I can go our separate ways.

There will be no remaining obligation as we seek to replace Thunder Tail."

"If Salamander is declared a witch?" Deep Hunter asked, apparently satisfied. "What then?"

"A witch who belongs to Owl Clan becomes their problem, not ours. I have spoken to Half Thorn. He will be happy to attend to it. After all, he has everything to gain."

Chapter Twelve

I n the light of a half-moon, Anhinga drove her canoe onto the muddy landing below Sun Town. Her stealthy arrival frightened a raccoon that searched in and among the beached canoes for bits of fish guts or other edibles left by the fishermen. The beast hurried away in its rolling waddle, lucky to have escaped. Raccoon had a succulent and sweet meat.

The night pressed warmly against the land, a blessing after the cold and drizzly winter. The presence of the raccoon made it doubtful that anyone was close enough to witness her return. For a long moment, Anhinga remained still and listened to the sounds of the night: Insect wings whirred around her head. Frogs croaked. Somewhere in the distance a bull alligator roared.

Nothing moved along the line of canoes. Many had been flipped over to keep water from collecting inside. The vessels reminded her of a school of sleeping fish.

She carefully stood, stepped out of the canoe, and dragged her slim boat onto the muddy bank. She bent and slung the loop of her daughter's cradleboard onto her shoulder. Then she reached for the fabric-wrapped bundle that lay in the bow. She handled it with great care. As she started up the slope she made doubly sure that her daughter's cradleboard hung as far as possible from the fabric bundle. She dare not even let them touch.

She slowed as she neared the top of the slope, hearing music coming from the Men's House. The clacking rhythm of hardwood sticks, rattles, and the thump of drums almost covered the sound of bare feet shuffling on cane matting. A heron-bone flute piped a delicate melody. Male voices rose and fell as they sang in accompaniment.

Light reflected in soft yellow from the building's roof openings. The east-facing window made a glowing square in the dark wall. Figures darted back and forth inside. She could see that they wore masks. Some had deer antlers, others birdlike heads. Still, others looked to be redheaded woodpecker, alligator, and dragonfly, all totems of war.

Let them Sing and Dance while they can.

War, like the dancers, wore many different masks.

A grim smile crossed her lips. Women weren't supposed to see any part of the men's secret rituals. She considered that as she turned her steps north toward the house she and Salamander had built. The mysteries of the Men's House had always intrigued her. They had more fun than the women did, the latter sitting around weaving baskets, making pigments, and gossiping while they changed absorbent and passed their moons.

I should have been born a man. But no, had she been, she would never have had the opportunity that now presented itself. A Swamp Panther warrior would never have been allowed—as she had—to walk freely among the Sun People.

What is it about them that they do not consider a woman to be dangerous? Arrogance? Stupidity? Or just a lack of respect for her and her kind? Certainly, their Clan Elders, also female, should have had the intelligence and resources to appreciate the threat she posed.

Then she recalled her uncle's insistence that she bide her time and endure the passing seasons among the Sun People.

How she had hated the wait. How smart her uncle had been. She now passed where she would, hardly garnering a second glance. She would have been forgotten but for her reputation for breaking Saw Back's face.

Thinking back, she didn't regret it. Of course, she would have been faceless, even more invisible than she was now. Over the moons, however, that act had brought her a curious sort of recognition. People made way for her, sometimes giving her a curt nod. Not friendly, just respectful. She decided she liked that, liked it a lot.

One day soon, she would be returning home. She would see that same look in the eyes of her people. If she managed to do this thing, if it unfolded the way she planned, it would stun the Sun People to the roots of their souls. Indeed, her descendants would speak her name with awe for generations.

All it would take was courage, and the hope that she didn't get caught before she could remove herself well beyond the Sun People's wrath.

As she walked past it, the Women's House was

silent and dark, although the faint smell of cooking cattail and smoke hung on the heavy air. A lone dog stood up in the doorway, shook, and growled at her. She made a soft cooing noise, and the cur trotted down the incline of the Mother Mound, its tail wagging. The animal appeared happy that she hadn't thrown an old cooking clay at it.

"How are you tonight?" she asked softly.

If she could trust her night-veiled eyes, the dog was a young bitch. She bounced and whined as she followed along behind. Like most dogs in Sun Town, she didn't receive kind words very often.

"Shsht! Don't do that!" She raised the bundle high as the dog grabbed it with its teeth and tugged. "That's poison! Not for you to be playing with!"

The bitch whined again and backed off at the harsh tone. Tail wagging expectantly, she stared up at Anhinga in the faint light of the half-moon.

"Go on!" She waved her away. "Go back to whoever was feeding you back there. You don't want any part of me."

Cowed, the bitch dropped behind, trailing by a short distance.

Anhinga walked past the borrow pit to her dark house. Swallowing hard, she removed the door and ducked inside. On stealthy feet, she crossed to Salamander's bed, feeling his empty buffalo robe.

Good. He's at Pine Drop's.

She carefully laid her sleeping daughter on the bench, felt for the small ceramic pot she knew was by the bed leg, and walked back to the square of light that marked the doorway. There, she found her fire-hardened digging stick where she had left it. With the pot in one hand, and the digging stick and her bundle in the other, she stepped out into the night. Haze softened the half-moon's face, dimming the brighter stars. From Wing Heart's house, Anhinga could hear the burr of the woman's snoring.

Anhinga laid the pot and fabric bundle on the ground. Pressing her breastbone against the end of the digging stick, she drove the sharp point into the soft earth and levered it up. It took her less man two fingers of time to dig a hole large enough to take the pot. Using only her fingertips, she placed the fabric bundle inside the pot and then capped it with a wooden plate that lay beside Wing Heart's loom. Lowering the pot into the hole, she scooped earth over it. The excess dirt she scattered around here and there. Finally, she laid a section of cane matting over the hump of earth and pressed it down to hide her handiwork.

In that instant, the image of Salamander's face flashed between her souls. Panther's blood, this was going to hurt him so. Only at that thought did her souls ache.

The crow caught Red Finger's attention when it swooped down out of the overhanging forest and clutched a lock of his graying hair in its feet.

Shocked and surprised, Red Finger ducked, then yipped at the pain as the gleaming bird pulled the length of hair out by the roots.

In anger, he almost capsized his canoe as he scrambled for his atlatl and darts. He sent a long dart flying after the bird, clawing for balance as his canoe wobbled with the force of his release.

The crow dodged artfully to one side, the dart sailing between the branches of a tupelo before arcing down to cut cleanly into the water.

Red Finger rubbed the top of his head, glaring at the circling crow.

"What do you want?"

The bird answered with a raucous call and dived at him again. Red Finger flattened himself into the bottom of his rocking craft and glanced up warily.

The crow had landed on a low-hanging branch. It stared at him with a curious brown eye, opened its mouth, and flicked a sharp-tipped tongue at him.

"Insolent bird." Red Finger carefully braced himself, easing his atlatl back as he fitted another dart into the nock. In a sinuous movement, his arm went back. The cast was liquid, fast, and accurate.

To his amazement, the crow bobbed down, flattening itself on the branch as the dart hissed within a feather's breadth of its shining back.

Caaaawwwww! The sound echoed through the swamp as the crow mocked him and bounced to yet another branch. There, it flapped its wings, teasing him.

Red Finger muttered under his breath and picked up his paddle. The cursed bird had to have been someone's pet. A fledgling stolen from the nest, raised and trained by some swamp hunter.

As he closed, the bird flipped off the branch and sailed farther into the swamp. Red Finger paddled after it, stopping on occasion to reach up and finger the raw place on his scalp.

For a hand of time, he followed the pesky bird.

Each time his interest waned, the crow dived at him, snatching at his hair, raising his ire to the boiling point again.

Thus, it was that by the middle of the day, he found himself deep within Swamp Panther territory.

The crow circled him, fluttering just out of reach. Red Finger used his atlatl to flail at it, hoping to smack the miserable pest from the sky. It avoided his wild blows with uncanny ease.

"What do you want of me?" he declared, half in anger, half in wary suspicion. Snakes! This wasn't a spirit bird, was it? Or, blood and pus, worse, it wasn't some creature trained by the Swamp Panthers to lure unwitting hunters into their territory where they could be ambushed and killed?

With that thought, he lifted his paddle, prepared to leave the accursed bird to its own devices, when he saw it wing to a cypress knee. Sunlight shone on its sleek black feathers. It studied him with an intelligent brown eye.

The crow bobbed its head, pointing its beak toward the brackish water.

"What do you *want*?" Red Finger glanced around, wary of a Swamp Panther ambush. Every direction he looked, he could only see the swamp, the surface of the water marred here and there by the normal rings left by water bugs, fish, and bubbles. Insects fluttered around him, and songbirds filled the spring-flush leaves with song.

Red Finger cocked his head as the crow plucked a white stone from the top of the cypress knee and dropped it into the water with a plop.

A stone? Out here? Atop a cypress knee?

He paddled forward, an eerie fear climbing his spine. No, this was no trained pet, but something else. He wasn't a man used to Power, but he could feel it swelling around him.

As the bow of his canoe slipped past the knee, the crow gave him a loud squawk, leaped into the air, and flapped through a ragged hole in the canopy above. Rays of vibrant color, reds, blues, and greens flashed off its wings.

Red Finger scratched his cheek in confusion. Then, bending over the side of his canoe, he looked down into the water. There, several hands below the surface, he could see a small round white stone. It was resting in what looked like a sunken canoe.

Chapter Thirteen

S alamander trotted down from the Bird's Head after his sunrise devotions. He felt a lingering sense of foreboding, partly from his disturbing Dreams the night before, partly from Night Rain's violent bout of morning sickness. Whereas neither Pine Drop nor Anhinga had been bothered much, Night Rain's first experience of pregnancy was proving to be downright miserable.

"Must be a boy," Pine Drop said as she cuddled her suckling daughter to her breast.

"That or a monster," Night Rain had insisted as she wiped her mouth and cast suspicious eyes on Salamander.

He had raised his hands in defense, and said, "I would have asked Power for another daughter. I'm in deep enough trouble with your uncle as it is. Knowing that I had produced another heir for his lineage might make him smile a bit more kindly when I'm around."

The round red-yellow sun seemed to drift off the

horizon and higher into the morning sky. The light made Salamander squint as he rounded the first ridge, where Cane Frog's house stood. The old Clan Elder hadn't emerged yet to greet the morning with her sightless eyes. Nor had Three Moss come to check on her mother and see to her needs.

He cast a cautious glance at the round Council House as he passed, knowing that soon, no doubt just before the solstice celebration, he was going to face expulsion. The topic of his witchcraft was now on every lip, some people even speaking openly of it.

How does a person prove he is not a witch?

How could he blame them? Last spring, he had been considered an odd boy, even despised by his mother. Within a turning of the seasons, his popular brother was dead, Salamander was Clan Speaker, with three wives, two houses, and an unheard-of alliance with the Swamp Panthers. People knew that he was tied up in the ways of Power, that he spent a great deal of time with the Serpent. He had helped prepare the bodies of the dead. Each morning found him alone at the top of the Bird's Head when normal young men were waking up in their wives' arms. If witchcraft didn't explain that, what did?

With those thoughts lodged in his head, he was surprised by a sudden prickling of unease. He stopped short, collecting his thoughts. He came this way every morning, following the trail that was beaten into the grass where people rounded the eastern end of the borrow ditch before climbing Owl Clan's first ridge.

The dog lay on its side in the weeds at the water's edge. From the way the vegetation was bruised, it was apparent that the animal had thrashed as it died. Even the earth was torn up where it had clawed frantically in its last moments.

Salamander stepped over and bent down. The animal, a bitch, was young. Her expanded nipples and fat sides indicated that she was just days shy of a litter. Her lips were pulled back, exposing foam-flecked teeth and gums. Even in death, terror reflected from her wide brown eyes, the pupils gray. Feces had been squirted onto the matted weeds behind her.

"What happened to you?" Salamander asked, his heart softening. He grabbed a foot, pulling the stiff animal over. She hadn't died that long ago. Not even the flies had found her yet.

Salamander made a face, feeling the presentiment that tingled along his soul.

"Why are you trying to warn me, little mother?" he asked gently. "What do you wish to tell me?"

He closed his eyes, trying to hear the dead dog's Dream Soul. With an aching longing, he listened and heard nothing.

Some people said dogs didn't have Dream Souls, but he didn't believe it. Too many times, he had seen the sleeping animals, their eyes twitching, their feet jerking, as they made muffled woofs. If they weren't Dreaming, running in the Dream world, what were they doing?

"I am sorry, little mother, but I will beware. Thank you for trying to tell me, even if I'm too stupid to hear."

He lifted the animal, feeling how stiff the body was, as if wooden beneath the thin hair. With great care, he bore the carcass to the drop-off overlooking Morning

Lake and laid it over the edge. The dead dog slid down along the steep embankment and lodged in some stalks of marsh elder that clung there.

Depressed, he turned his steps for home. Wing Heart sat at her loom despite the early hour. Water Petal—hunched at the side of the ramada—was graining a deer hide on a polished post set in the ground.

To Salamander's surprise, a third person sat in the morning sun just outside the ramada. It took a moment for the silver hair, the thick shoulders, and lined face to register. Thunder Tail wore one of his bear necklaces, which consisted of claws strung to either side of twin mandibles. A sleek cloak of black bearskin was draped over one shoulder.

Salamander walked past his house and over to the ramada. "Good morning, Council Leader. What brings you here?"

"Good morning to you, too, Speaker Salamander." Thunder Tail's serious face reflected the gravity of his visit. "I came to see Elder Wing Heart. It has been a while since I have had the pleasure of her company."

"She is no longer an Elder."

"She will always be an Elder to me, Salamander." Thunder Tail smiled precisely.

Salamander could see that his mother was oblivious to her guest. Her fingers continued to work the threads, arms rising and falling with a supple grace. Those vacant eyes saw nothing of this world but the fabric before her. Her head continued to move loosely as she dwelled on conversations no one else could hear.

"We thank you for your concern, Speaker. She didn't say anything to you, did she?"

Thunder Tail shook his head, pensive brown eyes on Salamander.

"I am sorry you didn't reach her. We remain hopeful. Water Petal and I keep believing that some familiar face will draw her back long enough that her souls could remember this world."

Thunder Tail gestured for Salamander to sit, then wrapped his thick arms around his knees. "I was a good friend of your mother's. She and I..."

"Yes, I know. You were lovers. She always spoke of you with great respect and admiration, Speaker. I'm sure that she is proud that you followed her into the leadership of the Council."

Thunder Tail studied him for a long moment. "You speak very well for such a young man, Salamander."

"I had good teachers." He indicated his mother. "I spent my childhood listening to her and Uncle Cloud Heron. Something of their skill must have rubbed off."

He hesitated. "I didn't just come to see Wing Heart."

"You are concerned about the talk of witchcraft," Salamander filled in. "Mud Stalker and Deep Hunter are going to introduce that claim at the next Council meeting, aren't they?"

"Are you so complacent that you do not understand the threat, young Salamander?"

"It isn't a matter of complacency, Speaker. I face the perennial problem of those accused of witchcraft: belief. No matter what I state in my defense, people will believe what they will believe. I am not a witch. I wish no one—even my enemies—ill. The more strident my voice is as I cry out my innocence, the more assured others will be that I am guilty of using Power for my own gain."

"And what gain is that, Salamander?"

He gestured around. "If I had that kind of Power, Speaker, I would return my mother's souls to this world. Owl Clan and the People have more need of her wits and knowledge here than do the souls in the Spirit World."

"Are you sure of that?"

"Yes, Speaker Thunder Tail. The Spirit World is already well served—it has my uncle and brother."

"Your mother never spoke very highly of you."

"Let us say that I wasn't what she expected in a son."

"But you ended up as Owl Clan's Speaker."

Salamander smiled wryly. "I think we both know how that happened. But, since it did, I will do my best for my clan, Speaker. I was unprepared for this. I can only hope that as time passes, I will do a better job."

"And the witchcraft?"

"Were I a good witch, my clan would be preeminent. I would be basking in the reflected fear and respect of my fellows. I would be plotting with Mud Stalker and Deep Hunter to replace you as leader of the Council. I would be surrounding myself with copper, stone, and exotic hides from the far reaches of our Trade. I think I would be busy destroying my enemies, making them die horrible deaths." A smile crossed his lips. "I ask you, do my enemies tremble at my name?"

"No, Speaker Salamander, they do not." Thunder Tail fingered the soft bearhide on his shoulder as he thought. His eyes kept straying to Wing Heart, and Salamander could see the hurt.

"She loved you," he said softly. "More than all the others."

Thunder Tail looked uncomfortable as he returned his attention to Salamander. "I don't know what good it will do in the end, Salamander, but for one, I don't think you are a witch. There is, however, something about you that worries me. When I am around you, I can feel it, a tension in the air, as if you are headed for some terrible fate."

"With all of my souls, Council Leader, I hope not. But I give you my word, I will do everything within my ability to keep from hurting the People."

"What of your barbarian wife? People would accuse her of witchcraft, too."

"Assuming that I knew how to recognize a witch, I've never seen it in her."

"And when she goes away?"

"She meets with her family."

"Does she plot against us?"

"Of course. We killed her brother and her friends."

"But you don't think she's dangerous?"

"Speaker, never, under any circumstances, believe that she isn't dangerous."

"Then why do you live with her? Surely not just for the sandstone."

Salamander chuckled softly, shaking his head. "It is a complicated thing to explain. I love her. She is my wife, and I enjoy the time I spend with her. Can you understand that? She does things for me, excites my souls when I look into her eyes."

"What of your other wives?"

"They are the same. Each one is different, each has her own qualities."

143

"But you can trust Pine Drop and Night Rain. You know they won't cut your throat in the middle of the night."

Salamander felt the prickle of warning again. "Speaker? Whatever made you say that? I can anticipate the threat Anhinga poses. She came to us as an enemy. It is those we trust the most who will drive the dagger deepest into our hearts."

Thunder Tail nodded in agreement, and a fist tightened around Salamander's souls.

Night Rain slipped as she followed her cousin, Water Stinger, down the path south of Sun Town. The trail was slick with mud from an afternoon rain shower. Water Stinger had appeared at her house as she patiently drilled stone beads while seated in the ramada's shade. The young warrior had been winded from a long run, and asked for her and Pine Drop.

"Sister is gone. You just missed her. She has taken a basket and gone to collect the first goosefoot greens."

"Then you come!" Water Stinger had insisted, practically dragging her after him as he headed south the way he had come. "It's important. Uncle wants you there."

So they hurried, taking a deeply worn path that led south along the steep embankment overlooking the bottomlands.

The way wound through trees that gave periodic glimpses of the cane bottoms where the channel was obscured by the spring flood. Water gleamed silver as sunlight was reflected through the vegetation. The whole world had taken on a blinding green, and the smell of blossoms carried on the air.

"What is it?" Night Rain placed a hand on her belly, wondering what a run like this would do to her queasy stomach.

"Uncle will tell you."

"Where are we going?"

"The landing just below Raspberry Camp."

She knew the place: the first camp south of Sun Town where the south channel looped back against a break in the high terrace. Not more than a half-hand's run away, people often camped there when they came from the outlying settlements. Close enough to allow easy access to Sun Town, it was far enough away to avoid the noise and confusion. Not all of the Sun People liked the bustling of Sun Town. She had relatives—people in her own lineage—who lived in the outlying camps, preferring the solitude of the swamps and forest to the city of ridges.

For her turn, Night Rain couldn't stand the slow pace of life in the camps and outlying settlements. After several days, the monotony, the limited companionship, and boredom set in. She swore she would pull her hair out if she couldn't return to Sun Town with its constant activity, games, feasts, and visiting.

Water Stinger surprised her when he directed her off the beaten route just outside of Raspberry Camp. Following a faint trail in the grass, he led her over the sloping embankment and down the steep incline. The way wound around roots of walnut, oak, and sweetgum. A spongy leaf mat muffled their steps as the path leveled into a brushy bottom.

Pushing through the willows and cane, Water

Stinger led her into a small clearing. There, the willows had been pushed flat, and several canoes dragged up onto the crushed vegetation.

To one side, Red Finger had his arms crossed. Uncle and Mother stood over a mud-stained canoe, faces grim in the morning light. Sweet Root's face reflected anger, grief, and frustration. Uncle just seemed to brood as he fingered the elbow of his ruined arm. Of them all, Red Finger had a look of satisfaction.

"What is this?" Night Rain asked as she stepped forward to stare down at the canoe. At first, she didn't recognize what she saw: A large yellow gourd with holes in it, bits of sticks and..."Snakes!" She placed a hand over her pounding heart. "Who is it?"

"Do you recognize the canoe?" Uncle asked softly.

She studied the craft, seeing the familiar lines. "It looks like Eats Wood's." She swallowed hard, leaning forward, fingers pressed to her breastbone. What she had first taken as sticks and a gourd were long bones and a skull. What might have been collapsed willow stays from a fish trap could only be the remains of a rib cage.

Looking more closely she could see that the body had been laid out, supine, the arms and legs straight. Muddy water had yellowed the remains. Waterlogged brown fabric about the waist had been a breechcloth. She could see the familiar turtle motif woven into the cloth. Eats Wood's mother was quite a weaver. While Night Rain couldn't be absolutely positive, she was pretty sure that that cloth had come from the old woman's loom.

"Where did you find him?" The fingers at her breast had closed into a knotted fist.

"Deep in the Swamp Panther's territory." Red Finger shifted. "Believe it or not, a crow led me to him."

"A crow?"

"But for the bird, no one would have ever found Eats Wood. His killers sank the canoe with his body in it. Once it was submerged, they wedged it under the roots of a cypress, where it wouldn't come loose." Red Finger shook his head.

"We were meant to find him," Uncle said as he massaged the scar tissue on his arm. "Your crow was a messenger. Power leading us to justice."

"You think the Swamp Panthers did this?" Night Rain asked incredulously. "Why would they hide the body?"

"They wouldn't," Sweet Root answered. "This isn't war, silly child."

"I don't understand." She was shaking her head, staring at the oblong hole in the top of Eats Wood's round skull.

Mud Stalker leaned forward, his hard brown eyes burning into hers. "We're talking *murder!*"

Murder? "Why would the Swamp Panthers murder Eats Wood?"

"They didn't," Sweet Root hissed. "If they had killed him, they would have taken his body to the Panther's Bones and strewn the pieces around like the animals they are."

"Think, Night Rain!" Uncle leaned closer, his eyes boring through her. "Who travels to the Swamp Panthers every moon? Who would have had a reason to hide the body instead of abusing it? Who would have done anything to *avoid* having to face us with our kinsman's death?"

"Snakes, you think Anhinga did this?"

"She's very good with an axe," Sweet Root reminded. "If you will recall, daughter."

Night Rain stared wide-eyed at the oblong hole in the top of Eats Wood's skull. "You think Eats Wood would have let her drive an axe into his head? He knew what happened to Saw Back. I heard him say he'd never be that stupid."

"Look at him, Cousin. Look hard, then you tell me what you think." Red Finger crossed his arms.

"There is a way to prove what we suspect," Uncle replied stiffly. "That is, assuming you still have any loyalty to your clan." He pinned her with his eyes. "How is it with you, Night Rain? Are you still Snapping Turtle Clan, or are you someone else? Someone who betrays her blood and kin. Someone without relatives?"

Her throat tightened, and she wished she were anywhere but here, looking down on these pitiful remains. "How can we be sure? I mean, how can we know that Anhinga did this? Only bones are left."

Red Finger bent down, picking up the globe of the skull. Muddy water drained from the big hole where the spine had been. It spattered off the damp wood and pattered onto her bare legs. She cringed at the feel of it on her warm skin.

Mud Stalker frowned, pained, as he studied the skull. "It doesn't take long for the crawfish, minnows, and bugs to clean up a body, does it?" He indicated the oblong wound in the top. "Here, Night Rain. This will tell us."

"How?"

"I want you to bring me Anhinga's axe." Mud

Stalker gave her a blunt stare. "You can do that, can't you? Borrow it? Sometime when she isn't looking?"

"I...Uncle, don't ask me to do this."

"You *owe* us!" Mud Stalker thrust his face into hers. *"We are your kin!"*

She stepped back, desperate to get away from him.

"Or do you serve someone besides your own flesh and blood?" Sweet Root asked. "Is it Deep Hunter? Salamander? Or perhaps that witch, Anhinga?"

"Have you forgotten your ancestors?" Red Finger asked, a sneer on his lips. "Would you rather serve strangers than your clan? Would you leave your cousin's, Eats Wood's, souls to wail over the injustice of his murder while you laugh with his killers?"

Night Rain couldn't catch her breath. She glanced from face to face. Water Stinger had stood to the rear, his expression brooding and angry.

"Do this thing," Uncle added in a softer tone, "and all will be forgiven between us. You and I will begin again on a new footing...as if the problem with Deep Hunter, and your betrayal, never happened." He paused. "Night Rain, do you understand the opportunity we are giving you?"

She bit her lip and nodded, feeling her heart thudding in her chest. "Yes, Uncle."

"Good." Mud Stalker took a deep breath, stepping back to look down into the canoe. "In the meantime, I think we should tell Pine Drop. Have her—"

"No," Night Rain whispered. "Don't tell her yet. Salamander will find out. She will demand an answer from him. Anhinga will find out, and her axe will be gone long before I can get to it."

"What makes you think Night Rain can manage

this?" Sweet Root asked Uncle in a caustic voice. "She couldn't even manage a meeting with her young lover without getting wound up in another's snare."

"I can *do* this!" Night Rain stamped her foot. "If it means fixing the damage I have done, I can." She took a breath of the muggy air and waved at a pesky fly that came to buzz around her ear. "I will get Anhinga's axe. No one will know. Not even Pine Drop."

Chapter Fourteen

Salamander saw morning come from his perch atop the Bird's Head. As he watched Sun Town in the hazy yellow light, he saw it as Many Colored Crow had shown him in the vision: abandoned, burned, and littered with rotting corpses and wreckage. That scene had filled his nightmares, and now it intruded into his waking thoughts.

The full moon hanging over the western horizon had depressed him further. When it came full again, it would coincide with the summer solstice. If his vision was correct, he had that long to find a solution. The tendrils of his souls could feel the strands of Power pulling tight.

After breakfast with Anhinga, he walked to the canoe landing where Yellow Spider worked on a new canoe. The sky that day had a hazy white cast, and the sun's heat beat down unmercifully. On Morning Lake, the milky brown waters shot beams of light from sluggish waves. They lapped at the muddy shore in irregular and weak splashes.

Salamander squinted his eyes at the acrid smoke that boiled out of the hollow cypress log. Yellow Spider had towed it in from the heart of the swamp several days ago. He had had his eye on this particular bald cypress for several turnings of the seasons. The trunk was straight, fine grained, and just the right diameter for a good Trade canoe. Last summer, after his return from upriver, he had ringed the tree by cutting through the bark. After killing it, he had allowed the wood to cure over the long fall and winter.

Now, the partially formed hull had been muscled up onto the beach, and the laborious process of burning out the interior had begun.

Salamander waved at a shining black fly that tried to suck sweat from his forehead. He watched as the pest rose, buzzing in a lazy circle—and was, in turn, snatched from the air by a long green dragonfly.

"Sometimes things do work out for the best," he called after the departing dragonfly.

"What was that?" Yellow Spider asked as he added kindling to a pile of coals in the hollow. Flames crackled as blue smoke rose in a smudge.

"Occasionally good comes of the right timing." Salamander changed the grip on his adze and began chipping at the charcoal inside the cavity. Making a canoe was an art that involved moving fire constantly up and down the interior of the boat. The burn had to be hot enough to char the wood, but not so hot as to split the grain. Easy at first when the log was thick, it became a great deal trickier when the hull began to thin.

For two days, Salamander and Yellow Spider had been at the chore while Bluefin made the Trade run for Swamp Panther sandstone. He chipped charcoal loose and flicked it back into the fire to be completely consumed. All in all, though slow, it was a great deal easier than hacking hard cypress wood out by hand.

Yellow Spider bent to his work, satisfied the fire was burning as he wished. For a time nothing but the hollow *thunk, thunk* of their adzes disturbed the morning. That, and more flies, drawn by their sweat.

Yellow Spider straightened and ran a hand over his damp forehead. "Did you know that Moccasin Leaf has been talking to people in the lineages?"

"She is saying that it is time that I was replaced as Speaker," Salamander replied flatly. "There is talk that I am not worthy of being Speaker. That I have been dabbling in witchcraft."

Yellow Spider nodded. "People are uneasy, Salamander. Some think you had something to do with your mother losing her souls. Others think you and Anhinga have forged some kind of destructive alliance, that you are plotting with her to harm the People." He shook his head. "I don't understand it. I've never seen you act like a witch."

"I frighten them."

Yellow Spider stopped short and stared. "I thought they just didn't like you."

"It's not that. I'm something they can't understand. They can feel the Power that has wound around me. It whispers to their souls, but they can't quite hear the words. They can feel the struggle about to be unleashed."

"What struggle?"

"For the future of the People. I am supposed to choose."

Yellow Spider's soft brown eyes looked puzzled. "I

don't understand. No one wants you to choose anything."

"Masked Owl does, and so does Many Colored Crow."

"So, choose one. Why should that be so difficult? People align themselves with Spirit Helpers all the time. I should be so lucky to have Power interested in me."

Salamander could only stare at his cousin. "You don't have the faintest idea what you are saying."

Yellow Spider waved at the noxious blue smoke that curled around him and tapped his chest. "I'd ask for prestige, a beautiful wife, and long, happy days filled with friends."

Salamander smiled sadly. "Then Many Colored Crow should have gone to you instead of me. He has offered me those things."

"So, why don't you take them?"

"Because if I do, Masked Owl will probably drill a hole through me with a bolt of lighting."

Yellow Spider squinted one eye. "You're right. Choose Masked Owl instead."

"If I do, all of this"—he gestured a big circle to include Sun Town—"will be gone by next summer solstice. Deep Hunter and Mud Stalker will turn the clans against each other, Cousin. Those of our people who are not killed outright will flee into the forests. The Dream that is Sun Town will die."

"You're right. Better that it's only you who gets drilled by lightning." Yellow Bird tried to make a joke of it but failed. "Sorry, Cousin."

Salamander took a deep breath. "When you boil the fat off the alligator, what you have left is a choice between my souls and the greater good. I could go off and Dream the One, my souls in bliss. Or I could become the greatest leader our people has ever known. Whichever way I choose, it will be at another's expense. Masked Owl said that if I choose Many Colored Crow's way, uncounted people will end up as slaves. If I choose Masked Owl's way, Many Colored Crow has shown me the destruction of our people."

Yellow Spider parked himself on the unfinished gunwale upwind from the fire. He flicked his adze as he asked, "I don't understand this. Why you?"

Salamander shrugged. "I don't think they planned it this way. Lines of Power have come together in a way that leaves Masked Owl and Many Colored Crow trapped in two possible futures. For them, it is one or the other. Because of the way the lines of Power came together, they just happened to cross on me."

"Like the lines on your chest?"

Salamander nodded, feeling the muscles in his back knot as he chipped at the charcoal. "Cousin, I want you to promise me something."

"Anything, Salamander."

"I have something in mind. Maybe it's a way out of this."

Yellow Spider glanced up, his face sooty from the fire. "Such as?"

"I can't tell you. You'll just have to wait and see."

"Salamander, maybe if you shared this idea of yours with someone, it might help."

He smiled wanly. "You will just have to trust me, Cousin."

"I'm not sure I understand what—"

"I need you to promise that you will support what

I'm about to do. I am going to ask you to do certain things for me. They will need to be done quickly and just as I say. I want you to tell me right now that you won't argue or make trouble for me."

"What you're saying doesn't make any sense."

"Neither will the instructions I give you. But believe me, it's the only way out."

"What is?"

"If this doesn't work, if the clans turn on each other, I want you to promise me something more."

"Of course."

"When it looks like fighting is going to break out, I want you to take some kinsmen and capture Pine Drop and Night Rain and my children. Take them far away. North to the Wolf People, or up to Spring Cypress among the Wash'ta, I don't care."

"What about Anhinga?"

"Send her south right away if anything happens to me. Saw Back and Deep Hunter will move on her immediately. You might have to bind and gag her, but get her out first thing. Deliver her to Jaguar Hide in person if you have to."

"And hope I get back alive," Yellow Spider muttered.

"He will let you go for keeping his niece safe."

"Then I take it you are going to choose Masked Owl?"

"I have something else in mind."

"What?"

"The price I have to pay," Salamander said pointedly.

"The way you're speaking is scaring me, Cousin."

"Not half as much as it scares me."

Pine Drop cried out, her body jerking her awake. She sat up, feeling for her daughter. The baby cried in the darkness as Pine Drop lifted her to a nipple and struggled to catch her breath.

"Are you all right?" Night Rain asked from her bed across the room.

Pine Drop blinked in the darkness, smelling the charcoal scent from the smoldering fire pit. "A Dream. By the Sky Beings, I've never had a Dream that vivid."

"What was it about?" Night Rain shuffled under her deer hide. Pine Drop heard her yawn.

"I was on the Bird's Head. Way up at the top. It was morning, the sun rising behind my right shoulder as I looked off into the West."

"The Land of the Dead?"

"Yes. The sky was lavender and pink, so wonderfully colorful, and someone was standing in the distance. Huge, as if rising out of the forest and towering over it. In spite of the light, he was shadowy, vague. Looking through the light was like looking through mist. I couldn't make out the face at first, and then I recognized him."

"Who?" Sleep filled Night Rain's voice.

"Salamander." Pine Drop shivered, remembering the sight.

"In the Land of the Dead?"

Pine Drop nodded in the darkness. "He was looking at me with such longing. I could see the sadness in his eyes. He reached out with one hand, but as soon as I started to reach back, he shook his head and lowered his arm."

"You mean, if you would have taken his hand, you would have been pulled into the Land of the Dead?"

"Yes. He wouldn't let me. Snakes! I wanted to, Night Rain. I wanted to like I've never wanted anything before."

"Wanted to be dead?"

"Yes, maybe. Pus and blood, I don't know. I just wanted to be with him."

"It's just a Dream, Sister. Go back to sleep."

"I can't." She paused, eyes searching the darkness. "I don't know how it happened?"

"How he died, you mean?"

"That, too, but no. I mean I don't understand how I came to love him so much. Remember when we were married? How horrified we were?"

"And how nasty we were to him."

"I would go back and change that if I could."

From the darkness, Night Rain said softly, "Me too."

"I never expected to fall in love with him." She shook her head. "What is it about him? He's not even a single turning of the seasons past boyhood, but he seems so much older. Why did Masked Owl choose him?"

"You really think that Salamander talks to Masked Owl, don't you?"

"Night Rain, I've seen things that I haven't told you about. I wasn't supposed to see him with Masked Owl, but I have."

"You were spying?"

"No. It's not that. I don't know how to explain it, but I know that Salamander is in great danger. I just don't know what to do about it. Night Rain, what if something happens to him? I've lost two husbands already. As much as I loved Blue Feather, I have come to love Salamander more. He is greater than any of us know. The Power that fills him frightens me, but at the same time, it thrills me. When I look into his eyes, there is something there, some patient caring that makes my souls yearn."

"I'm happy for you, Sister."

"I'm scared, Night Rain. Scared that something is going to take him away from me. I can feel it."

"Well, walk over to Salamander's and crawl into bed with him and Anhinga. At least you'll sleep."

"In the Dream, he was trying to tell me something. Why would he be in the Land of the Dead? That makes no sense."

After a long silence, Night Rain said, "Our husband isn't very popular these days."

Pine Drop asked sharply, "What do you know?"

"The same thing you do, Pine Drop. That something terrible is coming."

"Is Uncle behind it?"

"Uncle is behind a lot of things, but no. Everything is going to be all right. Either go to Salamander's or go back to sleep, Sister."

Pine Drop laid her head back against the wall and cuddled her daughter. Night Rain had never been any good at hiding things.

Chapter Fifteen

Mud Stalker seated himself across the fire from Cane Frog and Three Moss. He studied the old woman in the flickering yellow light. Not for the first time, he wondered what it was like to have darkness for a constant companion. The old woman's remaining white eye stared off into the night beyond the ramada. The empty pit of her other eye was a grime-rimmed hole. He had never had the courage to ask her what her souls saw. Did they only replay visions from the past, or did they make new images woven out of past and future, a sort of skewed pattern like a blind weaver might conjure?

Three Moss sat on the fabric blanket she shared with her mother and measured Mud Stalker with her flat brown eyes. She was intent on his expression as if she might decipher the real purpose of his visit to their ramada—and unfortunately, there was nothing wrong with her vision. Three Moss wore a fabric shawl over her shoulders, her skin greased against the mosquitoes that hovered in the air around them.

"What have you come to ask us for?" Cane Frog asked bluntly. She extended a hand, feeling for the warmth cast by the fire. "Can you see him, Daughter? Is the firelight good enough?"

"Yes, Mother." Three Moss reached out and placed her hand on her mother's bare shoulder.

"It has been a long time, Elder," Mud Stalker began in a noncommittal voice. "I thought it was high time that we visited and got caught up on things. I hear that the crawfish harvest has been exceptional this spring. I saw the latest catch down at the canoe landing this afternoon. Three Stomachs and Copper Toad brought it in. And then, earlier this evening, I could smell the aroma as they were boiled.

"I thought about sneaking in like a naughty child and spooning some out of the boiling pot when no one was looking." Frog Clan had a shallow lake in one of their holdings that reliably produced more crawfish than any other place known in the region.

"Yes, it has been good. We would be happy to provide you with some, Speaker." Cane Frog rubbed her wrinkled hand down the top of her leathery thigh. "It will be my pleasure to send a youngster over with a couple of bags full when the boiling is finished. We seasoned them with honeysuckle blossoms and some of those mustard leaves. It gives them a sweet and tangy taste."

"Snapping Turtle Clan will be obligated. For your fine gift we would reciprocate and send you a sack of hematite net sinkers. Some of my young men have just finished shaping a batch. We have a few more than we can use. It has been rumored that some of your fishermen are having trouble anchoring their nets. I saw some of Copper Toad's. He has ordinary rocks tied on with string."

"Ah." She smiled. "Yes. It has been mentioned that you Traded quite a bit of squash last winter for raw hematite to make net sinkers out of. Something about that deal Salamander made with those Wash'ta Traders last fall. People thought him a fool for stripping his clan of all their finery. Then, while his clan wove and crafted beautiful replacements through the winter, that same fool was judiciously giving away hides, stone, and dried buffalo meat to the needy. When people weren't approaching him for some of that Panther sandstone, that is."

"Yes, well, Speaker Salamander seems to have uncommonly good fortune." Mud Stalker smiled flatly at Three Moss to hide his delight that Cane Frog had brought up the very subject he wished to pursue.

"Good fortune? Is that what they call it?" Three Moss asked, the faintest hint of amusement curling her lips. "Many would like to say that Owl Clan has lost most of its prestige. At least, we hear that among the Speakers and Clan Elders and from those who are versed in the intrigues of the Men's House."

"And the Women's House, too, no doubt," Mud Stalker returned in a gracious voice.

"No doubt," Three Moss agreed, her round face betraying nothing. "So we find it curious that while the leadership speaks of Owl Clan's doom, people in the clans keep slipping over there for a piece of that Panther sandstone, or a buffalo robe, or a bit of tool stone from the far north. All the while, I keep tallying the amount of obligation that my clan has incurred to that young man. In another few turnings of the seasons or so, I'm afraid half of my clan grounds will be owed to Owl Clan."

Mud Stalker tried to read her expression. Was Three Moss for or against Owl Clan? He couldn't be sure.

Cane Frog surprised him when she said, "Quite the Speaker, isn't he?"

"Your pardon, Elder?" Mud Stalker asked.

"Salamander," she replied. "Let me guess, old friend. You didn't expect this, did you?"

"Expect what?"

"His success." Three Moss made no bones about it. "The amount of obligation he seems to accumulate."

"I can only be pleased with Speaker Salamander's success. His abilities reflect on my nieces."

Cane Frog erupted in a rasping laugh. "Indeed. A good reflection indeed. This time last summer, as I recall, my Three Stomachs and your Pine Drop were polishing the spear. A fine reflection indeed. In a more public display, people still wonder why he took Night Rain back after that fiasco last winter." She smacked her lips. "Touchy bit of business, that. Had tempers been allowed to flare, it could have become very nasty."

"Yes, well, responsible heads prevailed. Pine Drop, in particular, stands out in my memory. She counseled patience and restraint that day." Mud Stalker inclined his head pleasantly to Three Moss. The woman still had her hand on her mother's shoulder. Something about the way her fingers moved on the old woman's skin caught Mud Stalker's attention. Then, in a flash, he thought he understood. Did the younger woman signal to her mother? Was that why they always touched during the Council sessions?

"It was more than Pine Drop." Cane Frog sucked her lips back over toothless gums, and added, "Although I think she will make a very competent Clan Elder when she comes of age. Very competent indeed."

"Our lineage thanks you for your confidence in her. We are obliged."

"I think you are even more obliged to young Salamander for his eloquence that day, Speaker." Cane Frog tapped her right ear. "These have grown sharper since my eyes went away. They hear more than most people know. Your Salamander did more than his share in keeping the lid on an overflowing pot."

"Some would say he did almost too well," Mud Stalker replied offhand.

"Indeed?" Three Moss asked. "You *wanted* an ugly brawl with Alligator Clan to break out?"

He made a face at the incredulous tone in her voice. "Not at all, Elder. I am glad that the situation was resolved in a peaceful manner that satisfied all parties."

"Then what did you mean?" Three Moss asked.

"I mean it's curious, isn't it, that anyone's misfortune seems to end up as Salamander'sadvantage?" Mud Stalker tried to read Cane Frog's reaction in the firelight. The old woman's face might have been a mask.

After several heartbeats Cane Frog asked, "What do you want, Speaker? Talk to us in words that do not balance on the tongue like a magician's trick."

Mud Stalker fingered his scarred elbow and considered his next words. "Some people have begun to worry about Salamander's continued good fortune. Even my nieces cannot understand how he always seems to come out ahead. It is unnatural."

"We have heard the whisperings of witchcraft,"

Three Moss said. "We are still unsure what to make of it. Is it really witchcraft, or just the jealousy of others? What proof do you have?"

"Just look at his life over the last turning of the seasons. Think about everyone who stood in his way. Some, like his brother, have been killed, others, like his mother, have had their wits blunted. His barbarian wife walks freely among us, wielding her axe while she slips away to spoon poison about us into her uncle's thirsty ear. A suspicious young warrior follows her out into the swamp and disappears. People who oppose Salamander find themselves in very deep water."

"Ah, like his Clan Elder, Moccasin Leaf? Do you consider her elevation in Wing Heart's place a coup for young Salamander? Or do I recall a certain Speaker promoting her acceptance by the Council?" She didn't let him answer, stating, "Young Salamander is most unassuming for a witch."

"He seems innocuous, but when one looks past his misdirection and attempts at humility, they will find Salamander gathering ever more prestige and authority, especially, as you have noted, with the common people."

"So," Cane Frog cut straight to the hunt. "First, you placed him at the top, and now you want to remove him. Why, Speaker? Is it because he is better than you thought he'd be?"

"Oh, go ahead," Three Moss chimed in. "Speak to us with a clear tongue. There is no one to hear. Your words will be carried in silence between our souls."

"It's not a matter of me," he hedged. "Nor is it a matter of what my clan wants."

"Indeed?" Cane Frog asked. "And who else might it be?"

"All of us," he said pointedly, eyes making the challenge to Three Moss. "We have had Owl Clan's leadership for too many generations. On the whole, I admit, Sun Town has prospered. Owl Clan, in particular, has prospered mightily. My clan wasn't alone when it came to giving up certain resources because of obligation."

"You are referring to those lotus ponds that I ceded to Cloud Heron the time of the bad drought?" Cane Frog asked in irritation.

"That is but an example."

"How, Speaker, do you think you can badger Salamander into returning them? By simply accusing him of being a witch? Do you think he will surrender Owl Clan's assets just to make the charge go away?"

"I am not that simple." Mud Stalker watched the fingers move on the old woman's shoulders. When he smiled, Three Moss tapped with an index finger. He shrugged, as if absently, and watched the thumb and little finger move. Fascinating!

"Then how would a complicated man make such a thing happen?" Cane Frog was interested now, sensing for the first time, that some advantage might be in the wind for her and her clan.

"I don't just want to accuse Salamander of witchcraft, Elder, I want to convict him of it." Mud Stalker smiled again, seeing the first finger tap.

"Killing Salamander as a witch will not bring my root grounds back!" Cane Frog reminded shortly. "Nor will it cancel my clan's increasing obligation to Owl Clan."

"Moccasin Leaf would see Half Thorn take Salamander's place as Speaker for Owl Clan," Mud Stalker said firmly.

Cane Frog's wrinkles deepened as she made a sour face. "I've made cooking clays that were smarter than Half Thorn."

"That's just the point." Mud Stalker leaned back, a satisfied grin on his face.

"How would this be done? Would you deal with Salamander? Or did you have someone else in mind?"

"If he is declared to be a witch, he would be Owl Clan's problem. I happen to know that, odious as the duty would be, it would befall the Clan Elder to ensure that justice was done. I would imagine that someone like Half Thorn would use that opportunity to demonstrate his leadership abilities."

Cane Frog's expression seemed to sharpen, her lips pulling back and forth over her gums. Finally, she said, "If we were to support you in this, we would need a guarantee. Some assurance that our root grounds would be returned."

"Let me see what I can do. As I said, Moccasin Leaf would have a great deal of obligation to anyone who assisted her." Mud Stalker stood, seeing Three Moss's fingers rippling. "We may be dealing with an entirely new alignment of clans by the time the summer solstice feast is over."

"Just so Frog Clan isn't on the bottom," Cane Frog reminded. "If we are to be part of this, Speaker, we had better come out of it with renewed prestige."

"Give me your vote against Salamander, and you will, Clan Elder. I have great things in mind for the future of the People."

The backswamp slowly drained away during those last days as Mother Sun crept ever so slowly toward solstice. Each summer at this time shallow pools formed where fish thrashed, fed, and often became stranded. Knowing the lay of the low contours, a fisherman with a properly set net could drag the shallows, effectively sweeping up the bounty.

Salamander squinted as he stepped into a patch of sun between the shade of two sweetgum trees. In the knee-deep water, mud squished between his toes. The midday heat seemed to weight the humid air. Insects flitted past on silver wings, while birds and locusts called from the trees. He bent at the waist, struggling against the sodden weight of the net.

"Hot today," Pine Drop called from across the small pond. "I could almost wish for some of that miserable cold from last winter." She was struggling step by step, leaning as she pulled at the ropes that controlled the net.

Salamander watched her. Toned muscles slid under her smooth brown skin. He could see the strength in her arms and the swell of her thighs as she sloshed through the muddy brown water. Her broad shoulders tensed under the weight of the wet netting. Droplets of water mixed with perspiration as she bent her back, using her round hips for leverage. The top and bottom ropes had to be pulled correctly to create a pocket for the fish. Pine Drop held each rope in a knotted fist.

She glanced across at him, seeing the expression on his face, frowning. "What's the matter?"

"Nothing."

"Why are you looking at me that way?"

"You are so beautiful. I was just trying to understand, that's all."

"Understand what?" She seemed completely confused.

"How I could have been so lucky to have had you for a wife. I spend a lot of time watching you."

"I know. Sometimes it's disturbing. That look in your eyes, I mean. As if you're about to melt."

"You do that to me. If I have to melt for anyone, I would want to melt for you."

She smiled then—shy, but happy. Her teeth gleamed in contrast to her lustrous black hair. "Do you want to pull on this net instead of wasting the day staring at me like I'm a lost Dream?"

"You are a Dream." He leaned into the net, dragging it onward through the shallowing water and onto the muddy flats. As more of the netting was pulled from the water it grew heavier. He could feel the weight of the fish, their struggles carrying as vibrations in the netting. They thrashed in the shallows, hampered by the cords that bound them. He could see heads, tails, and fins protruding from the boil.

"Together now," he called. "Pull! Pull! Pull!"

With each gasp, they threw their bodies against the sagging net, dragging the catch onto the mud. In the process the netting twisted neatly, trapping the fish in the folds.

Lungs heaving Salamander laid his end down. Fish were writhing, gasping, slapping against each other. He could see catfish, bowfin, gar, bass, suckers, and buffalo fish in the mix.

"Good catch!" Pine Drop said between gasps as she walked over to stand beside him.

"I thought so when I married you," he said.

Her gleaming brown eyes reflected amusement. "What is it with you today? Do you want something?"

He saw delight shining behind a flawed mask of female cynicism. "I just want you. And my girls. I want everything to stay just as it is today and never change. I want to love you, and hold you, and watch my daughters grow. I want it so badly that it makes my souls ache."

She reached out, drawing him into her arms. He sighed at the heat of her wet body. Her breasts were against his. Damp strands of her hair clung to the side of his face. His arms around her, he reveled in her breathing, then detected her heartbeat as his ear pressed against her neck.

"You have me, Salamander. For as long as you want me."

"I have asked for too much."

"That's nonsense. I am staying with you. It is our decision and no one else's."

"I just wish the decision was ours."

She pushed him back far enough to stare into his eyes. "The clans cannot make us do what we do not wish to."

He reached up to finger a damp lock of her hair away from her eyes. "I do not worry about the clans."

"Then who?"

"Masked Owl."

He could see her doubt. "Salamander, why? I mean, I know you have visions. I know about you and Power, but this worries me. Why would Masked Owl harm you?"

"Because I cannot do as he asks."

"Why not?"

"If I follow the path to the One, I will lose you. I will lose everything. Like Wolf Dreamer, I will fall into the Dream and everything else will become meaningless."

"I don't understand."

He raised a sympathetic eyebrow. "I don't think anyone wants to be a Dreamer. The cost is so high."

"Why can't you stay just the way you are?"

"Because black clouds are gathering—among the spirits as well as among the clans. It is all coming together, Pine Drop."

A frown pinched her forehead as she nodded. "I know. Uncle is up to something. I think he's going to accuse you of witchcraft. I think he's been making deals."

"He thinks Snapping Turtle Clan will finally become preeminent." Salamander ran his finger down the side of her cheek. "It isn't going to happen that way, Pine Drop."

"How do you know?"

"I've seen that part of the future." He could see doubt firming her expression, and added, "You must trust me on this."

"Trust you?" Irritation tugged at the corners of her mouth.

"Have you done so poorly on those occasions when I asked you to trust me?"

"Snakes, no. But it leaves me wondering how someone as young as you can always be right. You're

W. Michael Gear & Kathleen O'Neal Gear

three summers younger than I! Where did you learn all this?"

"In the Spirit World," he replied uneasily. "The things I've seen—"

"You're not using those mushrooms again, are you?" Warning flashed in her eyes.

"No. Not recently. I don't have to. Bird Man showed me things."

"Bird Man? *The* Bird Man?"

"Before I choose one way or another, however, I have to go see someone in the Spirit World."

"You're not making sense!"

He let himself look into her eyes, seeing her souls as they tried to comprehend him. "She is older than the Hero Twins. She saved my life that time."

"The old woman you talked about?"

"Yes."

She shook herself, stepping away, looking at the fish as they gasped and flopped in the net. "I don't understand this, Salamander. I just don't want to lose you. I've come to love you. Do you understand? I'm afraid!"

"So am I."

"Well, let's stop it! Let's find a way to save you."

He hesitated before testing the idea on her. "Would you give it all up?"

"What?" The question had taken her by surprise.

"All of it," he insisted. "Could you give up Sun Town? Give up being Clan Elder someday? Your position in the leadership? Your clan? Would you just go away with me? Knowing that we could live the rest of our lives in peace? Raise our daughter?"

She gave him a blank look. "Just leave? Everything?"

He nodded.

"The clan *is* everything, Salamander. It's who we are. What we are. The clan is our blood and bones, our heart and lungs and souls. It is the air we breathe and the food we eat. It is our warmth and protection. Everything, the whole world, is determined by the clan. What we own, where we go, who we marry. The clan gives us our place in the world."

"Yes, it does."

"So, you're asking, could I give up the whole world?" He could see the confusion behind her expression.

"That's right. Can you give up everything for nothing."

She slowly shook her head. "I don't think I understand you. I don't think you can give up the world, Salamander. To do what? Just go off and live at the edge of the Earth? Be alone?"

"Totally."

"In other words, you're asking if I could give up being a person."

"It's a hard question, isn't it?" The answer—the one he had expected—was in her eyes. He smiled reassuringly at her and indicated the fish. "Come on, we'd better stun the ones that haven't died yet and lug them to the canoe. The thing about a big catch like this is that work is just starting."

But a great sadness lay between his souls. If Pine Drop, the bravest person he knew, couldn't even comprehend the question, how could he find the courage actually to do what she thought unimaginable?

Chapter Sixteen

N ight Rain tried for all the world to look
normal. Belted at her waist, she wore a
fabric kirtle with a prominent turtle design
on the front. A square bark hat perched on her head
with two long brown pelican feathers stuck into her hair
above her ears. A single round ceramic pot hung from
the net bag over her shoulders.

Ceramic vessels were light, easily made, and reli-
able containers. For a people who practically lived in
canoes, they served many purposes. Placed in a fire,
they could be used to boil liquids and cook soups. By
preheating cooking clays, they could become a portable
oven for the baking of foodstuffs, and when traveling,
fire could be built inside, and the pot changed into a
portable heat stove. Finally, when collections of
nutmeats, dried seeds, and other foodstuffs were stored,
pots could be sealed so that rodents and insects couldn't
gain access. Generally it was for the latter purposes that
people carried ceramic vessels. The trouble with boiling
water inside them was that given their poor firing, the

food often acquired grit and tasted muddy as the inside of the pot began to flake away.

So it was that Night Rain approached the Owl Clan ridges from the north, her ceramic pot bouncing just above her buttocks.

She kept her head down, trying for all the world to appear as just another young woman at her daily tasks. She watched the ground ahead of her and cast surreptitious glances from the corner of her eye. After climbing out of the deep drainage that bounded the northern side of the Owl Clan grounds, she threaded her way along the path past the ridges. To her left, under the embankment, Morning Lake looked silver in the afternoon light. To the right, the ridgelines of houses cast shadows in curving ranks. Smoke drifted skyward from tens of tens of fires as meals were being prepared in anticipation of the solstice.

People were everywhere, many having arrived from outlying camps and settlements for the solstice celebration. Most had moved in with relatives, bearing sacks full of dried, smoked, and cured fish, meat, and plant foods. Most of these would be succulent meals by the time the ceremonies started.

Night Rain passed the second ridge and turned onto the first. She walked right up to Salamander's door and leaned her head in.

"Hello? Anhinga? Are you here?"

Silence.

Night Rain ducked inside and squatted by the smoking fire pit. She laid her ceramic bowl to one side and slipped it out of the netting. Only then did she take a moment for her eyes to adjust to the dim interior.

She rose and stepped to the wall where the tools

lay. There, propped against the wall, were two stone-headed hoes, Salamander's axe and adze, several hardened digging sticks, an assortment of bow drills for fire starting and drilling holes in stone, bone, and wood, and finally, yes, Anhinga's axe.

Night Rain reached out, her fingers tracing the smooth wood of the handle. She grasped it, her gaze running the handle's length with its carved panther design. She studied the sharp greenstone head set into a notch in the wood and wound tightly with deer sinew. The freshly ground edge was sharp where she pressed her finger against it. Sharp enough to cut. How well Night Rain remembered the blood streaming down Saw Back's side in a slick sheet.

Could this be the weapon that knocked a hole into Eats Wood's head? She tried to remember the wound in the top of that mud-browned skull. Oblong, sinister. Just like this axe.

Night Rain made a face as she remembered this very handle slapping her cold buttocks as Anhinga drove her home under a load of firewood and humiliation.

What a child I was. The moons since that horrible event seemed to have run together, to have woven themselves into something else. Her life up to that day in the forest might have belonged to a different person—some child she no longer knew.

"But I still belong to my clan," she whispered, grasping the axe. She turned and hesitated—Salamander's face forming between her souls.

What if Anhinga *had* killed Eats Wood?

Night Rain reached out and encircled the axe head

with her thumb and forefinger. Did the cool stone seem to vibrate? Was it alive, harboring some sort of soul?

Eats Wood was a maggot.

The often-uttered cautions slipped out of her memory: *"I don't want you girls alone with him! Do you understand?"*

She could imagine Mother bending down, pointing a stern finger in her face. *"That boy is not to be trusted! Not even with kin! Snakes, not even the horror of incest would worry his souls if it meant the opportunity to stick himself into pretty girls like you."*

Night Rain's expression hardened as she remembered the way Eats Wood used to look at her. Something in those eager brown eyes had chilled her souls.

If Anhinga is proven to be the killer, she'll be banished at best. At worst, Uncle would manage to have her killed.

And Salamander? What would that do to him? How many times had Night Rain wondered at the love in his eyes as he watched Anhinga? Snakes, it would wound his souls if anything happened to her.

Night Rain bit her lip, considered, and carefully replaced the axe. The reason why would plague her souls afterward, but at that moment of decision, she grabbed up Salamander's axe instead. She slipped the handle into the kirtle's belt and turned back to the fire.

With a stick she scraped some embers into the pot before she tucked it back into the net bag. "I just stopped for some hot coals to take back. It was just quicker than building a fire at home," she would say if anyone asked.

With a final glance, she ducked out the door, and as

casually as possible, started across the plaza for her uncle's.

Mud Stalker smiled as he bent down in the dusk and lifted the skull from the mud-caked canoe. Behind him, beyond the screen of thick cane and willows, he could hear talking as people passed up the channel in a canoe. Still more arrivals headed for Sun Town and the solstice celebrations. Their voices carried anticipation as they neared their goal. Sweet Root and Night Rain stood across from him. His sister's eyes gleamed, while Night Rain's looked disconnected, lost in a tangle of conflict. Conflict over what? This was her chance to even the score and pay that barbarian witch back for the humiliation of that long-ago day in the forest. She should be happy to see her junior wife proven guilty of murder.

"Does it fit?" Sweet Root asked, leaning forward in the dusk to see better. She batted at the humming column of mosquitoes with an irritated arm.

"Just a moment." Mud Stalker turned the skull, feeling the cold bone in his hand. How did a human head become so light? He paused, staring into the empty eye sockets, seeing the Y-shaped holes at the back. Even if he could do it by a wish, he wouldn't will Eats Wood's eyes back into those orbits. The young man had been a disappointment from the days of his birth, and truth to tell, Mud Stalker had always accepted that someday Snapping Turtle Clan would have to pay for the boy's indiscretions.

"Better this way," he whispered softly to the grinning skull. "You are now serving your clan as you never would have in life."

"The axe," Sweet Root reminded as she lifted it from where it had rested on the canoe gunwale. "Does it fit the hole?"

Mud Stalker turned the skull until it faced her.

She lowered the sharp edge to the oblong wound. The axe made a partial fit. The length was right, but something about the width didn't work.

"Close," Sweet Root noted.

Mud Stalker frowned. "I don't know. The edges aren't quite right. This isn't anything I could take to the Council." He glanced to the side, seeing relief on Night Rain's face. What was this? She was truly relieved to discover that that Swamp Panther camp bitch hadn't killed Eats Wood? Why?

Unwilling to give up, Mud Stalker gestured with his head and when Sweet Root removed the axe, he turned the skull around. He would try everything just be sure that he hadn't missed some...Sweet Root nearly dropped the edge of the axe into the hole in the top of Eats Wood's head.

"Perfect," Sweet Root whispered, her eyes widening.

"I'll be," Mud Stalker breathed. "She *did* kill him. But she sneaked up and hit him from behind."

This time when he shot a glance at Night Rain, it was to find her expression betraying shock, astonishment, and disbelief.

Feeling weary to her bones, smelling of fish, and with every muscle aching, Pine Drop plodded to her doorway. A faint glow of sunset still shone in the northwestern sky. The night smelled of smoke, cooking food, and voices carried in the air. She could hear laughter, cheerful banter, and the soft murmuring of conversations. In any direction fires sparkled and illuminated thatch-roofed houses, ramada roofs, and countless people. So many people came in from the hinterlands. So many fires. The smoky air over Sun Town had taken on a reddish cast. Normally, she admired the sight.

She shifted her daughter with one hand and used the other to ease the tumpline from her forehead as she lowered the basket of fish that rode in the hollow of her back. Straightening, she winced and made a face at the stiffness in her back muscles.

Her house and ramada were dark, seemingly deserted. She walked to the fire pit on the north side of the ramada and bent down, her sleeping daughter cradled on her lap. With a stick she stirred the coals, finding a few gleaming red eyes in the heavy hardwood ash. From the tinder pile she placed some twigs on coals, shifted her daughter, and blew carefully until flames flickered.

Bit by bit she built up the fire until it cast a cheery yellow light to illuminate the insides of the ramada and the big wooden pestle and mortar.

For a long moment she sat, tired, and stared into the fire. How did a person give up being who they were? How could she just walk away from her world?

"Was he talking outside of his souls?" she asked her sleeping daughter. "What are we without our homes? Without our families, lineages, and clans?"

Her baby's face was a round golden brown globe in the firelight. Silky strands of black hair had escaped the fabric wrap. Her tiny mouth hung open under the smooth button of her nose. The tightly closed eyes reflected an innocent peace.

Had he been serious about just going away? What would that solve? The people who depended on him would just have to find someone else to depend on. Owl Clan would continue its decline, and Snapping Turtle Clan would continue to grow in prestige.

"Hello, Sister," Night Rain greeted from the night as she appeared from behind the house.

"Where have you been?"

"Uncle and Mother had some things for me to do," Night Rain said with a hollow voice.

Even weary as Pine Drop was, she looked up as Night Rain squatted at the fire across from her. Her sister's face reminded her of one of the Earth Monster masks the men wore on ceremonial occasions. It was something about the set of the mouth, the emptiness in the eyes.

"What's wrong?"

"There will be a Council meeting called tomorrow." Night Rain reached a stick from the woodpile and inserted the end into the flames. As it caught fire, she lifted it, watching the fire eat at the wood before it went out and smoked. Night Rain inserted the smoking end into the flames again to relight.

"You don't always look like you're sick to your stomach when the Council is called."

"Uncle orders that we both be there."

"Blood and pus, I've got a canoe load of fish to dry." She jerked her head toward the basket. "That's part of it. I thought I'd get them split tonight and partially dried before the flies got to them." She worked her hands, feeling the muscles in her forearms, hot and cramped. "But all I want to do is sleep."

"You should know something."

"I should know many things." She rubbed her tired eyes, aware of how her hand smelled of fish. "I should know who I am."

"What?"

"Who am I, Night Rain? What am I?"

"What brought this about?"

"A question that Salamander asked me today." She studied her sister, seeing the sick worry in her face. "Could you give up being you? Could you just walk down to the canoe landing and paddle away from here? Maybe go and live somewhere in the forest without any clan or family? Could you just go away, Night Rain, and never see your mother, your uncle, or any of your friends? Could you stop being you?"

"No! No one could! That sounds completely witless. We are who we are: Sun People, Snapping Turtle Clan."

Pine Drop nodded. "I thought so, too."

Night Rain's expression had tightened. "Is Salamander thinking about running away?"

Pine Drop shrugged. "I don't know. I don't think so. It was just a question he asked...like so many of the other questions he asks. What is it about him? He can look you in the eyes, that gaze all soft and concerned, and ask you a simple question. It upsets your souls so that everything that you are is turned upside down and spilled out."

Night Rain's chuckle held a bitter irony. "I don't

know, Sister. I don't know what to think of him." She paused. "He knew I was pregnant before I did. How could he know that?"

"How can he do a lot of the things he does? The man is a mystery!" She took a breath. "Night Rain, I have come to love him like I never thought I could love a man. When he's not around, I am obsessed with thoughts about him. I keep things to show him, just waiting to see his smile."

Night Rain nodded distantly. "I recall the day when we first married White Bird, and how horrified we were at the thought of ending up married to Salamander."

"After he asked that question today we were working on the fish, gutting them, packing them in the canoe, and the next thing I knew, we were touching. And the next we were on the grass. I will never forget that coupling. It was as if he was trying to make it last forever. In the end, when his loins let loose in mine, I would have sworn my body had exploded into beams of sunlight.

"And then?"

"And then, after I finally returned to my body and caught my breath, the baby was crying."

Night Rain smiled, teasing the fire with her burning stick. "Keep that memory, Sister. Hold it close to your souls like a precious stone."

"I will." She glanced at Night Rain, reading her troubled eyes. "What happened to you today?"

"I got out of bed. I shouldn't have."

"You get out of bed every day. Why should this one be different?"

Night Rain's shoulders jerked. "You are right about Salamander. Things happen to him. It's odd how coincidences are. Just after I got out of bed this morning, I saw Saw Back. Everything goes back to him and Anhinga's axe. It makes me wonder if I'm not just Power's tool."

"I have enough worries about Power. Don't you get involved in it, too."

"It's too late. I already am." She jabbed the burning stick angrily at the fire. "Somehow, we ended up talking about Salamander. Saw Back hates him. Hates me. Not only for being there that day, for witnessing what Anhinga did to him, but because I went back to Salamander."

"He's your husband, what does Saw Back think wives do?"

"He knows that Uncle would have let me divorce. He knows that Salamander kept him from taking his revenge out on Anhinga by defusing that Council meeting. But the irony this morning was that he made such a big thing about Salamander being nothing more than a boy promoted beyond his means."

"Salamander's age baffles us all," Pine Drop agreed.

"Saw Back called him a coward, said that he'd faint if he ever had to really fight another warrior for his life. That he couldn't kill a beetle with a pestle."

"Salamander isn't a warrior," Pine Drop agreed.

Night Rain gave her a hooded look. "Isn't he?"

"What are you talking about?"

"Red Finger found Eats Wood's body. He was in his canoe, sunk under some roots down in the Swamp Panther country. Salamander's axe fits the hole in Eats Wood's head. Our husband killed our cousin, Sister. That's why Uncle has called the Council meeting for tomorrow. He is going to accuse Salamander of murder and witchcraft."

"We have to go. Warn him."

"No, Sister. Uncle and Mother both have ordered us to stay here. At this house, until tomorrow when the Council convenes."

"Rot eat them, Salamander is our husband. I'm going to warn him!" Pine Drop stood on aching legs, swinging her daughter up to her hip.

From the darkness, Water Stinger stepped out, calling, "Pine Drop, I am here on both the Elder's and Speaker's orders to see that you stay home tonight."

Chapter Seventeen

Over the past turning of the seasons, Anhinga had become used to Sun Town and its marvels. She had never expected to be awed by the place again, but this was her first experience with the summer solstice ceremonies.

She sat in the shadows of the ramada and watched the tens of tens of tens of fires winking around the span of Sun Town. A thousand yellow eyes flickered and filled the air with the scent of smoke. The reddish tint they cast into the hazy sky amazed her. Sun Town was shining its own light into the night. She could imagine the Sky Beings circling, looking down, and gasping with delight as night and day blurred.

Wing Heart sat at her loom, humming to herself as she worked the threads and continued her endless weaving. How she produced perfect fabric in the faint reflection of firelight never ceased to amaze Anhinga.

People passed in a constant stream, most of them strangers, clan members from outlying camps and distant settlements, many of them from as far away as the gulf, two tens of days distant by canoe. They came bearing gifts: feathers, meat, and bones from pelicans, or plumage from rosy spoonbills, red egret, and purple gallinue, and fish like black drum, red snapper, barracuda, and even one odd flat specimen that had both eyes on one side of its head. Some came with the smoked crab, conch, and whelk meat, and some came to Trade tanned sharkskin. Other canoes arrived filled with dried yaupon leaves for making black drink, and others with items like stingray spines to be used as needles and awls.

Trade nourished everywhere. She had seen no less than five marriages brokered between the different clans. No sooner had she gone back to work before another greeting was called between old friends who hadn't seen each other for seasons. Until this day, she would never have believed so many people lived in the whole world! The numbers of the Sun People left her dumbfounded.

And I thought I could fight them? That by the six of us raiding them, we would pay them back for Bowfin's death?

What a fool she had been, and how wise her uncle was. Old weathered Jaguar Hide had truly understood. And now, so did she, in a way, she wasn't sure that even her uncle could.

She nodded, remembering his wisdom in sending her back to stay. He had said something about learning their ways, not just for the moment, but for the future when she returned to the Panther's Bones for good. Yes, she knew them now. Knew their strengths and weaknesses. Most of all, she knew that the Swamp Panthers could never challenge such immense strength.

So, how did her people prevail against so many?

She recognized Salamander before she could make out his features. It was the way he walked, the set of his shoulders, his movements. He had grown so familiar to her, become part of her in a most unsettling way. Panther's blood, wouldn't it be so much simpler if he just left with her? She could make a place for him among her people. He could be happy with her. They could live out the rest of their lives together, raise their children, and love each other until they grew old, knotty, and decrepit.

"Greetings, Husband." She rose, seeing that he labored under a burden. "What have you brought?"

"We made a good catch. Filled the canoe," he told her, fatigue riding his voice.

She caught the odor of fish as she walked up to him and helped him to lower a full basket to the ground. "What has been done with them?"

"We gutted them. They need to be smoked and dried. I don't know how long they will last, especially given the number of people who have come for the ceremonials."

"Husband, most of them arrived in canoes gunwale full of food. I've never seen so much to eat, or so many mouths to feed."

He bent over to hug her, and she felt the trembling in his muscles. When she wrapped her arms around him, it surprised her to find his body hot from exertion. She pressed him to her and sighed. "You feel good, Husband."

"So do you. I could keep you like this for days."

"Promise?"

"Yes, but it will make attending the solstice activities a bit awkward. People will point at us and talk."

"They talk anyway. Look! There goes Speaker Salamander and his barbarian wife. We are already the center of attention. You should have been here today."

"How is our daughter?"

"Fine. She slept, ate, and messed, and slept and ate and messed, all day long. I made three trips for firewood, figuring that as things get busy, we won't have much time. It's a long way to go, and believe me, everything close has already been scavenged for the fires. Even the big trees that fell last winter are being chopped up."

"Thank you," he whispered. "I don't know what I'd do without you."

"Poor man, you would have to make do with only two wives!"

He chuckled at that and patted her shoulders as she broke away. She strained to lift the basket of fish and waddled to the ramada. Throwing more wood on the fire, she started laying the fish out on the split-cane matting.

"What's cooking?" Salamander indicated the two earth ovens.

"Lotus root," she lied heartily. "What would people say if the Owl Clan Speaker ate anything else for the solstice?"

"They'd say that he was deranged." He lifted his arms, smiling in the firelight. "But they say that anyway."

"As I started to tell you, a stream of people have been here. They come in bits and dribbles, wanting to speak to you. Most of them want to get a look at me, to see the famous barbarian wife. Others want to see you, to see if it's true that the clan has such a young Speaker." She made a face. "And many come to see your mother. Mostly the older ones, the ones who knew her when she and Cloud Heron were laying the opposition low. They look, shake their heads, and drift off to Moccasin Leaf's to discuss marriages, bickering between the lineages, and grievances with other clans." She pointed to the glow of a huge bonfire two ridges away. "Half Thorn is busy strutting back and forth like a mating pigeon. You could go look, he has all of his feathers preened."

"I'll pass," he muttered, a heaviness in his voice.

She watched him from the corner of her eye. "What is wrong, Salamander?"

"I want you to promise me something."

"Of course."

"If things begin to go badly, I want you to dress in Owl Clan clothing. Something Mother made, and take our daughter. I want you to get into a canoe and paddle south to your family."

"What are you talking about?"

"I'm talking about your safety. It is summer solstice. Canoes full of strangers are everywhere. If you're dressed as Owl Clan, no one will notice. You are just one of many. By the time you are in Swamp Panther country, you'll be safe."

She cocked her head. "What do you know, Husband?"

"I know that you are in great danger." Pain reflected in his smile. "I've done a terrible thing, Anhinga."

"What?" she asked, her gaze darting to the earth

oven where the water-hemlock root roasted in a bedding of yellow lotus.

"I've been selfish. Kept you and my little girl here with me. I knew better. I should have sent you south during the past moon."

"You're being silly," she answered uncertainly. "We're a family, remember? We decided that night after the affair with Night Rain and Saw Back."

"He's yet another worry. You must leave in secret," Salamander warned. "And make three times sure that no one sees you leave, especially Saw Back. You, of all people, know how dangerous he can be. This time, I won't be there to save you."

She stopped short, the cold carcass of a bass in her hands. "What do you mean? Tell me, Husband. What do you know? What has Masked Owl told you?" She felt her heart skip with fear, and not over the poisoned roots she was cooking.

He sank down, his back against one of the ramada poles, his head tilted as he stared up at the palmetto roofing. "Sometime soon now, I am going to have to do something very difficult. I have no reason to believe that what I am planning will work. You have heard the witchcraft stories?"

"Of course. Half of Sun Town thinks I'm a sorceress. The other half thinks you are a witch. Let them stew. No one wants to make a witch mad. It has repercussions. Like Dancing on the Bird's Head during a lightning storm. You never know when the next bolt might blast you dead."

"I wish you wouldn't use that analogy." He glanced nervously at Wing Heart's shadow where she worked the dimly lit loom.

"Sorry."

"It's not a joke," he answered. "That's why I need you to promise. If I tell you to, you must leave. If I fail, they will come to kill you. Do you understand what that means?"

She nodded, sobered, memories of being bound to the pole at the Men's House still fresh in her nightmares. "Yes, Husband, I do."

"Then you will go if I ask? You will save yourself and our daughter?"

She nodded, meeting his eyes. They reminded her of dark pools of misery. "I will not let them cut me apart, urinate inside my chest, and feed bits of my body to the dogs."

He sighed then, body limp with relief.

Hope rose in her heart as she softly said, "You could come with me. They don't need you here, Salamander. You do so much for these people who despise you, who call you a witch and a fool. They think you are a joke, a spineless boy parading as a Speaker."

"Sometimes I think that, too," he answered.

"You are not, you know." She smiled, laid out the last of the fish, and reached out to grasp his hand. "You have the respect of my clan. Of my brother and my uncle. I *love* you, Salamander. I, for one, don't want to live without you."

His smile was wary. "I thought you came here to kill me."

She hesitated. What did she say? How did she handle this? "I did. I have no love for the Sun People. I never will. You know what they did to me—did to my friends. But I have a great love for you." She swallowed, hard, and added, "I wish I had never had our daughter."

"Why?" He looked truly hurt.

"Because then I could stay and fight at your side," she said proudly. "If Half Thorn came for you, he would find two warriors ready to defend you rather than one."

"Warrior?" He stared off into the distance, no doubt remembering the blow that dispatched Eats Wood.

"Warrior," she affirmed. "Come with me, warrior. In time we can work something out, some means whereby we can see Pine Drop and Night Rain."

"We?" he asked with mild curiosity.

She shrugged, as if it were nothing. "Well, somehow, over the moons, I have come to like them a little. It wouldn't displease me to see them periodically."

"Your secret is safe with me."

She gave him a slow smile, hoping against hope. "Will you come away with me?"

"Funny, isn't it? I asked that same question of Pine Drop. Not meaning quite the same thing, but with the same result. She, too, said no."

"I don't understand."

"It would be so easy, and at the same time, so hard. We could all escape the pain, Anhinga. All we have to do is give up our responsibilities. Why is that so hard? Why is it easier to stay and die than it is simply to stop being ourselves to become someone else?"

She stared at him, frowning, hearing the importance of his words but not quite understanding the weight of the ramifications.

He pointed at Wing Heart. "Isn't that what Mother did? She gave up. Her souls left her body so that they didn't have to face the pain and disappointment. Pine Drop won't stop being who she is to run off with me. I won't stop being who I am to run off with you." A faint smile bent his lips. "You won't stop being who you are to stay here with me."

I won't stop being who I am? What is he talking about? And then her gaze slipped to the covered earth ovens with their simmering cache of hemlock-laced yellow lotus root. She felt a tingle race across her skin. Panther's blood! He couldn't know, could he? If he did, why didn't he stop her? Challenge her over it?

She could feel his knowing stare burning through her skin as she avoided his gaze. *It's your nerves. If he knew, he'd never allow you to get away with this!*

She took a breath, trying to think of what to say, but her response was cut off when Yellow Spider appeared out of the night, saying, "Salamander? There is news. Mud Stalker and Deep Hunter are calling the Council to session tomorrow morning."

"I see."

Anhinga saw the slow spread of misery in his expression.

"It's serious," Yellow Spider added, his muscles bunching under his smooth brown skin. "I have contacts, people who are obliged from the Trade White Bird and I brought down river. They are going to accuse you of witchcraft tomorrow."

"I have been anticipating that." Salamander's fists opened and closed. "Cousin, no matter what, I want you to remember your promise to me that day at the canoe landing. Will you do as I ask, not as your heart demands?"

What was this? Anhinga turned her eyes on Yellow Spider. He was fidgeting, rocking his weight from foot to foot. A faint nod was his only answer.

"Good," Salamander said with a sigh.

"What are you going to do?" Anhinga asked.

Salamander's lips twitched. "I am going to try to save myself and the clans," he answered. "As we were just discussing, sometimes in order to save yourself, you must give up everything. Timing will be the most important thing." With that, he pushed himself to his feet, looking completely haggard.

"What are you going to do?" Yellow Spider demanded.

"For the moment"—silver fish scales glittered on Salamander's hand as he rubbed his face—"I am going to see Speaker Thunder Tail. After that, I have a stop to make at the Serpent's. Then, if I can, I am going to try and get a full night's sleep."

Wing Heart's voice caught them by surprise. "If there is any trouble, you be sure to alert Speaker Cloud Heron. He'll handle it."

"Yes, Mother." Salamander sounded like his souls were bleeding. "I will do that first thing."

"I'm coming with you," Yellow Spider said, and for the first time, Anhinga noticed the axe hanging from his hand.

"Me too!" Anhinga cried. She hadn't made two steps before Salamander's hand caught her elbow.

"No, please," he said gently. "If you would help me, be here when I return. I won't be able to sleep tonight unless you are here to hold me."

The fear in his voice paralyzed her. She stood rooted as her husband and his kinsman walked off into the night.

Chapter Eighteen

D ew gave the world a grayish tint in the pale light of dawn. Salamander prodded the smoking fire with a stick as he looked out past the pestle and mortar to the plaza. The grass had been beaten flat by the Northern Moiety players as they prepared for the game, now only three days away. Fingers of silky mist wound around the Women's House where it perched atop the Mother Mound. They drifted over the plaza and slipped between the houses like ghostly serpents on the prowl. The Bird's Head was sheathed in gray, a Spirit figure dominating the west.

He could feel the last tendrils of the Dream, like the dawn mist, slowly fading away. The vision had been so clear. He could still see the images old Heron had shown him of the coming day.

He had used the smallest sliver of mushroom. It had been enough to open the doors of his Dreams. He had reached Heron, Danced with her, and she had let him see.

Salamander poked at a coal and sniffed at the mint

tea that steamed in a stone bowl at the fire's edge. In the growing light, he could make out the latest of his mother's fabrics, a white, red, and purple design that sported a red potbellied owl with huge eye disks in the center.

Salamander stared into the round black eyes she had woven into the fabric. Was he still seeing through the fast-shrinking tunnel brother mushroom had opened, or was the creature really alive?

"So, we have come to it, haven't we?"

The weaving remained mute.

"Today, I shall make my decision. You and Many Colored Crow must wait to see which of you I choose. Or will you take that chance? What if you just killed me? Would another be more compliant to your wishes than I am?"

The owl's large eyes pried at him, trying to see into his souls.

Salamander stepped over and inspected the fabric. He ran his fingertips over it, feeling the softness. Mother had used carefully separated flax fibers. As far as Salamander could tell, she had finished last night before retreating to her bed. Using a sharp stone flake, he cut the threads and lifted the fabric from the loom. After one last admiration, he draped it over his shoulders, then resettled himself at the fire to keep track of his tea.

His eyesight blurred with bits of the vision old Heron had granted him. The day's events unfolded like a lotus flower. He saw Pine Drop, her eyes blazing righteously as she faced the Council. Saw Back stood guard in the darkness, his souls wreathed in hate and anger. Anhinga pointed at two ceramic pots decorated with interlocking owls. Mud Stalker smiled at him in triumph. He saw the craftiness in Deep Hunter's eyes. Half Thorn gleefully clapped his hands, crying, "I win! I am to be Speaker!"

Salamander blinked hard to fracture the vision. He glanced back at his house, satisfied that Anhinga still slept soundly. After completing his errands the night before and tucking his daughter in, he had taken her to his bed. For a hand of time, they had alternately held each other and coupled until she had fallen into a deep and exhausted sleep.

It was afterward that he had lifted the thin bit of mushroom to his lips and begun calling for old Heron.

The mint leaves swirled slowly in the hot water, the fresh tang flavoring the very air. In the growing light, Salamander could see that the water had turned amber. Satisfied, he used an old rag to wrap his hand and moved the stone bowl to one side. Then he opened the little pouch and sprinkled a powder into the steaming liquid, making sure to keep his nose upwind of the rising steam.

He had realized that the tea was necessary to his plans when he noticed the missing axe and fitted it to the vision. Its spot in the collection of tools was ominously vacant. Coupled with the silence, he could guess at the reasons for Pine Drop's absence.

"It will be better this way," he told the morning, and glanced eastward. A glowing iridescent rose light surrounded by a softening lavender filled the northeast beyond the mist-shrouded trees across Morning Lake. Brother mushroom tugged playfully at his souls, smearing the colors in the sky.

Salamander smiled, imagining the view from the Bird's Head. It was going to be a glorious morning. He wondered how many of the people in Sun Town would take the time to enjoy it.

Mud Stalker smiled and stretched as he sat up on his bed. He could hear the murmur of voices outside, and the angle of light through the door told him that Mother Sun was nearly two hands high above the horizon.

"Is it morning?" Three Moss asked as she rolled onto her side and slitted her sleep-heavy eyes.

"It is." Mud Stalker bent his head back, feeling the bones in his neck crackle and the muscles pull.

Three Moss stretched before she threw back the elkhide, wiggled past him, and stood. The nipples on her full breasts looked like burnished copper. The width of her hips compensated for her thick waist, and the gleaming black wealth of pubic hair reminded him of bear fur.

"Would you like to eat with Mother and me before the Council meeting?" Three Moss watched him as she caught up her loose hair and pulled it back into a shock behind her head. She smiled as his gaze fixed on her taut breasts. "I would think you hadn't been with a woman for moons, Speaker. Had you forgotten what a woman's body is like?"

He chuckled. "I had indeed. Moons, yes. It's been even longer than that."

"I enjoyed myself," she told him evenly, eyes measuring. "Myself, I would have no objection to sharing a bed with you every so often."

"And your husband?" He raised an eyebrow.

"He is a hunter who prefers the swamp—and I

think he spends a great many nights in beds that aren't warmed by my body."

"I see."

"For now, just consider the advantages that might be of benefit to your clan. After today, I would expect Snapping Turtle Clan to have a great deal of prestige. Frog Clan, with my influence, might be a solid ally for you, Speaker. I can't wait to tell Mother that Moccasin Leaf has agreed to return our root grounds. It will make her most happy. Almost as happy as I was several times last night."

He nodded. "I, too, enjoyed last night. At my age, and for as little practice as I have had in the last turning of the seasons, it was a delightful reminder that I'm not decrepit."

She laughed at that. "No, indeed you are not."

"But I will pass on breakfast. Give my regards to the Clan Elder. I have some things to see to before the Council meets. This is too important to allow anything to go amiss."

She nodded as she found her kirtle, wadded on the floor where it had been hastily discarded the night before. Her eyes held his as she slipped it on. "Why do men always give a woman that look when she dresses?"

"Because deep in our souls we see it as an ending rather than a beginning," he replied. "Endings are always laced with regret while beginnings are sprinkled with hope."

She stopped at the door, one hand on the cane-pole frame. "This is just the beginning, you know. After Owl Clan, you still have to unseat Thunder Tail. Deep Hunter will be thinking the same thing."

He nodded. "I have plans for him."

She smiled. "Will I see you tonight?"

He stood, making a face as his bones complained. With his good hand he recovered his breechcloth and belt. "If all goes as I hope, I was thinking of feasting the Council tonight. Invitations have already gone to the Clan Elders. Had you not been otherwise occupied last night, you would have heard."

"I see." A smile. "And after the feast, what? Politics with the Speakers?"

"Some. But after that, perhaps I would be interested in discussing some things with a Clan Elder's daughter."

"Yes, well, after last night it will be interesting to see just how long you can still paddle in my canoe, Speaker."

"Let's hope I'm not *that* decrepit."

And then she was gone.

He stood for a moment, frowning down at the smoldering embers in the fire pit. Cane Frog was old. How many seasons did she have left anyway? Was it worth a marriage to Three Moss? Or would his interests be better served with a different alliance? Perhaps one of Deep Hunter's nieces? True, they were all currently married, but as he had come to understand so well, things could happen to a husband. Only this time, no crow was going to lead any hunter to the body.

Each time Pine Drop shot a glance in Water Stinger's direction, she fumed. How dare her mother and uncle treat her like a common captive? By blood and pus, she was their daughter! A woman married to a Speaker, one who had provided her lineage and clan with an heir! Yet here she was, treated like an errant child, who, if she pushed the issue, would end up in public humiliation when her kinsman physically prohibited her from leaving her house.

Her fire popped and crackled in the bright morning light as she continued the chore of smoking the last of yesterday's catch of fish.

It was but two days to the beginning of the solstice ceremonies. Sun Town had become a hive. People kept passing and calling solstice greetings to her. Some she knew, others were strangers. She played the game, keeping her voice light as she called polite responses. Reading their expressions, she realized that no one but her seemed aware that something sinister and brooding was being hatched. That gave her pause.

Night Rain ducked out of the house wearing a white kirtle belted at the waist. Her thick hair was parted, appropriate to her married status and pulled back over her shoulders. She had inserted long white heron feathers at an angle over her ears. As attractive as she looked, a single glance at her eyes would have been sufficient to discourage anyone from approaching her.

She walked over and crouched beside Pine Drop—so close that their thighs were touching. "We're still captives."

"Water Stinger insists on watching my every move." Pine Drop reached over and tucked the cloth around her baby's face where the infant slept in the cradleboard. "I threw a cooking clay at him when he insisted on following me down to the borrow pit. I *don't* need my cousin peering up my rear as I squat."

"He is under Uncle's orders." Night Rain made a face. "But I'll take a cooking clay with me next time."

"I got my revenge when I changed Tadpole after her feeding."

"Tadpole?"

"It seemed more fitting for a little girl than Mud Puppy. Not only is she Salamander's child, but each time Uncle hears the name, it's going to drive him wild."

"When did you decide this?"

"Last night. She's old enough for a name, Night Rain. It's been three moons since she was born. If her souls haven't settled into her body, they never will. I think it's safe to name her now."

Night Rain ground her teeth as she studied Water Stinger. The young warrior leaned insolently against the house wall ten paces distant, face expressionless, arms crossed as he watched them.

"Why do you think Salamander killed Eats Wood?" Night Rain asked bluntly.

"*If he* killed Eats Wood—and we still don't know for a fact that he did—I would wager a moon's food that he had a good reason. Snakes! I wish I could just talk to him!"

"Did he ever flatly deny it?"

Pine Drop had been considering just that. "Now that you mention it, no. Thinking back, he very cleverly evaded the question. I need to talk to him."

"Uncle doesn't trust us when it comes to Salamander."

"You were there. Did the axe really fit the wound?"

"Perfectly." Night Rain shook her head. "I can't believe I did this to him. If I'd taken Anhinga's axe like

Uncle wanted, it wouldn't have fit. The shapes are different. I looked at them very closely."

Pine Drop studied her sister. "I still don't understand why you did that."

Night Rain's shoulders rose and fell. "I don't either. Isn't it silly? I just want everything to be like it was. I want us to be a family. You, me, Anhinga, and Salamander. I should hate them, but somehow I don't. How did that happen?"

"You were happy," Pine Drop said. "We all were. Salamander made it happen."

"I didn't want to see him hurt." Night Rain lowered her head and squeezed her eyes shut. "I always do the wrong thing! I always hurt the people I love. What's the *matter* with me?"

"Do you follow your clan, or your heart?" Pine Drop asked absently. "That's partly what Salamander meant yesterday." She took a breath, coming to a decision. "All right, are you up to stopping this silliness?"

Night Rain wiped at tears that dampened her eyes. "What did you have in mind?"

"A way to save us, if you don't mind lying a little. It is sure to enrage Mother and Uncle. It may have terrible consequences for us. Uncle might even cast us out of Sun Town for it."

Night Rain was looking half-sick. "Why don't you tell me what you're thinking before I have to decide."

"I killed Eats Wood."

"*What?*"

"Uncle wants us at that Council meeting. He wants us to see Salamander charged with murder as well as with witchcraft. We are to be witnesses to his disgrace and humiliation. That way, we will be docile nieces the next time he needs to marry us off for the clan's benefit."

"You mean to say that in Council? That *you* killed Eats Wood?"

Pine Drop peered coolly into her sister's shocked eyes. "Think about it. A clan is responsible for the behavior of its own. Eats Wood was a walking spineless leech. A wiggling bloodsucker who would have eventually glutted his appetite on some young woman. He was trouble waiting to happen. We agree on that, right?"

"Yes."

"Well, our story is that he came on me in the forest just after Tadpole was born. He wanted to taste my milk, wanted to slide into my canoe as he watched my naked baby's body."

"That's *disgusting!*"

"As disgusting as a man can get," Pine Drop agreed. "I had Salamander's axe that day. I had taken it from his house while I was on the way to gather firewood." Her lips quirked. "Our family has a history of getting into trouble when we're after firewood."

"Not funny."

"When I finally realized that Eats Wood wasn't just making crude jokes, I was so upset and distressed that I crashed the axe through his head."

"From behind. That's the only way the axe fits."

"From behind," Pine Drop agreed, fitting that new fact into her story. "Let's see. He turned toward Tadpole, who was on the ground in her cradleboard, and I struck."

"So, how did he end up in a canoe under a root down in the Jaguar Hide's swamp."

"Because I asked Salamander to help me dispose of

the body. You, Salamander, and I carried him to the canoe landing one night, and Salamander took him away. You and I had no idea where, and we didn't ask."

Night Rain looked horrified. "You would do this? Say this?"

"And you will say that it is the truth."

"Why?"

Pine Drop smiled. "Because, like you, I want to be happy again. I want to spend the rest of my life with the man I love."

"You might be giving up the chance to be Clan Elder."

"You can take my place. Most of the blame will be mine."

Night Rain gaped. "You would actually do that?"

Pine Drop nodded. "I know my husband. Whatever he did, it was done to protect someone, to keep them from harm. No matter what, Night Rain, he will not be given a fair chance in the Council. You and I both know that."

Night Rain nervously chewed her lip, her brow lined. "Uncle will know it's a lie. He will wonder why I didn't say something or do something when I brought him the axe. Snakes! He still thinks it belongs to Anhinga."

"It was an easy mistake to make," Pine Drop said simply. "You were upset at having to steal Anhinga's axe. You ducked into Salamander's house, grabbed the first axe you found, and ran. Uncle may not believe it, but the Council will."

"Snakes, I'm already feeling scared," Night Rain muttered. "I've never done anything like this before."

"If we don't save him, Night Rain, we will hate

ourselves for the rest of our lives. Do you want to live with that?"

"No, Sister. I'm with you all the way."

"Hello the camp!" a pleasant male voice called.

They turned to see Yellow Spider walking up with a drinking gourd cupped in his hands. "Salamander sends his greetings! He made tea this morning, and since there was extra, he wanted you to have this."

Water Stinger stepped forward, a keen expression on his face.

Pine Drop jumped to her feet, hurrying to meet Yellow Spider before Water Stinger could come close. She smiled into Yellow Spider's strained face and took the gourd. In a loud voice, she declared, "Thank you, Yellow Spider." In a hushed rash, she whispered. "You must tell Salamander to trust me today like I once trusted him!" With her eyes, she burned emphasis into each of her words.

"He told you to remember him fondly as you share it." Yellow Spider replied bluffly, playing his part with difficulty. The faint wink and slightest jerk of his head in acknowledgment filled her with relief.

"Would you care to join us?"

Water Stinger was now too close for subterfuge.

"I have things to do." Yellow Spider touched his forehead in respect. "But thank you for your kind offer."

"Give our husband our regards," Night Rain called in a too-shrill voice. "We will see him soon."

Yellow Spider managed a quick glance at Water Stinger, read the man's aggressive posture, and nodded before he turned on his heel and strode away.

He sent us a gourd full of tea? What is this all about?
Pine Drop evaded Water Stinger's eyes and retreated to

W. Michael Gear & Kathleen O'Neal Gear

the ramada where she squatted beside Night Rain. Lifting the gourd, she sloshed the liquid and sniffed. The soothing aroma of mint filled her nose.

"He sent us tea," she said as she studied the gourd container. "Isn't that just Salamander's way? The whole world is about to fall on him with claws and fangs, and he sends us tea."

Night Rain took the gourd and drank. "It's good, too. Try some."

Chapter Nineteen

Anhinga was wrapping clean moss around the baby's bottom when Salamander ducked through the door. He stepped over and smiled down at his daughter. Anhinga tied the thongs that bound the little girl in the fabric wrap.

"She's beautiful, isn't she?" Salamander said with longing.

"She has her mother's looks and her father's souls," Anhinga replied and straightened. She lifted an eyebrow at the roll of clothing in his hands.

"For you." He extended them. "If you would put this on before you leave, anyone who sees you, even from a distance, will believe you to be a member of Owl Clan."

She read the tension he tried so hard to hide. "It has really come to that?"

Hating to, he gave her a short nod.

"You and I, Husband, are not like the others. We know that life is neither fair nor predictable." She ran her fingers along his face as she stared into his eyes.

"Perhaps Power places us where we are for specific reasons, as your Masked Owl would have you believe. I will go the moment Yellow Spider assures me that Saw Back is otherwise occupied."

"Thank you," he said unsteadily.

"You made me promise," she recalled. "And now I will make you promise something."

"What is that?"

"Come to me." She bent down and kissed him gently on the lips. "You are the bravest man I know. If you live through this, I will be waiting for you at the Panther's Bones."

"I promise. If I live, I will come to you," he whispered. "Never forget my love for you."

From outside, Yellow Spider's worried voice called, "Salamander?"

"It is time." He turned reluctantly, then looked back, haunted eyes pleading with hers.

"Go, my husband," she told him simply. "Or come with me now, and we will leave this all behind us."

"We are who we are," he whispered and ducked out the door.

For a long moment, Anhinga's heart seemed to sink right through her body and into the muddy earth. She closed her eyes, feeling the hammering of loneliness closing around her.

How long she stood, she couldn't say. Then a voice penetrated her benumbed souls. "Salamander?"

Her frantic thoughts searched and placed a name with the voice. "Little Needle? Is that you?"

A round and youthful face appeared in the doorway. "Has Salamander gone to the Council?"

"He has." Anhinga smiled at the boy. "But he asked

me if I saw you, to ask you for a favor. He would like you to do something for him."

"He's Clan Speaker," Little Needle answered. "He can just order it."

"That's not Salamander," she told him warmly, "and you know it."

Little Needle smiled with an apparent wistfulness. "I know."

Anhinga pointed to the two large ceramic pots resting on cane matting beside the door. "Do you see those pots? The ones with the owl designs on the side? They need to be delivered, Little Needle. One needs to be placed at Speaker Deep Hunter's fire, and the other set inside Mud Stalker's doorway. You are *not* to do two things. First, you are not to sneak a taste! Do you understand?"

At the boy's solemn nod, she added, "And you are *not* to mention this to anyone! Not to the Speakers, and certainly not to Moccasin Leaf. Salamander wants to tell the Speakers of this special gift in his own way. Do you understand why that might be?"

Little Needle, big-eyed, jerked another nod.

"Good. Salamander thinks very highly of you, you know."

"I know." His voice sounded small.

"If you could place those pots without being seen, it would make the surprise even bigger. Could you do that?"

"I think so."

"Good." She smiled at him, thought for a heartbeat, and reached for the little red chert owl that Salamander had been carving. Finished, but for the polishing, the little potbellied figure was cool in her hand. "In return for your service, I want you to have this. It's to remember Salamander by."

Little Needle studied the little owl she dropped into his hand, and tears welled in his eyes. "Thank you, Anhinga. I'll do it." He swallowed a sob. "For him. No one will see me, I promise."

A terrible battle raged in Mud Stalker's souls as he surveyed the huge crowd that had gathered around the Council House. He wanted to pace back and forth irritably, to release the rampant energy that powered his bones and muscles. But he dare not. He had waited all of his life for this moment, planned of it, Dreamed of it. If Snapping Turtle Clan was to be ascendant, he must show himself and Sweet Root as controlled, steady, confident, and worthy of leadership.

His souls screamed to be about this last great task. He nodded to people as he met their eyes, keeping his face calm and possessed. He kept his bad arm cradled, struggling to project the countenance of a serene Speaker faced with a difficult task. The mighty weight of the clans was poised, watching, waiting with him.

Where are Pine Drop and Night Rain? The question ate at him as he looked at Sweet Root. His sister stood to one side, her back resting against one of the poles. She had a sour look on her face, her darting eyes betraying her growing anxiety.

Mud Stalker turned, looking across at Owl Clan's contingent. Moccasin Leaf's face was pinched, her eyes glittering. Beside her, Half Thorn had a stupid smile on his lips. He was greased, dressed in a fine white breechcloth with a purple-dyed cape over his shoulders. He had stuck so many white heron feathers into his hair that he looked like a bristly flower.

That is the man I am going to make Speaker of Owl Clan. Not even the elevation of Salamander had filled him with such disgust. *Ah, Wing Heart, if only your souls had stayed around to see this. But, perhaps it is better that they have fled. As great as you were, it is better that you have escaped the humiliation.*

At Alligator Clan's spot, Deep Hunter fretted. He reminded Mud Stalker of a male dog standing over a pile of scraps. He was anxious to growl and show his teeth, but he was unsure at whom to snap. Colored Paint was talking in low tones to Sour Mouth and Saw Back in the shaded rear where the rest of the lineage leaders were gathered.

Mud Stalker centered his attention on the young warrior with the misshapen face. Saw Back's eyes might have been hot stones. He kept smiling in that lopsided manner he had adopted, and his gaze kept turning to Owl Clan, as if in anticipation of his enemy's arrival.

In Frog Clan's spot, Three Moss was leaning to speak into her mother's ear, her hand on the old woman's bare shoulder. It would speak volumes through the silent movement of fingers against the old woman's skin on this day.

Clay Fat looked miserable, as if he'd eaten something for breakfast that disagreed with him. Clan Elder Turtle Mist's head was tilted his way, her mouth moving as she spoke in obvious irritation. Clay Fat was the only unknown. He might vote either way. Not that it mattered, with Cane Frog in hand, Mud Stalker had his majority.

Eagle Clan's Thunder Tail sat beside Stone Talon, a brooding darkness behind his stiff face. He seemed not to see or hear anything but the plodding thoughts slipping between his souls.

Enjoy yourself today, Leader, it will not be many moons from now before I take your place.

A stir in the crowd was the only warning before Salamander pushed through the throng and walked into the eastern entrance. A sudden hush fell on the Council House as all eyes turned toward him.

Salamander seemed unreasonably calm, as if he had no idea what lay in store for him. He wore a simple brown breechcloth while a spectacularly dyed fabric draped from his shoulders. Wing Heart's work, most definitely. Mud Stalker could almost feel the owl's eyes staring back from the design.

To Mud Stalker's surprise, Salamander called some sort of greeting to Saw Back. The latter just glared in return.

A half heartbeat later, Salamander nodded to Yellow Spider, and the warrior slipped away through the crowd.

What was *that* all about?

It was then that Water Stinger appeared at his elbow. "Speaker?"

"Yes, what is it? Where are Pine Drop and Night Rain?"

"Sick, Speaker."

Mud Stalker blinked, trying to absorb the information. "What do you mean, sick?"

Water Stinger looked truly mystified. "They were fine until a half hand of time ago. Then, all of a sudden, Night Rain threw up. A moment later, so did Pine

Drop. I put them in their beds, but they are not well. Their eyes are all wrong, their pupils have grown large. The worst thing is, Speaker, they are delirious, talking to people who are not there."

"What?"

"I think it is some kind of fever, but their bodies are not hot, and they aren't sweating. It's just the opposite. They feel cool to the touch, breathing slowly. You would think they were more corpses than alive."

"Attention! Your attention, please! I think we are all here," Thunder Tail called as he stepped out into the open by the smoldering central fire. "This Council has been called to deal with a most serious matter."

Mud Stalker pushed Water Stinger away in irritation, trying to recapture the string of his thoughts. "We'll have to do without them. Go, Cousin. Be ready for my signal." He stepped forward, waiting to be acknowledged by the Leader.

Thunder Tail raised his voice, trying to be heard by as many as possible. "It has been alleged by some that Speaker Salamander of Owl Clan has been involved in witchcraft, his spells and attacks having been leveled against not only his own relatives, but others as well."

A ripple of conversation rolled through the crowd. Mud Stalker tried to keep the smile of satisfaction from his lips.

"That is not the only charge." Thunder Tail looked from face to face around the Council. "Speaker Salamander's third wife, the woman known as Anhinga, is believed to have murdered a young man named Eats Wood, a member of the Snapping Turtle Clan."

Another eruption of conversation followed.

"These are serious charges!" Thunder Tail gave Mud Stalker a hard stare. "Who makes these charges?"

Mud Stalker and Sweet Root stepped forward, crying in unison, "We do!"

Deep Hunter also stepped out, not to be left behind, and cried, "Alligator Clan makes these charges."

"As does Frog Clan!" Cane Frog's reedy voice barely carried across the circle.

To everyone but Mud Stalker's surprise, Moccasin Leaf strode out and cried, "So does Owl Clan!"

All eyes turned to Clay Fat, who stood uncomfortably and stepped out from under the palmetto-and-cane roofing to squint in the sun. "Rattlesnake Clan is unsure. We would hear the evidence."

Mud Stalker had been hoping for just that request. He raised his hand high over his head, the signal to Water Stinger. "Snapping Turtle Clan will address the murder of our young warrior first." Give them a brutally murdered corpse to start with, and the less substantive charges would follow of their own accord.

A buzz of voices and a stirring of the crowd preceded the six strong young men who came forward at a trot. Between them, they bore Eats Wood's mud-caked canoe. Red Finger came striding along behind, a cardinal-feather cloak over one shoulder, his creamy white breechcloth swinging with each step. Sunlight glistened on his gray hair.

The canoe was borne through the eastern entrance and laid carefully on the ground at Mud Stalker's feet.

Mud Stalker glanced around the Council. "I would have this Council recognize my cousin, Red Finger. It was he who found Eats Wood's canoe."

As Red Finger recounted his story about the pesky crow, Mud Stalker's souls delighted at the expressions he saw in the audience. People were truly captivated and awed.

Red Finger finished and produced the little round white stone. He held it between thumb and forefinger as he turned so that all could see it.

Mud Stalker cried, "What are we to learn from this? Power wanted Eats Wood's murderer found!"

He glared hard at Salamander, expecting to see some reaction: embarrassment, guilt, confusion, something. The young Speaker just stood as if listening to a discussion of the weather.

Mud Stalker gestured with his left hand. "When my kinsmen returned with the canoe and Eats Wood's bones, we were at a loss. Why would this have happened? Who would have hidden his canoe and his body in the Swamp Panther lands? Why there?" He turned his head, directing everyone with his hard stare.

Salamander waited with his head cocked, paying attention, but unconcerned.

"Following the trail to its logical end," Mud Stalker continued as he stepped carefully back and forth behind the canoe, "we sent my niece, Night Rain, to obtain the Swamp Panther woman's axe."

He bent down and picked it up from the bones within the canoe.

Sweet Root lifted Eats Wood's skull, saying, "If you will look, you can see the fatal wound. Here." Her brown finger pointed to the oblong hole in the round dome of the skull. "Not only was Eats Wood murdered by this axe, but if you will notice, he had to have been struck down from behind!"

Mud Stalker aligned the axe just so, while Sweet Root placed the skull so that all could see the perfect fit. At Clay Fat's scowl, Mud Stalker said, "Oh, don't worry. You will all have plenty of time to see how well this fits."

Clay Fat shook his head. "You might have used Anhinga's axe *after* you found the skull. This proves nothing!"

"Look at the mud in the wound!" Sweet Root cried. "If you crush a dirty skull, the bone breaks cleanly and has a different color. You know that." She pointed at Saw Back. "It's not as if we don't know this woman's handiwork with an axe!"

"Agreed! *Agreed!*" Deep Hunter cried. "We would have dealt with this once before, but for certain interference with this Council."

Again, all eyes turned to Salamander. His expression was thoughtful, his eyes almost dreamy, as if he had seen this all before.

Clay Fat muttered under his breath and shot a worried look at Salamander.

"Does the Speaker for Owl Clan have *anything* to say about this?" Thunder Tail asked gravely.

In his preoccupied manner, Salamander stepped forward. He paused for a moment and studied the axe in Mud Stalker's hand. The way he smiled, it might have been a private joke.

In a firm voice, he said, "That is not Anhinga's axe."

Mud Stalker realized he was staring—dumbfounded as the rest. "What? Night Rain herself took this axe from your house!"

"That is not Anhinga's axe," Salamander repeated. "If you are familiar with her axe, it has a series of panthers carved into the handle in an interlocking design."

"Then whose axe is it?" Deep Hunter demanded.

"It is my axe," Salamander said casually. "For reasons of her own, Night Rain took my axe from the house that day."

"Anhinga killed Eats Wood with your axe?" Mud Stalker wondered.

Salamander smiled as if in benevolence to a simple fool. "Anhinga killed no one, Speaker."

"Wait!" cried Clay Fat as he stepped out, one hand up. "Yes, that axe fits the hole in the skull. But, let us keep in mind, there are many axes! Axes, by their nature, are all roughly the same size. What if we tried fitting every axe in Sun Town to that wound? How many matches would we have? Tens of tens? More? This proves nothing!"

"It proves *everything!*" Mud Stalker thundered back.

"Speakers, please!" Salamander stepped forward, his hands up. "Let me speak."

Thunder Tail jerked a nod. "The Owl Clan Speaker has the right to speak."

Salamander threw a fond smile in Clay Fat's direction. "I thank you for your open mind, Speaker Clay Fat. It is refreshing to find yet another individual who thinks in terms of the People before he thinks of his own personal gain. For that, I am truly obliged in my souls."

"Who killed Eats Wood?" Mud Stalker shouted.

"Hush!" Thunder Tail ordered.

Salamander turned, his head cocked. In the open circle, he didn't look like much—just a short, skinny young man with large, dreamy eyes and a knowing expression. "For reasons which need not concern this Council, I killed Eats Wood, Speaker."

Mud Stalker stopped short. "Why?"

"As I said, my reasons do not concern this Council. Further, I take full responsibility for my actions. Speaker Mud Stalker, I will see you later to discuss a mutual settlement for Eats Wood's death." He looked at Thunder Tail. "May I continue and address the other more serious charge of witchcraft?"

"You may," Thunder Tail said with a wary gravity.

Salamander walked around the fire pit in slow steps, expression pinched, as though searching for the right words.

When he finally looked up, he said, "Speakers, Elders, there are those among you who will be anxious, sit here in Council for hours telling stories about the reasons for my brother's death, about my mother's curious soul loss, about my dealings with Jaguar Hide, and so many other things. If we go through with this, you will hear how I sit atop the Bird's Head every morning to watch the sun rise. You will hear that I helped the Serpent with the care and preparation of the dead. Depending on how far some people are willing to go in pursuit of my destruction, there may be even wilder stories to be told." He looked at them, one by one, and added, "I don't care."

"What do you mean, you don't care?" Deep Hunter asked irritably.

"What I said, Speaker." Salamander turned to face him. "I don't care." A pause. "Let us speak honestly, shall we? This Council meeting is really about who will replace Owl Clan in the leadership. Removing me and placing Half Thorn in the Speaker's position will benefit both Snapping Turtle Clan and Alligator Clan. I have heard that Moccasin Leaf will return Frog Clan's root grounds in return for her vote to convict me of witchcraft." He faced Cane Frog, saying, "I congratulate you in getting your root grounds back, Elder."

Mud Stalker barely noticed Three Moss's fingers playing on the old woman's shoulder.

"What are you saying?" Clay Fat asked. "That declaring you a witch is part of a deal?"

"I am saying that I quit," Salamander replied. "If this is allowed to ferment, it will spoil. What we do here today will affect the future. If I act one way, I can destroy the clans. If I act another, Mud Stalker and Deep Hunter will be at war within a turning of the seasons. We are that close to disaster! So, I will choose a third way. I will just give up the Speakership."

"What?" Thunder Tail asked, looking confused.

"Last night, when I asked you to allow me to speak uninterrupted, Leader, it was to give me the chance to tell my enemies that they win. Rather than fight them in a destructive and divisive battle that, innocent or not, I cannot win, I will give up everything. It is my only defense, Speaker."

"Defense how?" Clay Fat asked. "It sounds more like a confession!"

"Agreed!" Deep Hunter growled.

Salamander made a calming gesture. "A *real* witch is interested only in harming others, in accruing wealth, prestige, and authority. A witch wants admiration, respect, and status more than he wants life. That, or he wants revenge."

"Revenge for what?" Thunder Tail asked.

"That is a very good question, Speaker." Salamander stopped to stare down at Eats Wood's bones. "Revenge for what was done to my brother? How does one get revenge on lightning? Masked Owl killed him to keep him from planting those goosefoot seeds and changing the People. Revenge for my mother's soul loss? Do you take revenge on a woman because she can't stand her grief? Or perhaps I might want revenge for having been made a Speaker?" He gave Mud Stalker a thin smile. "Indeed, there might be some merit in that." A pause. "No, not even for being thrust into this position. I certainly wouldn't want revenge for having to live with my three beautiful wives."

"Then why are you casting spells?" Sweet Root asked.

"*I have cast no spells!*" Salamander spread his arms wide in a gesture of innocence. "Clan Elder, you have committed yourself to this course of action. Deals have been concluded. Promises made. You and the others have invested so much in this that though I am *not* a witch, you must declare me one. A fine predicament you find yourselves in. How do you declare Speaker Salamander to be a witch when he isn't?"

He held up a hand, stifling Sweet Root's outburst, and cried, "To solve this problem and release you from the trap you laid for yourselves, I will leave Sun Town forever. As soon as I settle my obligation to Snapping Turtle Clan, I will be gone. It saves you the odious chore of having Half Thorn murder me. It keeps peace between my lineage and his. It ensures that there will be no whispers through the coming seasons that you murdered an innocent man."

"Why?" Deep Hunter asked. "It means you will lose everything."

Salamander's eyes expanded like dark pools. "Yes, Speaker. I lose everything. I willfully and freely lose so that, unhindered, you may pursue your schemes in search of prestige and authority."

"You can't just let them win!" Clay Fat protested.

"Old friend of my mother's," Salamander said warmly, "I can, and I must. I have seen the future, and I know the price I must pay to save it. I ask you to vote to recognize Half Thorn as Speaker of Owl Clan until this Council is called tomorrow."

"*Salamander!*" Water Petal cried in disbelief, pushing past the stunned Moccasin Leaf. "What are you doing?"

He smiled at her. "Saving us all, Cousin. When Masked Owl called on me to make one choice, and Many Colored Crow called on me to make another, I could accede to neither."

"What are you talking about?" Mud Stalker asked as he stepped forward and spun Salamander around.

The youth's eyes might have been watching him from a midnight eternity. "There will be no cities of stone built by the People. But we will not be Dreamers locked away in the One, either. The Brothers will continue to squabble, but they will do so at another place, in another time."

"What is he saying?" Sweet Root demanded.

"*Hear* this!" Salamander cried, breaking away. "*Remember* these words! Tomorrow, when this Council meets, I ask you to recognize the voices of reason. Our strength has always been found in harmony among the clans. Your responsibility is simple! Just do what is right for the People." With a sad smile, he added, "May the rest of your solstice celebration be filled with joy."

In a lower voice, he said, "Speaker Mud Stalker, I will join you for your feast tonight if that is all right. We can discuss Eats Wood and what is a proper settlement for his death."

Mud Stalker was still gaping as Salamander touched his forehead in respect and walked out the western exit. The crowd parted for him like a wave as he passed.

"What did he just do?" Deep Hunter asked.

"I haven't the faintest idea," Cane Frog answered.

"What about Eats Wood?" Sweet Root demanded.

Thunder Tail gave her a scathing look and said, "That is between you and Salamander. It is no longer the business of this Council."

"I win!" Half Thorn clapped his hands gleefully. "I am to be Speaker!"

Chapter Twenty

When Salamander arrived that evening, the inside of Pine Drop's house was lit by faint flickers of fire from the central hearth. Someone had been coming to check on both women, to assure the baby had been freshly changed, and he assumed, fed by a wet nurse. Where he crouched at the bedside, Salamander could hold each of his wives' hands. The chill in their flesh cooled his hot palms.

He took that moment to study their faces, knowing how they were locked in the Dream. They were both so beautiful. How had he ever been so lucky to have been the subject of their smiles? He would carry the feel of their warm bodies against his even after his souls finally journeyed to the Land of the Dead.

"Relax," he whispered. "Don't be frightened. You are Dreaming. I used a potion of morning glory in the tea and covered it with the taste of mint. I knew what you would try to do. I couldn't let you claim to have killed Eats Wood. It would have ruined both of you.

Your clan would never forget, never forgive. In the end, it would have cost you everything. I couldn't allow that. Not when I love you both so much."

He thought he saw a faint frown on Pine Drop's brow. "I give you my Dream for the People. Take it and make it yours. You shall become a great Clan Elder. I have seen these things come true."

Night Rain's lips twitched when he turned to her.

"You shall become the greatest of them all, Night Rain. Your sons will take the Trade across the whole world. Generations will speak your name with respect."

Night Rain sighed from deep in her Dreams.

"Take good care of my sons when they are born. I wish that I could stay and watch them grow. I wish that so much that my souls ache with the longing. But I have to finish my affairs with your uncle."

He smiled down at them, their soft skin under his fingers. "I have to leave now. In the meantime, I want you to fly. Just relax. Set yourselves free. Open your wings and drift into the air. Soon, we shall all be flying together."

Did he see a faint smile on their lips?

His daughter lay in her cradleboard, dark eyes watching him. The infant's arms were free, and she reached out with chubby hands, grasping for Salamander.

"I shall miss you, too, little one," he replied softly. "I just came to tell all of you that leaving you behind is the hardest thing I will ever do."

He bent, touching his lips to Night Rain's, then Pine Drop's. Finally, he stood, stepped over to his daughter, and traced his fingers along the softness of her rounded cheeks. "Live long and well, little one.

When you feel a warm caress in your Dreams, it will be me."

Then he ducked out into the night, walking in the shadows at the edge of the borrow pit, smelling the rank water. He kept his head down, aware of the fires and the crowds of people moving back and forth between the houses.

"For everything, there is a price." Heron's words rang in his souls.

They would live because of him, because of what he was about to do. When solstice came next summer, Sun Town would be alive, vibrant, and children would be playing and laughing here. His wives would be smiling, and his children would not know fear, hunger, and grief.

As he had known they would be, several young warriors were posted around Mud Stalker's house to keep off the curious on this most important night.

"It is Salamander," he said to Water Stinger. "I have come to make a settlement with Speaker Mud Stalker."

Saw Back, a looming shadow in the darkness, said, "I want you to know, I personally am going to be dealing with you later tonight. Following that, I am hunting down that Swamp Panther bitch to pay her back. And, the day after solstice, the clans are going south to raid. Owl Clan will no longer control the sandstone. We have a debt to settle with Jaguar Hide."

Salamander told him. "What you do after this night is no longer my affair. My business here is with the Speakers and Elders."

"Pass," Water Stinger told him coldly. "I, too, will be waiting to deal with you. And, while you are in there, know that I was Eats Wood's friend."

"Yes, he has found a great many friends in death, hasn't he?" Salamander felt the man bristle in the darkness as he passed.

Without ceremony, he ducked through Mud Stalker's door to find the interior well lit by the central hearth. Mud Stalker and Sweet Root sat at the back. Cane Frog and Three Moss to the right, while Deep Hunter, Colored Paint, Moccasin Leaf, and Half Thorn were to the left. All of them looked up as Salamander settled himself at the last open space between them.

"We expected you to have run by now," Mud Stalker greeted jovially.

Food had just been set out. Two large ceramic pots were filled with baked lotus roots. A steatite bowl rested at the side of the fire, black drink steaming its invitation. The bark platters and gourd cups that were being passed back and forth had stopped short at his arrival.

"Good evening," Salamander greeted, nodding from one to the next. "Please, do not let me interrupt. Continue with your feast."

Mud Stalker scooped up some of the root paste. "What did you do to yourself today, Salamander?"

"What I had to, Speaker. Just as I have since the moment you made me Speaker."

"You are Speaker no longer," Half Thorn remarked arrogantly.

"No. I am nothing now."

"Did you really kill Eats Wood?" Mud Stalker demanded. "Or was that a trick to save your barbarian bitch?"

"I could not let him cut my unborn daughter from Anhinga's raped and murdered body, Speaker." Salamander hesitated, seeing the design on the clay-tempered pot beside the fire. The interlocking owls couldn't be mistaken. There, beside it, stood its twin. He smiled, feeling the last pieces of the future falling into place.

"Where is Anhinga?" Deep Hunter demanded. "We went looking for her today. No one has seen her."

"She is far to the south." His gaze remained fixed on the two pots. "After tonight, the ghosts that plague her will be laid to rest."

"What is this about?" Cane Frog asked, her single white eye on Salamander. "Why did you just give up that way?"

Salamander watched Moccasin Leaf scooping the thick root paste from the pot and piling it on her wooden plate. "I had a vision after the Serpent's cleansing last winter. Brother mushroom is not to be treated lightly. Some of you will remember when I was so sick? I fell so deeply into the tunnel, I couldn't find my way back. There, in the Dream, I was dying."

"I don't understand," Half Thorn muttered.

"You never will," Salamander replied. "A Spirit Helper came to me, Danced with me. She showed me bits and pieces of the future. Seeing is tricky. A great many things may change. People make decisions that alter the way events may unfold."

"Now we are to believe that you are a seer?" Sweet Root asked derisively as she scooped some of the paste into her mouth.

"We have already discussed belief once today, Clan Elder. You may believe what you wish."

"So"—Deep Hunter waved a taunting hand—"tell me of this future you saw."

"There were so many futures," Salamander said

carefully. "Different visions of what might be. That is one of the lures of the One. When you Dance, you see different futures as you spin about. But, to get back to your request, we could have followed Many Colored Crow's vision and made Sun Town influential beyond your most exotic imaginings. It would have happened under a great leader who bound our entire world together through Trade and war. Sun Town would have grown to cover a huge area. Other towns would have been built up and down the length and width of the river—as far as canoes can travel."

"A great leader?" Mud Stalker asked. "Just one?"

"All that authority," Salamander agreed, "all placed in one person who passed it on to his heir."

Mud Stalker was smiling grimly, seeing himself in that place.

"What about this other future?" Cane Frog asked.

"Other futures," Salamander corrected. "In some, my decision would have driven the clans into open warfare. Within moons, bodies would lie among the houses, and in the ensuing battles, the clans would be split, dispersing and raiding each other until Sun Town is only a memory. A no-man's-land where we kill each other on sight."

"Never," Colored Paint muttered under her breath. "Stop trying to frighten us."

"Alligator Clan would win anyway," Deep Hunter cried, smacking a hand to his thigh. He dipped a handful of pasty root from one of the jars and sucked it from his fingers, heedless of the hot stares of the others.

"What future did you choose?" Three Moss asked, glancing meaningfully at Mud Stalker.

"I chose a third way. I stopped at the Serpent's last

night and obtained a bit of mushroom. Just enough to open the tunnel. Old Heron answered my call, and we Dreamed. Peculiar, isn't it? So many lines of Power, so many paths to the future ran through me. With one decision I would have been the greatest Speaker ever, uniting the People under Owl Clan. With another, I could have Danced and Dreamed the One. This place, and our People, would have evaporated in a few turnings of the seasons. They hadn't counted on my finding a third way."

"You?" Deep Hunter laughed. "The greatest Speaker ever?"

Salamander ignored him. "Tomorrow, a new Council will be chosen. The lesson that we have taught them will survive for another five or ten generations, and then, as Morning Lake fills with mud, and the beliefs that we learned here spread, the people will slowly move away. In the end, Sun Town will be left to the forest, and the center of our world will move to other places and other peoples. Clans, peoples, and leaders will rise and fall. The meaning of our earthworks will change. Great Dreamers will carry the words of Masked Owl and Many Colored Crow across the land. Old Heron will sit in her cave, and watch the Tree of Life grow as she Dreams the One."

"So," Mud Stalker asked, "tell me, *Seer*, which clan will be preeminent in the next turning of the seasons?"

"Until Thunder Tail dies, Eagle Clan will be preeminent. Following that, Clay Fat will lead the Council until his death. Only then, after many turnings of seasons, will he be followed by Clan Elder Pine Drop."

Both Mud Stalker and Deep Hunter erupted into

guffaws, slapping their legs, as they eyed each other like kestrels over a grasshopper.

Of them all, only Cane Frog, perhaps seeing more through her blind eye, remained serious. "Why, Salamander? Why would any of us in this room vote Clay Fat into the leadership?"

"You won't. Tomorrow, you will all be dead." Salamander smiled ironically. "That is the lesson that we will teach this day. Harmony between the clans must be maintained. Fortunately, there are young leaders ready to fill our positions."

"Our positions?" Half Thorn asked. "I am already Speaker in yours."

"Yes." Salamander nodded pleasantly. "Enjoy it while you can." He indicated the pot before him. "May I share your bounty, Speaker?"

"By all means." Mud Stalker gestured with his good hand before he scooped more from the pot. "You know, Salamander, that despite your announcement today, we can't just let you go. It isn't just the matter of Eats Wood, but as we were discussing before your arrival, we cannot allow you just to wander about."

"We would be uncomfortable," Deep Hunter added, "knowing that you were out there, talking to people, giving them ideas."

"We are afraid you might find allies," Cane Frog explained. "Bring them back to challenge the authority of the clans."

Moccasin Leaf gave him a humorless smile. "We are sorry, Salamander, but you are too dangerous. Of course, the people, Water Petal, and Yellow Spider, will think that you left in secret. Water Stinger and Saw Back will make sure that no one discovers your body."

He nodded, feeling a stone-heaviness in his heart. "Well, I shall hope that this last meal will be as good as it looks."

Mud Stalker smiled past hard eyes. "It is excellent! A solstice gift. I found it here upon my return. And then Deep Hunter brings a pot just like the first. Yellow lotus, our traditional feast, but seasoned heavily with mint, honeysuckle, and some strange tang that I cannot identify."

"Water hemlock," Salamander supplied with a numbness in his souls.

"Hemlock? The poison?" Moccasin Leaf cried, then burst into peals of laughter. "I see, you made a joke, Salamander. A grand joke indeed."

"Yes. A joke worthy of Masked Owl himself," he answered and used his fingers to dip into the rich mixture of roots Anhinga had baked. Before the first debilitating cramps, he would make sure that he took an ample serving out to share with Saw Back and Water Stinger.

A hard day's paddle to the south, Anhinga bent over a handful of flickering fire that guttered in the ceramic pot she carried. Moths continued fluttering out of the darkness to circle her fire until the heat and flames engulfed them.

"He will be coming to us, little one," she told the infant at her breast.

Anhinga smiled at the thought. "You should know, Daughter, that Salamander is the most cunning of all men. He will come to us. You will see. His enemies will not defeat him in the end."

She turned her head, looking back in the direction of Sun Town, imagining the countless fires and the masses of people preparing for the celebration.

And there, among them, Deep Hunter and Mud Stalker would be feasting. Bowfin, Mist Finger, and the rest would finally allow her to dream in peace.

Anhinga ran a finger along her daughter's cheek, an empty sadness deep in her breast. The elation she had expected didn't rise to bubble and froth between her souls. She had struck the Sun People, obtained her revenge. It left her hollow.

"As the endless seasons pass, little one, it shall be my secret." Anhinga looked out at the black night. "If they accuse me, I shall deny it. It is the price I shall pay for success."

She did not see the looming shadow of the great barred owl who sat in the tree above her, watching, guarding, and mourning.

Epilogue

Pine Drop was having one of those aggravating days. They happened sometimes. A full turning of the seasons had passed since she had set fire to both her mother's and uncle's houses. A full cycle since Mother Sun had fled south and come back north—since the day she had watched fire consume Salamander's house and bones. That day after solstice had been marked by so many funereal fires. Bobcat, responsible for the ceremonies, as well as the preparation of the dead, had been sorely pressed to manage it all.

Had it been that long since she had held Salamander? Felt the hammering of his heart against hers? The hollow wound in her souls felt as painful as if it had been yesterday. But life went on.

As on this troublesome day.

That morning she had caught Tadpole splashing her hands in the large hide bag where the acorns were leaching. Pine Drop had looked just in time to make a desperate dash and pull the child back as she bent down to drink a mouthful of the poison-laden water.

Little Mud Puppy, three moons old now, had been squalling from his cradleboard like a wounded bobcat every time she turned around. Feed him as she might, the tiny infant burped, went to sleep for a couple of fingers' time and woke up squalling again.

Water Petal had been by to see if anyone had seen Wing Heart. The old woman had taken to rambling aimlessly around Sun Town. Where once she only talked to Cloud Heron and White Bird, now she was heard muttering to Salamander, too. That latter was particularly upsetting for both Pine Drop and Night Rain.

That morning a canoe load of Swamp Panthers had arrived from the Panther's Bones. Anhinga and Striped Dart had sent requests for certain fabrics in Trade for the once-a-moon shipment of sandstone. It might have originally been Owl Clan's Trade, but Anhinga preferred to deal with Pine Drop because of their former relationship. And, fulfilling what had become a ritual between them, Anhinga had sent Night Rain another bundle of firewood as a gift. When the canoe left, it carried a stone-headed axe from Night Rain in return.

Pine Drop had been interrupted no less than five and ten times that morning to settle petty little squabbles between the lineages, and one major one that involved Frog Clan.

"Pine Drop?" Night Rain's urgent voice called from outside.

"What now?" she cried, exasperated.

"Come quick!" Night Rain stuck her face in the doorway. "Canoes! Tens of tens!"

"Whose?" Pine Drop asked, a hand to her aching back as she straightened. Wisps of loose hair tickled her face.

"Barbarians! Traders! With bulging canoes! They have entered Morning Lake and headed for the Turtle's Back before even announcing themselves!"

"Where is our husband?"

Night Rain gave a faint shrug. "Headed for the canoe landing, no doubt. You'll find him there—along with everyone else in Sun Town. I just asked Little Egret to keep track of my son. She will probably watch your children, too." And then she was gone.

Pine Drop ducked out into the mottled sunshine created by a cloud-dotted sky. Little Egret sat next to a cradleboard under the ramada. Night Rain's baby boy gurgled and cooed from its restraint. "Cousin, could you watch my children? I must see to the Traders."

"Yes, Clan Elder," the girl replied.

Pine Drop fought the urge to run—that being inconsistent with her status. She joined the flow of excited people, fending off questions, as they passed the ridges, rounded the Men's House, and walked down to the canoe landing.

Recognizing her, people touched their foreheads and stepped back, allowing her to pick her way through the beached canoes to the waterfront. Council Leader Clay Fat had beaten her there, and was staring out from under the flat of his hand.

"Who are they?" Pine Drop asked—and fought to keep her jaw from dropping. So *many* canoes! It took her three tries to count them all. Three tens and four!

All filled with oddly dressed strangers who wore their hair in buns. Sun Town had never seen such a thing.

"What is this?" Yellow Spider asked, elbowing his way to her side.

"Traders? Barbarians."

"Does anyone recognize them?" Water Petal asked as she pushed next to Yellow Spider.

"I do," Yellow Spider said warmly. "I see old friends out there. Come, let's take a canoe and greet them."

"Take a canoe out to the Turtle's Back?" Water Petal shot him a worried look.

"The water's too deep to wade. But you could swim out if you were determined not to take a canoe." Yellow Spider turned, searching the faces around them. "Little Needle! Go and find the Serpent, we have a cleansing to attend to." He smiled at Pine Drop. "Help me push this canoe out."

She looked at him askance as Night Rain slipped through the pack to join them.

The fact that they took Sour Mouth's canoe—because it was the closest—gave Pine Drop a feeling of satisfaction. The man had a bobwhite's brains when it came to sense.

I am not prepared for this. I look like I've been processing food all day long. "Quick," she asked, "do I have smears all over my face?"

"You're beautiful," Yellow Spider called from behind her."

"Don't give her airs," Night Rain shot back. "She's hard enough to deal with as it is."

Nevertheless, Pine Drop took a moment to reach over the side and scoop up a handful of water to sponge her face with. She smoothed her hair and wished she'd taken the time to grab a cloak.

Yellow Spider's sure strokes guided their canoe across the intervening water and onto the bank just down from the rows of Trade canoes on the beach. Pine Drop stepped out, helping to drag their craft ashore. Then she took her place at Yellow Spider's side as they walked toward the gathered strangers. A smaller group stood off to one side, dressed differently, as a tall, young woman spoke to two men in low tones.

A big fellow stepped out from the big group. Muscles packed his sweat-gleaming skin. In guttural pidgin, he called, "Yellow Spider! By the Wolf, it's good to see you again!"

"Hazel Fire! My kinsman!" Yellow Spider burst out, and charged forward, clapping the man in a violent embrace.

"Wolf People! Yes! That *is* Hazel Fire!" Water Petal cried before hurrying forward. "And there is Gray Fox, and I'd know Two Wolves anywhere."

Pine Drop waited her turn, and Night Rain at her side, was introduced to a great many young men with odd-sounding names.

"And these people," Hazel Fire added, pointing, "met us on the river. They, too, were coming to bring Trade."

Pine Drop turned her attention to the party at one side. Indeed, they were dressed differently, wearing carefully tailored hide tunics designed with quillwork. Pine Drop stepped forward, calling, "Welcome to Sun Town."

"It's good to be home," the young woman replied. Tall, attractive, she stood beside a muscular man and surveyed the crowd onshore. Her gaze had centered on Clay Fat, a frown lining her forehead. "My husband and I have come to Trade with Speaker Salamander, of the Owl Clan. Is he here?"

"You don't speak like a barbarian," Pine Drop observed. Why was she so familiar?

The attractive woman turned her gaze back from Clay Fat, her eyes measuring. "I would hope not, Pine Drop."

"Spring Cypress?" It took her a moment to place the face.

"The same, but I am of the Wash'ta now. You may have met my husband, Green Crane." She pointed behind her, "And back there is Always Fat, returned for more Trade."

"You are married to Green Crane?"

"She is, and with great status, thanks to Salamander," Green Crane told her in Trade pidgin. "We have canoes full of Trade to give to Salamander."

"As do we," Hazel Fire called. "I swear, we have stripped our country for you. Stone, furs, medicines, copper, dried meats, exotics from the far north, stone hoe blades, points, siltstone, you name it! It is all Salamander's."

"Salamander's?" Night Rain asked, hiding a stricken expression. "Why?"

Hazel Fire extended his hand. A small carved stone owl was pinched between his thumb and forefinger. "When we left here, two summers ago, he saw into the future and gave us a warning. We heeded his words. And used our warriors"—Hazel Fire made a slashing motion—"to open the river. Our Trade will flow freely now."

Yellow Spider shot Pine Drop a quick look and said, "My cousin, Salamander, is dead. An accident at last summer's solstice ceremonies. Water hemlock, we think. Someone wasn't careful when they were harvesting lotus root. I am Speaker for Owl Clan now. Water Petal is Clan Elder. In Salamander's name, we bid you welcome."

Hazel Fire seemed stunned. Spring Cypress and Green Crane, too, might have just been slapped, given their expressions. Spring Cypress looked down at her palm. Pine Drop could see the small red stone owl resting there.

She stepped forward, souls whirling as she reached up to touch the little stone owl that hung from her neck-lace. "I am Clan Elder Pine Drop, of Snapping Turtle Clan. In Salamander's name, we bid you welcome. Before my sister and I married Speaker Yellow Spider, Salamander was our husband." A pause. "My husband."

"How?" Hazel Fire demanded. "Power filled him! He spoke with the animals! How can someone who can see the future be killed by such a simple thing?"

"Because of the little stone owl you bear, you will hear what I have never told to a living soul. He died to save the People." She had their attention now. "That night, I was sick, my souls floating outside of my body. The Serpent had come, listened to my heart, looked into my eyes, and felt how cold my skin had become. He told people that I was dying. My souls saw a great many things that night. I spoke with Many Colored Crow and Masked Owl. They told me what Sala-mander had done and why."

Hazel Fire shifted, shooting a nervous glance at Yellow Spider, then back at her.

"I flew that night," she told them. "Across from me in the sky, I could see Night Rain, sailing through the air on owl wings. Then, out of the clouds, I heard Salamander's voice say, 'It is all right, my wives. I have fixed everything. I am going now.' At the sound of his voice, I knew he was dead. The last thing I heard was the echo of First Woman's voice, calling him to her cave."

She smiled, feeling the tendrils of Salamander's Dream spinning through time to this place. "I felt his touch that night, as did Night Rain. And in that instant, I understood. From that moment on, I spoke with Salamander's voice. So, hear him, when I bid you welcome to Sun Town, the center of the world. You are part of his Dream, and we are obliged by your presence."

A look At Book Four:
People of the Raven

New York Times bestselling authors W. Michael Gear and Kathleen O'Neal Gear present a gripping tale of survival, ambition, and conflict in ancient America.

As melting glaciers reshape the rugged Pacific Northwest, the Raven People struggle to adapt to a world where familiar landscapes vanish, and survival becomes more perilous with each passing day. Mammoths and Mastodons have disappeared, and the Raven People fear they may be facing extinction. At the heart of this struggle is Rain Bear, chief of Sandy Point Village, who must balance the survival of his people with a decision that could bring either hope or destruction.

When Evening Star, a mysterious red-haired woman, stumbles into Rain Bear's lodge, the stakes skyrocket. A fugitive from the brutal North Wind People—their sworn enemies—she warns of a coming war. Rain Bear faces a brutal choice: shelter her and risk an all-out assault from the North Wind People, or send her back to almost certain death. As tensions escalate, Rain Bear must decide whether to prepare his people for a fight they may not win or to seek sanctuary elsewhere, knowing that any choice could shatter them.

Set against the majestic yet unforgiving beauty of a changing world, *People of the Raven* is a thrilling saga of endurance, sacrifice, and loyalty. Will Rain Bear's courage be enough to secure a future for his people, or will their legacy be lost to the ravages of time?

AVAILABLE FEBRUARY 2025

About W. Michael Gear

W. Michael Gear is a *New York Times, USA Today,* and international bestselling author of sixty novels. With close to eighteen million copies of his books in print worldwide, his work has been translated into twenty-nine languages.

Gear has been inducted into the Western Writers Hall of Fame and the Colorado Authors' Hall of Fame —as well as won the Owen Wister Award, the Golden Spur Award, and the International Book Award for both Science Fiction and Action Suspense Fiction. He is also the recipient of the Frank Waters Award for lifetime contributions to Western writing.

Gear's work, inspired by anthropology and archaeology, is multilayered and has been called compelling, insidiously realistic, and masterful. Currently, he lives in northwestern Wyoming with his award-winning wife and co-author, Kathleen O'Neal Gear, and a charming sheltie named, Jake.

About Kathleen O'Neal Gear

Kathleen O'Neal Gear is a *New York Times* bestselling author of fifty-seven books and a national award-winning archaeologist. The U.S. Department of the Interior has awarded her two Special Achievement awards for outstanding management of America's cultural resources.

In 2015 the United States Congress honored her with a Certificate of Special Congressional Recognition, and the California State Legislature passed Joint Member Resolution #117 saying, "The contributions of Kathleen O'Neal Gear to the fields of history, archaeology, and writing have been invaluable..."

In 2021 she received the Owen Wister Award for lifetime contributions to western literature, and in 2023 received the Frank Waters Award for "a body of work representing excellence in writing and storytelling that embodies the spirit of the American West."

Bibliography

Alden, Peter. 1999. *National Audubon Society Field Guild to the Southeastern States.* Alfred A. Knopf. New York, New York.

Amos, William H., and Stephen H. Amos. 1985. *The Audubon Society Nature Guides Atlantic & Gulf Coasts.* Alfred A. Knopf. New York, New York.

Brecher, K. S., and W. G. Haag. 1980. "The Poverty Point Octagon: World's Largest Prehistoric Solstice Marker?" *Bulletin of the American Astronomical Society.* 12:886.

Brian, Jeffrey P. 1988. *Tunica Archaeology.* Papers of the Peabody Museum of Archaeology and Ethnology No. 78. Harvard University Press. Cambridge, Massachusetts.

Brown, Calvin S. 1992. *Archaeology of Mississippi.* Reprint of 1926 edition. University Press of Mississippi. Jackson, Mississippi.

Bruseth J. E. 1980. "Intrasite Structure at the Clairborne Site." *Louisiana Archaeology.* 6:283-318.

Byrd, Kathleen M. 1991. *The Poverty Point Culture: Local Manifestations, Subsistence Practices, and Trade Networks.* Geoscience and Man 29. Louisiana State University Press. Baton Rouge, Louisiana.

Coffey, Timothy. 1993. *The History and Folklore of North American Wild-flowers.* Facts on File. New York, New York.

Connaway, John M., Samuel O. McGahey, and Clarence Webb. 1977. *Teoc Creek, a Poverty Point Site in Carroll County, Mississippi.* Archaeological Report No. 3. Mississippi Department of Archives and History. Jackson, Mississippi.

Duncan, Wilbur H. and Marion B. Duncan. 1988. *Trees of the Southeastern United States.* University of Georgia Press. Athens, Georgia.

Fagan, Brian M. 2000. *Ancient North America,* 3rd ed. Thames and Hudson. New York, New York.

Foster, Steven, and James A. Duke. 1990. *Eastern/Central Medicinal Plants.* Peterson Field Guides. Houghton Mifflin Company. Boston, Massachusetts.

Fritz, Gayle J. 1997. "A Three-Thousand-Year-Old Cache of Crop Seeds from Marble Bluff, Arkansas." In *People, Plants, and Land-*

scapes: Studies in Paleoethnobotany, edited by Kristen J. Gremillion, pp. 42-62. University of Alabama Press. Tuscaloosa, Alabama.

Gibson, John L. 1980. "Speculations on the Origin and Development of Poverty Point Culture." *Louisiana Archaeology*. 6: 319-348.

--. 1987. "The Poverty Point Earthworks Reconsidered." *Mississippi Archaeology*. 22(2): 14—31.

--. 1991. "Catahoula—An Amphibious Poverty Point Manifestation in Eastern Louisiana." In *The Poverty Point Culture: Local Manifestations, Subsistence Practices, and Trade Networks,* edited by Kathleen M. Byrd, pp. 61-88. Geoscience and Man No. 29. Louisiana State University Press. Baton Rouge, Louisiana.

--. 1996. "Religion of the Rings: Poverty Point Iconography and Ceremonialism." In *Mounds, Embankments, and Ceremonialism in the Midsouth,* edited by R. C. Main-fort and R. Wailing, pp. 1-6. Arkansas Archaeological Survey Research Series No. 46. Arkansas Archaeological Survey. Fayetteville, Arkansas.

--. 1998. "Broken Circles, Owl Monsters, and Black Earth Midden: Separating Sacred and Secular at Poverty Point." In *Ancient Earthen Enclosures of the Eastern Woodlands,* edited by R. C. Mainfort and L. P. Sullivan. University Press of Florida. Gainesville, Florida.

--. 1999. *Poverty Point: A Terminal Archaic Culture in the Lower Mississippi Valley.* 2nd ed. Anthropological Study 7. Department of Culture, Recreation, and Tourism. Louisiana Archaeological Survey and Antiquities Commission. Baton Rouge, Louisiana.

--. 2000. *The Ancient Mounds of Poverty Point: Place of Rings.* University Press of Florida. Gainesville, Florida.

Gibson, J. L., and J. W. Saunders. 1993. "The Death of the South Sixth Ridge at Poverty Point: What Can We Still Do?" *SAA Bulletin.* 11(5): 7-9.

Haag, W. G. 1990. "Excavations at the Poverty Point Site: 1972-1975." *Louisiana Archaeology.* 13:1-36.

Hillman, M. M. 1990. "1985 Test Excavations of the Dock Area of Poverty Point." *Louisiana Archaeology.* 13:1-33.

Hirth, K. G. 1978 "Interregional Trade and the Formation of Prehistoric Gateway Communities." *American Antiquity.*43(1):35-45.

Hudson, Charles. 1976. *The Southeastern Indians.* University of Tennessee Press. Knoxville, Tennessee.

--. 1979. *Black Drink: A Native American Tea.* University of Georgia Press. Athens, Georgia.

Jackson, H. E.. 1991. "Bottomland Resources and Exploitation Strategies During the Poverty Point Period: Implications of the Archaeological Record from the J. W. Copes Site." In *The Poverty Point Culture: Local Manifestations, Subsistence Practices, and Trade Networks,* edited by Kathleen M. Byrd, pp. 131-158. Geoscience and Man 29. Louisiana State University Press. Baton Rouge, Louisiana.

--. 1991. "The Trade Fair in Hunter-Gatherer Interactions: The Role of Intersocietal Trade in the Evolution of Poverty Point Culture." In *Between Bands and States,* edited by S. A. Greg, pp. 265-286. Occasional Papers 9. Center for Archaeological Investigations, Southern Illinois University at Carbondale. Carbondale, Illinois.

Kidder, Tristram. 2002. "Mapping Poverty Point." *American Antiquity.* 67: 89-101.

Lazarus, W. C. 1958. "A Poverty Point Complex in Florida." *Florida Anthropologist.* 6(l):23-32.

Mainfort, Robert C, and L. P. Sullivan. 1998 *Ancient Earthen Enclosures of the Eastern Woodlands.* University Press of Florida. Gainesville, Florida.

McEwan, Bonnie G. 2000. *Indians of the Greater Southeast.* University Press of Florida. Gainesville, Florida.

Morgan, William N. 1999. *Precolumbian Architecture in Eastern North America.* University Press of Florida. Gainesville, Florida.

Neuman, R. W., and N. W. Hawkins. 1987. *Louisiana Prehistory.* Department of Culture, Recreation, and Tourism. Louisiana Archaeological Survey and Antiquities Commission. Anthropological Study 6, 2nd ed., revised. Baton Rouge, Louisiana.

Pearson, James L. 2002. *Shamanism and the Ancient Mind.* Altamira Press. Walnut Creek, California.

Penman, John T. 1980. *Archaeological Survey in Mississippi, 1974–1975.* Archaeological Report No. 2. Mississippi Department of Archives and History. Jackson, Mississippi.

Purrington, R. D. 1983. "Superimposed Solar Alignments at Poverty Point." *American Antiquity.* 48:157-161.

Purrington, R. D., and C. A. Child, Jr. 1989. "Poverty Point Revisited: Further Consideration of Astronomical Alignments." *Journal of the History of Astronomy.* 13: 49-60.

Sassaman, Kenneth E. 1993. *Early Pottery in the Southeast.* University of Alabama Press. Tuscaloosa, Alabama.

Schlotz, Sandra C. 1975. *Prehistoric Plies: A Structural and Comparative Analysis of Cordage, Netting, Basketry, and Fabric from*

Bibliography

Ozark Bluff Shelters. Arkansas Archaeological Survey No. 6. Arkansas Archaeological Survey. Fayette Ville, Arkansas.

Smith, Brent W. 1974. "A Preliminary Identification of Faunal Remains from the Clairborne Site." *Mississippi Archaeology.* 9: 1-7.

--. 1976. "The Late Archaic-Poverty Point Steatite Trade Network in the Lower Mississippi Valley." *Louisiana Archaeological Society Newsletter.* 3:6-10.

--. 1981. "The Late Archaic-Poverty Point Steatite Trade Network in the Lower Mississippi Valley: Some Preliminary Observations." *Florida Anthropologist.* 34: 120-125.

Smith, Bruce D. 1992. *Rivers of Change: Essays on Early Agriculture in Eastern North America.* Smithsonian Institution Press. Washington, DC.

Swanton, John R. 1979. *The Indians of the Southeastern United States.* Reprint of the 1946 Bureau of American Ethnography Bulletin No. 137. Smithsonian Institution Press. Washington, DC.

--. 1998. *Indian Tribes of the Lower Mississippi Valley and Adjacent Coast of the Gulf of Mexico.* Dover reprint of 1911 edition. Dover Publications. Mineola, New York.

--. 2001. *Source Material for the Social and Ceremonial Life of the Choctaw Indians.* University of Alabama Press. Tuscaloosa, Alabama.

Thomas, Cyrus. 1985. *Report on the Mound Expeditions of the Bureau of Ethnography.* Reprint of the 1894 Bureau of American Ethnography No. 12. Smithsonian Institution Press. Washington, DC.

Thomas, Prentice M., and L. J. Campbell. 1978. *The Peripheries of Poverty Point.* New World Research Report of Investigation No. 12. New World Research. Pollack, Louisiana.

Tiamat, Uni M. 1994. *Herbal Abortion Handbook.* Sage-femme! Press. Peoria, Illinois.

Vogel, Virgil H.. 1970. *American Indian Medicine.* University of Oklahoma Press. Norman, Oklahoma.

Webb, Clarence H. 1968. "The Extent and Content of Poverty Point Culture." *American Antiquity.* 33:297-321.

Webb, Clarence H., and J. L. Gibson. 1982. "Studies of the Microflint Industry at the Poverty Point Site." In *Traces of Prehistory: Papers in Honor of William G. Haag,* edited by F. H. West and R. W. Neuman, pp. 85-101. Geoscience and Man 22. School of Geoscience. Louisiana State University Press. Baton Rouge, Louisiana.

--. 1970. "Intrasite Distribution of Artifacts at the Poverty Point Site, with Special Reference to Women's and Men's Activities." *Southeastern Archaeological Conference Bulletin.* 12:21-34.

--. 1982. *The Poverty Point Culture.* Geoscience and Man 17. 2nd ed., revised. Geoscience Publications, Department of Geography and Anthropology. Louisiana State University Press. Baton Rouge, Louisiana.